To Arizona 66 To Oklahoma 66 Gallup New Mexico 66

The Law and Dan Mesa
East Meet West

ARIZONA RANGERS

SANTA CRUZ COUNTY DETACHMENT
NOGALES, ARIZONA

The Law and Dan Mesa

East Meet West

Dan Sears

iUniverse, Inc.
Bloomington

THE LAW AND DAN MESA
EAST MEET WEST

This is a work of fiction. All of the characters, names, incidents, organizations, and dialogue in this novel are either the products of the author's imagination or are used fictitiously.

iUniverse books may be ordered through booksellers or by contacting:

iUniverse
1663 Liberty Drive
Bloomington, IN 47403
www.iuniverse.com
1-800-Authors (1-800-288-4677)

ISBN: 978-1-4759-3016-0 (sc)
ISBN: 978-1-4759-3018-4 (hc)
ISBN: 978-1-4759-3017-7 (ebk)

Printed in the United States of America

iUniverse rev. date: 05/31/2012

This book is dedicated to those who enforce the law. As someone once said, "It is a dirty job, but someone has to do it." The law is what we live and die by, whether it be God's law or man's. Without law, there would be total chaos. Without officers of the law to enforce the law, society could not exist. The line between enforcement of the law and revenge becomes very slim at times. The idea of justice can become somewhat suspect.

Chapter One

Captain Robert Emmett of the Richmond, Virginia, Police Department has just gotten to work for the midnight shift and is sorting through the messages and letters. Captain Emmett is a veteran police officer of twenty-five years on the force. He finds a message from the commander of the Arizona rangers stating that a Sergeant Daniel Mesa will arrive to escort William J. Ranson back to Nogales, Arizona, to testify against Carlos Meana, a local trafficker in illegal aliens and murder for hire.

> Sergeant Dan Mesa will arrive on August 12 to escort Ranson back to Nogales. Please accord him all courtesy and assistance. We are forever in your debt.

A Colonel Grant signed the message.

Captain Emmett curses and yells for the Desk Sergeant saying, "Sergeant Anderson, get Ranson ready to go back to Arizona. The rangers are sending one of their people to pick him up."

Sergeant Anderson hesitates and asks, "Captain, do you mean the Texas Rangers?"

Captain Emmett smiles and says, "No, I mean the Arizona rangers. They still exist, sergeant, and we will meet one in a few hours. His name is Daniel Mesa, a sergeant."

Ranson is brought upstairs and put into the holding cell. He is a tall slender man who is upset and nervous. He is contantly looking around as if he is expecting something or someone.

"Why am I being put into the holding cell?" he asks. "Where am I being sent?".

"You are being returned to Arizona, to Nogales," Sergeant Anderson says. "One of the rangers is coming for you."

"What is the name of the ranger?" Ranson quickly asks.

"A Sergeant Dan Mesa," Anderson replies.

"Oh no, not him. Please? That ranger is one of the meanest people in Arizona. He never smiles, and he has killed probably ten men. He actually stood in the middle of the streets and had a shoot-out with another guy. He is fast with guns, sticks, or anything. Why did they send him?"

Anderson looks at Ranson and asks, "Does he know you?"

"No," Ranson says, "but Sergeant Dan Mesa is a cross between Langford Peel and Bill Tilgman. He got into a fight with a fella I know in Phoenix. This guy weighs around two hundred pounds, and Mesa weighs about one fifty, but it didn't matter. He beat that guy something terrible and never received so much as a bruise. Then he bought him a drink and walked out of the bar."

Sergeant Anderson walks into the captain's office with a frown on his face and relates what Ranson has just told him.

A patrolman, Jim Hennessey, is listening and says, "You know, there was a Captain Daniel Mesa who was assigned to Turkey during the Gulf War, and he was 'Hell on Wheels.' They tried to kill him several times, and he survived each attempt. He also served in Vietnam, and rumor has it he killed a few people during the fall of Saigon in 1975. There were many rumors about him. He was a good officer. He was also enlisted at one time—a staff sergeant, I believe. He was respected, but he never got close to anyone. It was as if he was afraid."

Captain Emmett turns to Hennessey.

"Stick around," he says. "I want you to tell me if he is the same person."

In Baltimore, a father and son are saying good-bye to each other. They are standing in the hallway and both have tears in their eyes.

Dan Mesa hugs his son.

"Devlin, Daddy has to go back to Arizona today," he says. "I've had a great time visiting you and your mom. Maybe you can visit me at Christmas, if Mommy doesn't mind?" Garnett has been watching them and finds it difficult to what she sees.

He turns to Garnett, who says, "Of course, he can visit at Christmas. It will give me a chance to visit some friends in Las Vegas."

"Garnett, I want to say thanks for letting me visit. I needed a break after that last incident. I am happy that we are at least friendly toward each other. I still . . . Anyway, I'd better get started for Richmond."

He hugs his son and walks away a little sadder but a little happier too.

Captain Emment later tells a friend, "In walks this guy who is about five feet five inches tall, weighing about a hundred fifty pounds, wearing jeans, a green western shirt, a Ranger Star, brown boots, and a gray western hat. He looked totally out of place in Richmond, Virginia,"

Mesa walks into the police station and speaks to the desk sergeant.

"I am Sergeant Daniel Mesa of the Arizona Rangers," he says. "And I am here to escort William J. Ranson back to Nogales, Arizona. I have the necessary papers for extradition. Your commander should have received a communiqué from the rangers' commander, Colonel Grant."

"Ranger," the sergeant says, "Captain Emmett is waiting for you in his office. I'll show you in."

"Thank you, sergeant."

As Mesa walks through the area, he notices people staring at him. Suddenly, he realizes they are looking at the way he is dressed.

"I am from Arizona," he says, "and this is how we dress."

The sergeant takes Mesa into the captain's office.

"Sir," he says, "this is the Ranger you are expecting."

"Thank you, sergeant. Welcome to Richmond, Virginia, Ranger Mesa. I received the message from your colonel, and we have Ranson ready for extradition. We should have you ready to go in less than an hour. Is that okay?"

"Yes, sir, that is very good."

A voice behind him says, "Captain Mesa, how are you?"

Mesa turns and immediately recognizes retired Master Sergeant Jim Hennessey.

"Hello, sergeant," Mesa says. "It has been a while. I am happy to see you. Captain Emmett, Sergeant Hennessey was an excellent trooper in the air force, and from appearances, I'd say he is the same as a policeman."

"Thank you, Captain Mesa, for the compliment," Sergeant Hennessy says, smiling. "And I try my best to do my job. Captain, how did you wind up as a ranger? I didn't know Arizona had rangers."

Mesa smiles.

"When I retired, I started teaching high school ROTC, and a friend told me about the rangers. I was able to help them in an emergency, and they hired me. That is the mini version of it. I love my job; it fits my personality."

"It is good to see you again, captain."

Hennessey shakes Mesa's hand and departs.

Suddenly, Captain Emmett says, "Now I know who you are. You are the ranger who tracked that Jackson fella and wound up in a fight and a shoot-out in the streets of Albuquerque, aren't you?"

Sergeant Mesa's whole demeanor changes, and the captain sees his sudden alertness.

"Hold on, sergeant; no need to fear. We are all friends here. It's just that you don't see those kinds of things too often. I saw it on Ted Koppel's *Nightline*. You are some kind of folk hero."

"Captain Emmett, I would appreciate it if you kept that quiet. People don't like to have people like me around. They consider me to be too violent. In reality, I just do my job as is required of me."

"Ranger, I'd say you are damn good at it. I wish I had two like you and Hennessey. He has a lot of your traits. He is one darn good policeman."

Mesa attempts to change the subject, asking, "Captain, is there a place where I can get breakfast? I haven't eaten yet."

"Yes, there is a cafeteria upstairs. By the time you finish your breakfast, Ranson will be ready to go."

Meanwhile, Carlos Meana is holding court in his palatial home in northeast Tucson. The house is located in the hills surrounded by a tall brick wall and security cameras. Antonio Blackbear, his faithful friend is by his side.

"Carlos, what are we going to do about William J. Ranson? If that guy goes to court and testifies, it could hurt us. Let me take him out, please?"

"Antonio, we will wait and see how it plays out. I know the rangers will be escorting him back to Nogales. I don't want to cross them unless I have to. There is one ranger I don't want after me. I am not afraid of him, but why borrow trouble before it is necessary? We will wait for now," Carlos says. "Now, tell me about that shipment of illegals coming in. Have we enough locations to send them and do we have enough transportation?"

"Boss we have around two thousand units," Antonio briefs Carlos, meaning people "that need to be sent out. California needs around five hundred at fifteen hundred dollars each which equals seven hundred fifty thousand dollars. North Carolina needs five hundred units, which makes one thousand five million. Texas wants five hundred units, and Louisiana wants five hundred, making a total of three million dollars for this month alone. What do you think, boss?"

Antonio, a tall handsome Mescalero Apache, is wanted in Texas, New Mexico, and of all places, Arkansas. He was vacationing in Hot Springs when he was cited for having a concealed weapon. He shot a policeman in the foot and escaped. The policeman survived, and the state issued a warrant for his arrest for assault of a police officer.

Carlos beams.

"I like dealing in illegals a lot better than drugs," he says. "This drug business is too dangerous. With illegals, I am at least giving them a better life. Drugs only destroy. If it proves to be worth the effort, I am giving up the drug trade and going full-time into illegals. That way, the federal boys won't be on my case as hard. I can get politicians and the big ranchers and farmers on my side."

"Boss, I like the way you are thinking. I too would love to give up the drug business. I can easily justify dealing in illegals, but not so with drugs. Let's make this trade in illegals work."

Carlos likes the idea more than he lets on, because he has ideas of becoming legitimate and making inroads into politics through the back door. He wants to be advisor to the big boys—judges, senators, and such. These are bold ambitions for a glorified drug pusher. Carlos knows that the killing of Ranson is essential, but he will hold off until absolutely necessary. It would be better yet just to kidnap him. *Yes, kidnap William J. Ranson and put him on ice*, he thinks. *If that is done, then no one has to die.* Killing can be so messy, yet it has solved a lot of problems, like that friend of Dan Mesa's Carlos killed many years ago. He was too smart for his own good. But Mesa has suspected that Carlos was responsible; Carlos knows that Mesa will one day come for him.

"Antonio, do you still have that friend in the ranger headquarters in Tucson? If you do, then find out who is escorting Ranson back from Richmond and let me know."

"Boss, I already know that," Antonio says. He seems anxious to please his boss. "The escort will be Ranger Dan Mesa, that gun slinging ranger who killed Jose a few weeks ago. What's up, boss?"

Carlos thinks it would be great to kidnap Ranson and kill Mesa at the same time.

"Antonio," he says, "put together a two-man team and have them kidnap Ranson as they leave the police station in Richmond. If Mesa is accidentally killed, that will be okay too. Maybe you are right. Maybe getting rid of Ranson is the thing to do."

"Carlos, I don't mean to tell you what to do," Antonio says, "but killing Dan Mesa is not in our best interest. He is a hard man to kill, and if he is only injured, we both know that, as soon as he finds out who is behind the kidnapping, he will come for us. I recommend we just kidnap Ranson and leave Mesa be."

"Antonio, Mesa is a threat to everything I am trying to do. I can't let him stand in the way. One of these days, he will figure out who had that ranger killed. When he does, he will destroy me unless I destroy him first. I want you to contact our friends in DC and have them take care of both Ranson and Mesa. Make sure there isn't a paper trail or any other trail back to us. Do you understand what I am asking?"

"Sí, patron, entiendo."

In Washington, DC, anything can be had or done if the money is right. Poverty in DC is a constant thing, and it spills over into Baltimore. There is an area of Baltimore named Cherry Hill that is primarily rundown projects and shabby stores. Most of the inhabitants have just given up on the dream of owning their own homes. They are just surviving from day to day. The sounds of police sirens, loud voices, and loud music are the texture of Cherry Hill.

Raymondo Sandoval and Jefferson Mitchell are products of this particular segment of humanity. They are two young men—one Puerto Rican and the other African American—who have reached the conclusion that the only way to escape to a better life is to take advantage of others. Both have police records and are convinced they are people to be reckoned with.

They receive a phone call from Vermenti Pellegrinni, another victim of circumstances as he refers to himself. He is well-known by the Council on Criminal Behavior and by the DC and Baltimore police departments. He is suspected of having killed at least two other members of the mob and the firebombing of at least five mob-owned nightclubs.

The phone call Mitchell and Sandoval receive orders them to go to Richmond, Virginia, and kill William J. Ranson and Ranger Daniel Mesa as they depart the Richmond Police Department. They are supplied with pictures of Ranson and Mesa; the mob has a plant in the Richmond Police Department.

Dan Mesa is deep in thought when the waitress asks, "Sir would you like a refill of coffee? Man, you were deep in thought. I had to ask you three times if you wanted more coffee. Your expression was one of torment. You will have to forgive me, because I am a psychology major at the university; sometimes I get carried away with my knowledge of psychology or lack thereof."

Mesa smiles and says, "No harm done. I was just thinking of a friend who was injured protecting me. How much do I owe you?"

When she tells him, he pays the bill and leaves hurriedly.

By coincidence Mitchell and Sandoval are seated in the same restaurant.

Mitchell stops the waitress and asks, "Who is that fellow who just left? He surely doesn't seem to be from these parts."

"He is an Arizona ranger," she says. "He is the one they did that feature about on Ted Koppel's *Nightline*. Remember that fight and shoot-out in Albuquerque, New Mexico, about two or three weeks ago?"

Mitchell and Sandoval gets up and leaves without comment. They goes outside and watches as the ranger returns to the police station. Mitchell gets into a tan and white Ford Explorer with Washington, DC, tags.

"Mitchell looks at Sandoval and says; "Well, I'll be damned. How lucky can we get? Let's pull over there in front of the station and look for a back entrance."

Sandoval and Mitchell find the rear entrance for detainees and position themselves for the hit.

Inside the police station, Ranson is removed from the holding cell and is prepped for departure. Dan Mesa puts on his body armor and accompanies Sergeant Hennessey to the waiting police car. As they exit the overhang, a shot rings out, and Sergeant Hennessey falls. Mesa grabs Hennessey's weapon and returns fire, hitting Mitchell twice once in the stomach and once in the leg. Sandoval fires and misses. Mesa fires hitting Sandoval in the arm. Sandoval escapes.

Mesa turns his attention to Hennessey and Ranson. Ranson appears to be dead; he received a bullet to his chest. Hennessey has taken one in the shoulder.

Immediately, police cover the area. Captain Emmett runs to Mesa and sees what has happened. He orders the area sealed for one square mile.

"Sergeant Mesa, what happened?"

Mesa spins around gun poised with a look of animal anger. His eyes are black and sparkling. Captain Emmett realizes that the man he is facing is more dangerous than anyone he has met recently.

Mesa suddenly relaxes, lowering his weapon and explains. "Sir, as we walked out, a shot rang out, and Sergeant Hennessey went down. I grabbed his weapon and returned fire, stopping one of the assassins. I hit the other one in the arm. When I looked at Ranson, he appeared to be dead. How did anyone know we were taking him back to Arizona?"

"Sergeant, let the medical team take care of Hennessey. We'll follow them to the hospital. I thank you for saving my sergeant's life. We'll talk to the assassin now, because it doesn't look as if he is going to make it."

Death is a sad sight, something that shouldn't happen but does much too often. Dan Mesa has seen too much of it and has been involved in too much of it.

Captain Emmett kneels down to talk to the assassin.

"Look, fella, you don't have long in this world, so tell us who sent you and for what reason."

With tears in his eyes, he says, "I don't want to die. *Please* help me."

We will, just tell me who sent you and why."

"We were sent by Vermenti Pellegrinni to kill Ranson and the ranger. He received his orders from someone in Arizona. Now help me . . ."

Mitchell's breathing slows done. His body starts to shudder and suddenly he dies.

Captain Emmett checks Mitchell's pulse and turns to Mesa shaking his head and says, "Someone wanted both of you bad.

Pellegrinni is well known on the East Coast as a member of the mob. He has a stable of trained assassins. Someone is paying big money to have you killed."

"But, captain, how did anyone know I was here? I have spent the last two weeks with my ex-wife and son in Baltimore. There must be a traitor in the rangers somewhere. I had better call my captain."

When the phone rings in Captain Johnson's office in Nogales, Sergeant Savalas answers the phone and calls for the captain.

"Captain Johnson, Sergeant Mesa is on the phone."

Captain Johnson picks up the phone.

"Hello, Dan, what's up?"

"Sir, Ranson was shot a few minutes ago as we were leaving the station. According to one of the assassins, the targets were Ranson and me. They were hired by some guy named Vermenti Pellegrinni out of DC, and his orders came from Arizona. Sir, how did anyone know I was here to pick up Ranson? We have a leak somewhere."

"Dan, are you okay? Is Ranson dead?"

"Yes, sir. Ranson is dead. And they shot a police sergeant I knew from my military days. I shot and killed one of the assassins, but before he died, he gave up the information I'm passing on to you."

"Okay, Dan. I will contact Colonel Grant and let him know. Get back here as soon as possible."

In Tucson, Carlos Meana has received news of the botched assassination and is raging.

"What have you people done, Antonio? Can't you carry out a simple mission? Those idiots in DC hired two amateurs to kill Ranson and Mesa. They got Ranson and shot a cop in Richmond. Mesa killed one of them, and the other was wounded. I don't know if talked before he died, but you can be sure of one thing: if he did talk, Sergeant Dan Mesa will be after us. I am going to take a long vacation in Switzerland, and I suggest, Antonio, that you visit your family on the reservation for a while. Contact DC and tell them to disappear for a while."

Lieutenant Colonel Garnett Williamson-Mesa, a doctor of pediatric surgery, is making rounds in the hospital at Johns Hopkins University when she hears the news of the shoot-out in Richmond.

"Dr. Mesa," a nurse says to her, "do you know a Sergeant Dan Mesa of the Arizona rangers?"

"Yes, I know Daniel Mesa. He is an Arizona ranger and a retired air force captain. Why are you asking?"

"Doctor, there was an attempted assassination of a prisoner and an Arizona ranger in Richmond, Virginia. The prisoner was killed and a police sergeant wounded. Apparently, the ranger shot and killed one assassin and wounded the other. The second assassin got away. According to the news, this same ranger was involved in a shooting in Albuquerque, New Mexico, where he shot and killed a fugitive who had robbed a Wells Fargo armored car and killed four guards, a policeman, and a city marshal."

Dr. Mesa turns pale and sits down, shaking. The nurse runs to her aid.

"Dr. Mesa, are you all right? Can I get you something?"

"No, Alma. I'm all right. I thought I'd left Dan Mesa and the rangers behind me. That man is so stubborn! He'd rather be a ranger and chasing criminals than be here. He could be a college professor or work for some big company, but he is still playing Cops and Robbers in Arizona and now in Virginia."

The news flashes on again, and the news correspondent is saying, "This is June Parks of ABC News with a follow-up on the shooting at a Richmond police station. I have Captain Emmett of the Richmond Police Department. Captain Emmett, what can you tell us about the shooting?"

Captain Emmett dreads talking to reporters, but June Parks is one he respects, so he decides to answer.

"June, we are still investigating the shooting. It seems as though the target was Sergeant Daniel Mesa of the Arizona rangers and a prisoner he was taking back to Arizona. We suspect it was a professional hit. The prisoner was killed, and one of our policemen was seriously injured. Thanks to Ranger Mesa, we were able to identify some of the people behind the shooting."

"Captain, this Ranger Mesa seems to always be in the line of fire. He was involved in a shooting in New Mexico a few weeks ago. How does this situation sit with you?"

"Sergeant Mesa is a good cop, and he did what any good cop would have done. He attempted to protect and serve."

"Thank you, Captain Emmett. This is June Parks for ABC News."

Nurse Alma Brown is very perceptive and can tell that there is more to this than meets the eye. She decides to ask another question.

"Dr. Mesa, is this ranger your brother?"

Dr. Mesa smiles and says, "No, Alma, he is not my brother. He is my ex-husband and Devlin's father. He was visiting us and was supposed to leave today. He never mentioned that he was here to extradite a prisoner. He probably didn't want to burden me with his problems. He is a good man, but he can be so stubborn."

As Dr. Mesa walks away, she mutters to herself, "Dan Mesa, you really piss me off at times. Why can't you just stay out of my life?"

At the police station, Ranger Mesa is facing the chief of police, a Colonel Matthew E. Lee. Colonel Lee is upset. His face is beet red and the veins in forehead is popping out. He stands toe to toe with Mesa.

"Ranger, I want you out of my city before this day is over," he tells Mesa. "I have a wounded policeman, a dead citizen, and a dead assassin. Just who the hell are you?"

Captain Emmett intervenes quickly saying, "Sir, allow me to close the door and I will explain a few things. Chief, first off, none of this is Sergeant Mesa's fault. Sergeant Hennessey's wounds are serious, but he will recover fully, and as for Ranson, he was injured. We just said that to keep the media from printing it in the paper. Ranger Mesa believes there is a leak in his unit and doesn't want the traitor to find out that Ranson is still alive, so we faked his death. He was shot, but the vest he was wearing protected him."

The chief looks at Emmett and Mesa and sits down and relaxes a bit.

"Okay, captain, that is a good idea. Maybe I did fly off the handle a little. So what is the next move?"

At this point, Ranger Mesa says, "Chief, we need to get Ranson back to Arizona without attracting any attention. I propose to take him out dressed as a policeman. Then I will have him change, and we'll depart your city. I know a man who will fly us back to Arizona in his private plane—that is, if he is still talking to me. He is my ex-father-in-law, Major Jonathan Horatio Williamson, retired.

"Major Jonathan Horatio Horn Blower Williamson is a World War II and Korean War veteran. He is one of the Tuskegee Airmen and a member of the Ninety-Ninth Pursuit Squadron. He saw limited action in World War II. When the war ended, he went back to college using the GI Bill and joined the army ROTC. After graduation, he went active in time to be sent to Korea as an infantry soldier.

"He received the Silver Star for bravery under fire. The North Koreans surrounded his unit, and he held out for a week without relief and finally fought his way out, losing half of his unit. He called in an air strike on himself rather than surrender but manage to escape before the strike hit. In another incident, Major Williamson single-handedly held off the enemy, killing one hundred fifty North Koreans and allowing his unit to successfully pull back. He later escaped without injury.

"That is my ex-father-in-law. Today he is retired and lives in Baltimore and spends part of the year in Douglas, Arizona. I love him and Nadia dearly, but due to the divorce they aren't exactly happy with me."

CHAPTER TWO

In Baltimore, Maryland, at the home of Garnett's father, the doorbell rings, and Major Williamson answers the door.

Upon seeing Dan, he says, "Hello son, how are you? It has been a while since we've talked. I see you've changed a bit."

"Yes sir. I guess this job makes one older and sadder. I visited Garnett and Devlin, and they are great. He is growing into a handsome, smart boy. I am so proud of him, and she has done a super job raising him.

"Dad, I need your help badly," Mesa continues. "I guess you heard about the shoot-out in Richmond. As you are aware, I was involved in it. It was a hit carried out by the mob, and it was meant for Ranson and me. Apparently, someone in Arizona is trying to take me out, and I know who it is. It's Carlos Meana and his mafia."

Jonathan motions for Dan follow him in to the house. Major Williamson is of medium height and build but presents a picture of a man who is used to giving orders. The house is a Brown Stone, one that was built in the early nineteen twenties. He motions for Dan to sit down. "You do know that is why Garnett moved back here. She wanted you to leave the rangers and that entire killing business. Didn't you get enough of it in Vietnam and the Gulf War? I still believe you should have moved here with her. You could have done well here. Okay, what can I do to help you?

"Sir, I can't fly Ranson back on a commercial flight. There is a traitor in our organization, and they are passing information to the mob. I need to get him back to Tucson without anyone knowing. We have him listed as having been killed, but he is still alive. Can you fly me back to Tucson or at least to Albuquerque? Then I can rent a car and drive the remainder of the way."

"Dan, it looks as if you have yourself a bit of a problem. Have you contacted your boss in Nogales?"

"Yes sir, but I am not sure where the leak is. It could be in Nogales or Tucson. I plan to call him at home tonight and tell him the whole story."

Nadia, Jonathan's wife and Dan's ex-mother-in-law walks through the front door. When she sees Dan, she smiles. She is a tall slender lady could easily grace the pages of a fashion magazine. She is also a respected doctor.

"Dan, it is good to see you," she says. "What brings the famous Dan Mesa to Baltimore and in uniform? I saw you on the news a few weeks ago. You were involved in that shoot-out in New Mexico. I am happy that you weren't hurt. You lead a dangerous life."

"Yes, ma'am, I do. But sometimes, it is just the way things are. I know you guys aren't too keen on me, but I need your help. I was telling Dad about my situation."

"Son, how about going back to Arizona traveling in a motor home?" Jonathan asks. "The way I see it, no one would expect you to be traveling in that manner."

"You know that is not a bad idea," Nadia says. "I have too much time on my hands. I'd like to go back to Arizona, and Jonathan, you owe me a vacation. I will need to call the hospital and let them know where I will be for the next couple of weeks. I am officially retired, but I still need to keep them informed of my location."

Nadia is a thoracic surgeon assigned to Baltimore General and a very intelligent lady, who was once a high school biology teacher. Rumor has it she once saved the life of a student by cutting a hole in his throat to allow him to breathe. After that, she decided to go to medical school and become a doctor. That was about thirty years and several operations ago. Garnett, her daughter, decided that becoming a doctor was okay after that.

Dan Mesa is aware that the proposal has merit and, after due consideration, decides to go with it.

"Dad, these people can be dangerous; I don't want the two of you exposed to danger. Also, Garnett would kill me if anything happened to you, and Devlin thinks the world of his granddad and grandmother."

Nadia smiles and comments that she would never do anything to put Jonathan or herself in danger. Then they get busy planning their trip to Nogales.

"How serious are Ranson's wounds?" Jonathan asks.

"Well, he was shot in the left shoulder and the bullet has been removed. He is conscious and talking. Mom, I know you are a doctor, but is this something you are qualified to handle?"

"Sure. A bullet wound of that nature is fairly simple medicine. You have to be alert to infection, as in any wound. But I'll carry everything needed to treat him, and that way, we won't have to stop and purchase anything, which will attract attention."

They decide to take the less obvious route of I-64 through West Virginia into Saint Louis, then Highway 67 south through Arkansas, I-40 to Flagstaff, and then I-15 to Tucson. Jonathan figures I-15 will be less traveled to Tucson than I-10, which goes straight to Tucson.

Dan calls Captain Johnson at his home to explain the situation.

In Nogales, it is a hot day with no rain in sight—a typical August evening. It seems that, when the mercury rises, tempers also rise.

The city police and the rangers are investigating two murders involving illegal aliens and one kidnapping. The kidnapping involves two of the local tribes, which brings in the rangers and the federals. Captain Johnson is fed up with the FBI. It is his opinion that the FBI doesn't know their butts from a hole in the ground."

Captain Johnson's phone rings, and Mesa is on the line.

"Sir, Sergeant Mesa here," Mesa says. "I am still in Virginia, and we have a problem. Ranson is not dead. I said that to throw our mole off. He has a slight flesh wound. Sir, I can't return Ranson by commercial plane or any other public transport; the risks are too great. My ex-father-in-law has agreed to drive us back in his motor home. It would be risky flying back to Tucson. I believe someone is watching me and knows everything I'm doing, and that is why I called you at home and not at work. I propose that I drive him back. What do you think about it?"

Captain Johnson is quiet for a while before saying, "I don't like it. I don't like having you on the road alone with a fugitive. If something happens out there, you don't have anyone to back you up."

"Sir, I believe I have a solution," Mesa says. "I have a friend in the FBI in Washington, DC. He will be able to do something. I will call you back."

Mesa turns to Jonathan and says, "Dad, how about going with me to the FBI building to see a friend? He is an old air force buddy."

He agrees, so they leave for Washington. Dan Mesa is anxious about seeing his old friend. Scotty Ortiz is an ex-air force chief master sergeant who left the air force and joined the FBI. He is a very secretive sort of fellow who knows where the bones are buried, and he and Dan have been friends for a lot of years.

The Hoover building is located at 935 Pennsylvania Avenue in close proximity to the Capitol Building. Jonathan and Dan arrive at the entrance and ask to speak to Agent Scott Ortiz. Mesa identifies himself as an Arizona ranger.

The phone rings in a spacious office where Ortiz is working.

"Special Agent Ortiz speaking. How can I help?"

"Scotty, Dan Mesa here. How the heck are you?"

Scotty jumps up from his chair, excited, and yells, "Dan Mesa, where the heck are you?"

"I am downstairs with the guard, and I need you to come down and get us. Can you do that or send someone down for us?"

Scotty is beaming.

"I will send someone down for you right now," he says. He hangs up and turns to his assistant. "Annette, will you please go down to the guard station and escort Ranger Dan Mesa and his guest upstairs?" He is an old friend.

"Is he a Texas ranger?" Annette asks.

"No, wrong state. He is an Arizona ranger and darned proud of it. I haven't seen.him since I left the air force. He was a captain in the military police. When he retired, he became a ranger. I've kept up with him over the years, and he is something as a ranger. Do you remember that incident in Albuquerque last month? Well, that ranger was Dan Mesa, my dearest friend? Now, please hurry down and escort them up."

Annette arrives at the guard station and sees two men. One is dressed in a sports jacket and tie, but the other one stands out. He is dressed in jeans, a green western shirt with a brown western tie, brown boots, and a gray western hat. There is a star on his chest. He is a small man as far as size goes but a big man in his demeanor.

"Ranger Mesa, I presume," she says.

"Yes, I am Dan Mesa, and this is my father-in-law, Jonathan Williamson."

"Agent Ortiz sent me down to escort you to his office, so please follow me."

When they arrive on the fifth floor, all eyes are on the cowboy. Annette escorts them to Scotty's office. Annette sits down and is delighted to watch two old friend greet each other.

"Daniel Mesa, how the hell are you, old buddy? It has been a few years since we have seen each other."

"Scotty, it is good to see you," Dan says. "I try to keep up with you, but man, you are constantly moving and changing residences. Once you were in San Antonio, then Kansas City, and the next thing I know, you are in DC with the big boys. Oh, let me introduce you to my father-in-law, Jonathan Horatio Williamson."

Scotty beams and says, "Sir, I have heard about you all my life. My father was in the Korean War and always talked about 'Jonathan Horatio Williamson' and your exploits at Kunsan and Pusan. He says you saved the day."

"Please express my thanks to your father," Jonathan says, smiling. "All of us were heroes that day."

Scotty turns to Dan.

"Now, what brings you from Arizona to DC?" he asks. "I kept up with you too. Man, that was some performance in Albuquerque a few weeks ago. You know something? I'd hate to piss you off. You could be a force to reckon with."

"Scotty, I need your help. I was sent to escort a prisoner who is a witness in a murder trial back to Tucson. The bad guys found out about it and have already tried to kill him and me. There is a traitor somewhere in the rangers in Tucson, and they know my every move. If I fly in, they will be waiting for me, so I have decided to drive back. Dad has agreed to drive us back in his RV, and I need you to ride shotgun with me. I know what you can do with those hands and feet of yours. I have seen you in action, and you were the European champion. I don't want to put Dad and Nadia at risk, so will you help?"

"Dan, I need a break from this crazy town," Scotty says, "so you have yourself a shotgun rider. Now, tell me what I am getting myself into."

Mesa explains the details to Scotty while Jonathan listens.

Finally, Jonathan says, "Dan, what have you gotten yourself into? This sounds like mafia-type stuff. The rangers are definitely keeping you busy these days. You just finished that situation with Jackson down in New Mexico. When do you get a break?"

"Well, Dad, according to the captain I have had my break with this trip. He told me this was just a simple trip without any problems. He will owe me big-time for this. Scotty, those would be assassins came from the Cherry Hill area of Baltimore City. I'd like to go to that area and find out exactly who those guys really are. Can we do that?"

Scotty ponders for a moment before saying, "Dan, Cherry Hill is a dangerous area; you never know what will happen there. We could wind up fighting our way out. Are you sure you want to do that?"

"Scotty, I have been fighting since I was a kid. When do we start?"

Jonathan looks at Dan and Scotty and comments, "You two are crazy. Take me home before you two start on your adventure. I am too old to be taking part in that type of activity. I hope you fellows will be extremely careful."

Mesa and Ortiz take Jonathan back to Baltimore and proceed to Cherry Hill. They arrive at 17452 Emory Lane, the home of Maria Sandoval, the mother of Raymondo Sandoval. They sit and observe for thirty minutes, and no one arrives or departs.

Ortiz slowly gets out of the car, and Mesa follows.

"Dan, let me do the talking. Sometimes federal cops can get more done."

Ortiz knocks on the door and waits as a very beautiful, middle-aged lady answers the door.

"Good day, señora. I am Agent Scott Ortiz of the FBI, and I am looking for the mother of Raymondo Sandoval."

"That will be my sister Maria," she says. "I am Jodia Sandoval. I will get Maria. If you are the FBI, then who are you?" she asks, pointing at Mesa.

Mesa realizes she is talking to him.

"I am Sergeant Daniel Mesa of the Arizona rangers," he says.

The lady departs and returns with Maria Sandoval. Ortiz smiles and introduces himself.

"Señora, I am Scott Ortiz of the FBI, and I am looking for Raymondo Sandoval, your son. He was involved in a shooting in which a prisoner was killed and a policeman injured. He was traveling with Jefferson Mitchell. Mitchell is dead, and Raymondo could wind up dead as well unless he gives himself up."

Maria looks at Scott and says, "Señor, I haven't seen my son since two days ago, and he was talking about all the money he would have. I suspect Raymondo is in big trouble and I told him so, but he only smiles and says he is doing it to get money for the family. I don't need that kind of money, and I told him that if he did bad things he shouldn't come home ever again. He's not home."

"Mrs. Sandoval, Raymondo and Jefferson are working for the mafia, and that is very bad business, so please be careful. If you have any problems please call me at any time. Here is my phone number at work and my cell number. If Raymondo calls, tell him I came by and that he is in serious trouble. Thanks for talking with us and good-bye."

"Jodi turns to Maria and says, "That Scott is a handsome fellow but that ranger guy has the look of the Lobo, the hunter. He is a very dangerous man but a good man I believe. He would be good for you but not so good for Raymondo. We must keep them apart."

"Jodi, I don't need a man in my life. I had one and he was totally useless and I have been alone for a long time and I am probably not so good company for such a man as the ranger. He is very handsome but he is not the "playboy" type. He is a man who has seen much trouble and heartbreak I think."

Mesa and Ortiz return to Jonathan's house.

Meanwhile, Raymondo has contacted Pellegrinni and is telling him what has happened.

In Vermenti's office, Raymondo says, "Mr. Pellegrinni, we shot Ranson, but in doing it Mitchell was killed, and we accidentally shot and injured a policeman. That ranger fellow is hell on wheels. He killed Mitchell and came close to killing me. He shot the heel off my boots. I don't want to tangle with him again."

Pellegrinni laughs and says, "You completed the assignment, and now I want you to disappear for a while. I don't want the police to find you, so here is the money I promised you and Mitchell. He isn't here to claim his part, so it goes to you. I suggest you send some of it to his mother as a gesture of caring. He was your friend."

"I believe I will visit Puerto Rico for a while. Mom has family there. Thanks, Mr. Pellegrinni. If you need me again, just ask."

Raymondo is a member of the mafia and one of the bad boys who will wind up with a bullet in his brain or blown to bits. So goes the life of a hit man. He takes his money and goes straight to the airport to take a fight to San Juan Puerto Rico.

The phone rings in Tucson and Carlos answers.

"This is Carlos."

"Carlos, your problem with Ranson has been taken care of; however, you are aware that one hand washes the other, so we may one day ask a favor of your organization."

"Yes, I am aware, and that will not be a problem. Please express my appreciation to your company for helping us out in our time of need."

Antonio is listening in and asks Carlos after he hangs up, "Boss, does that mean we are on the hook for them?"

"No, it only means that, one day, we may have to return the favor. The main thing is that Ranson is dead and can't testify against me."

Chapter Three

Lieutenant Alana Osborne of the rangers has been discharged from the hospital and is at home. She is a friend of Dan Mesa who was injured in a gunfight. Her sight has returned but only in one eye, the right eye. Doctor Vansant, the optometrist, is briefing her and her mother.

"Alana, although your sight has returned in the right eye, it may not be permanent. I am giving you a prescription for a solution to put into your eyes twice each day. It will cause temporarily blindness for about five minutes, and then your sight will return. You will be able to function as normal. One day, you will lose sight in the right eye. Do you have any questions?"

"At least I have sight for now," Alana says, smiling. "How long before I lose sight in my right eye?"

"That is something I don't know. I do believe you will get some sight back in your left eye as well."

"Doctor, I can see some light right now."

Dr. Vansant beams and says, "Lieutenant, you continue to amaze me. You have a desire to recover greater than anyone does. What is the motivation?"

"There is this certain ranger, named Dan Mesa, who is the source of this great desire," her mother, Matilda, says.

"Oh, don't pay her any attention, doctor," Alana says.

Dr. Vansant looks puzzled and asks, "Who is this Dan Mesa?"

"He is a very close friend of ours and someone Alana has very strong feelings for," her mother says. "He is the one who came in with her the night she was injured. She had a temporary loss of her memory and couldn't remember him when she came out of the coma. She regained her memory but lost her sight, so she hasn't told him about any of this and he doesn't know she has regained her memory."

Vansant shakes his head and says, "I understand why you did what you did, but he deserves the right to know." He pauses and snaps his finger saying, "Oh my goodness! He is that fellow they had on the news that was involved in that shoot-out in Albuquerque with Jose Jackson. That is the Dan Mesa you are speaking of?"

"Yes, doctor. He is the one and only Sergeant Daniel Mesa. He is someone who deserves some happiness after what he has been through. I'd rather lose him than to be a burden to him."

"Alana, don't you believe he has the right to make that decision? He sounds like the kind of fellow who'd never give you up if he knew the circumstances. Give him a chance to decide," Dr. Vansant says. "I must make my rounds, but I will check in later today."

After the door closes, Matilda says, "Honey, you have to decide what is best for you. No one can tell you what the best thing is. Whatever you decide, I will be here for you."

"Mom, I love him dearly, and one day, I will call him and tell him. I just don't know how to face him now."

In Amado, Sonia is preparing for work when she suddenly sees Dan's picture. It all comes back and settles on her shoulder like a weight. She looks at her reflection in the mirror and sees a beautiful, sad face, one that should be happy but isn't. She remembers the day he left and how sad his face was and tears begin to fall. She says to herself, *I love him so very much, and I am afraid to let him know*. In her mind, she knows there has to be a middle ground where they can meet and be happy. It is just a matter of finding it.

At Jonathan's house in Baltimore, Dan is making preparations for the trip to Arizona. Nadia has packed all the food requirements, and Jonathan adds a large bottle of Brandy. As an afterthought he packs his old assault rifle with extra ammunition.

"Jonathan, why are you taking that old thing?" Nadia asks.

Jonathan smiles and says, "Honey, I don't know what we will face, but I plan to be prepared. Whatever happens, I want you to be safe. I haven't spent nearly enough time with you. I want to be a very old man and still madly in love with you."

At that moment, Garnett walks in. She turns and walks right into Dan Mesa. She stammers, and he just smiles.

"I understand," he says and turns and walks away.

Garnett suddenly remembers the good times they had together. She remembers days and nights in the Bahamas, a boat cruise in Turkey, a dinner in Belgium, and other pleasant times. Then she recalls the nights and days she spent alone while he was away in Greece, Turkey, Greenland, Saudi, or some other forgotten place. Maybe things could have been different, but she knows Daniel Mesa better than anyone does, and she knows how eccentric he can be and how he doesn't fit into any neat category. Dan Mesa is an enigma. Somewhere deep down in the recesses of her soul, she loves him dearly, but she will never take him back. He will always be a part of her life, though, because every time she looks at Devlin, she sees Dan.

Nadia watches Dan as he walks away and sees him wipe his eyes. His usual erect pose has sagged a little, and she knows he is slowly falling apart. She follows him outside, and as he turns toward her, he smiles that Mesa crooked smile and says, "I guess I must have gotten some trash into my eye."

"Dan, you don't have to pretend with me. I know how much she means to you and how it haunts you. You need to find someone to belong to. It is hard for you to let go of her, I know. Son, some things can't be fixed. I love you as if you were my blood, and I feel your pain. Jonathan knows this isn't your doing. He just loves her more than anyone except me."

Dan's face shows all the hurt and pain he has faced these past few years. Suddenly, he feels very cold and alone.

"Mom, I just don't know how to face life without her and Devlin," he says slowly. "I met two women I like in Arizona. One saw me kill a man in self-defense and couldn't handle it. Her husband was a policeman who was killed in the line of duty. The other one is a ranger who was accidentally shot when we were having dinner by two assassins sent to kill me by Jose Guittierrez-Jackson's family. She lost her memory and doesn't remember me and now thinks I am a trigger-happy cop. I am running out of places to go and people to go to. I only want to be happy with someone who wants me."

"Dan, you have paid a heavy price in your life—Vietnam, the Persian Gulf, and twenty years of military life—and it has left you with very little in the way of tangible items. You do have a lot in that you are making a difference as a ranger and you love it. Don't give up on life and love. It is out there somewhere waiting for you. You just have to keep your eyes open. Devlin thinks you are the greatest; you are his idol. He tells everyone about his dad, the ranger."

Dan slowly smiles and says, "Thanks, Mom, for being there and caring about me. You don't know how much it has meant to me."

"Dan, how do you see your life in the future? Have you looked that far ahead?"

"Mom, I have been living from day to day these last few years. I believe my life is too difficult to look at it in the light. My private life is so difficult until I try not to look at it too closely. I don't have any plans for marriage right now. I want to see Devlin grow up and turn into a handsome, good young man."

Scotty walks out then and says, "Mr. Williamson is ready to load up the RV."

Jonathan asks Dan when and where they will pick up Ranson.

"Dad, we will have to go back to Richmond and pick him up at the police station in Richmond. They are holding him there under an alias."

Garnett comes out with Devlin to say good-bye.

Devlin looks at his dad and says, "Dad, be careful and take care of Grandmother and Granddad."

"I will, son. You take care of your mother for me and be a good boy. I love you dearly. Give me hug. Now, you hug Mom for me and tell her I love her. Good-bye, Garnett."

She looks at Dan and just waves good-bye.

When the RV has been loaded, they proceed on their way. The trip to Richmond is uneventful. Upon arriving at the police station, Dan checks in with Captain Emmett.

"Captain, these are the plans for transporting Ranson back to Tucson," he says. "We will travel by RV, and the license number is ML371 Maryland. It is registered to Jonathan Horatio Williamson of 3234 Sequoia Boulevard, Baltimore, Maryland.

"We will travel on I-85 south until it meets with I-64, continue west on I-64 until it meets with I-40, and continue on I-40 to Flagstaff. In Flagstaff, we will take I-15 to Tucson, and that is the end of the line. I have a feeling that reaching the end of the line is going to be difficult. I don't believe we have fooled them at all. The leak is still there, and we don't know who it is."

Captain Emmett scratches his head and says, "Ranger, I agree. You and Agent Ortiz had better be damned careful. You will most certainly be on your own. I wish I could help you, but there isn't anything I can do except wish you well. Do you have all the equipment you need? Do you have body armor and plenty of ammo?"

"Yes sir, we are heavily armed, and we have enough ammo to start our own war. I just hope we don't have to use it. I don't trust Ranson. He does know that we are the only things saving him from death, so hopefully he will play along with us. Jonathan is an old soldier, and he knows how to take care of himself. The only flaw is Nadia, and she will not leave Jonathan. They have been married for fifty-two years; they are inseparable. She is also a doctor, so she just might come in handy if someone is injured. Before this is over, I have a feeling we are going to need her skills. Captain, if you ever get down to Nogales, look me up. Please say good-bye to Sergeant Hennessey for me."

Sergeant Mesa climbs into the RV and begins what will be a hair-raising trip to Tucson, Arizona.

In Yuma, Alana is adjusting to being partially blind. Her sight is slowly returning, and she goes in to work each day. Matilda drives her to work and picks her up each evening. Major McMasters has purchased a special keyboard with large letters just for her.

He sticks his head into the room and says, "How is my favorite lieutenant?"

"Good morning, sir," she says. "I am well and working on some case files I left unfinished. I just want to say thanks for keeping me on as a ranger. I would be lost without you guys."

"Lieutenant, you are a good cop. With or without your sight, you are one of the best. You and Dan Mesa have instincts like no one I know. Have you spoken to him since he left? I don't mean to pry into your affairs, but Alana you are a good friend, and Lucy and I worry about you. You are a like a little sister to me."

"Major, thanks for caring. Tell Lucy I am well and I will see her this weekend. As for Dan, no I haven't spoken to him. He doesn't know I have regained my memory. I said some awful things to him when he was here. I called him a trigger-happy cop. Major, when he left, he was so close to falling apart. He killed a man who was once his best friend, and the girl he loved let him go because he killed a man who was trying to kill him in her presence. His wife left him after almost twenty years of marriage. He has had a hard time, and I don't want to mess up his life any more than necessary."

"Alana, I have known men like Dan Mesa before. They have a hard exterior, but inside they suffer a lot. They are the ones who save us from ourselves. They do the things no one else can do. They usually die alone on some battlefield with just God and their memories. It is amazing that men like them have close relationships with God. They really are good men for the most part. Don't let Dan become one of those men. He deserves better. He has given a lot to this country and has gotten very little back," he says. "Well, I have to go and call the colonel, something about a prisoner being transported back from Virginia by one of the rangers. I'll look in on you later."

Alana feels the weight of the world on her shoulders. She knows that everything the major has said is true, but how does she rectify all that is wrong? She has dreams about this ranger and can't get him out of her mind, but still she can't convince herself to call him.

Back at the ranch Matilda is thinking of the lonesome handsome ranger also. She wonders what she would do if she were in Alana's position. Would she call him and tell him how much she loved him and ask him to come back? Suddenly, she picks up the phone and dials his cellular number.

Jonathan is driving west on I-85 when the phone rings.

"Dan, your phone is ringing."

Dan Mesa picks up the phone.

"Sergeant Mesa here."

"Dan, this is Matilda calling. Where are you and what are you doing?"

"Hello, Mrs. Osborne. Is everything okay? How is Alana? Is something wrong?"

"No, Dan everything is okay. Alana is recovering and is doing fine. She has returned to work on limited duty. Dan, I have some good news. Alana has regained her memory, but she is partially blind in one eye and may lose her sight altogether. She doesn't know that I am calling you, so please don't let her know I called. She is afraid to call you because of how she acted when you were here. She also doesn't want you to know she is blind."

"Mrs. Osborne, you don't need to worry. I will never let her know that you told me. I am returning from a long trip and won't be home for a while. I am on an assignment and can't talk about it on this phone. When we stop for the night, I will call you if possible. Better yet, call Captain Johnson, and he will explain. Take care of Alana for me. One of these days, if all goes well, I'll show up at your door."

"Dan Mesa, you are welcome at this house at any time. You are missed here. Take care of yourself. That last case of yours scared me to death. Don't become a dead hero. I like you the way you are. Good-bye."

After he hangs up, Nadia asks, "Dan is everything okay? Who is Mrs. Osborne?"

Jonathan says, "Nadia, don't be nosy. Stay out of the man's business."

"Jonathan, I am not being nosy just curious. So, Dan, who is Alana?"

Dan Mesa smiles.

"Mom, she is a friend who was shot by an assassin sent to kill me. She took a bullet meant for me. Matilda Osborne is her mother. Alana is the lady I spoke to you about. She lost her memory due to the bullet wound to her head. She didn't remember me when she regained consciousness. She referred to me as a trigger-happy cop. Her mom just informed me she has regained her memory but is partially blind in one eye and may lose her sight completely. Alana doesn't want me to know any of this. Mrs. Osborne is very concerned about Alana and about me too, I guess."

Nadia is aware of Mesa's inner turmoil. She smiles and says, "Son it will all work out for you. Just trust in God and keep doing what is right. Jonathan, as you can see, I am only being a concerned friend."

"Nadia, the world needs more people like you. It would be a much better place to live. That is why I love you so much, my dear."

Agent Ortiz just smiles at Dan.

"Dan," he says, "you are a most fortunate man. Always remember that it is a fortunate man who has friends who worry about him."

The motley crew continues down the road.

Meanwhile, back in Tucson, Carlos Meana is in conference with his people.

"Amigos, I have news that Ranson is not dead and Ranger Daniel Mesa is transporting him back to Tucson. We know the route he is taking and that he is traveling by personal vehicle, an RV. Antonio, I want you to put together a group you can trust to get the job done. I want you to lead them and take care of Ranson and Ranger Daniel Mesa. I want Mesa dead."

Juan Reynosa, a member of Carlos' group, says, "Señor Meana, killing Ranson is not a problem, but killing a ranger is a different story and especially Ranger Mesa. Mesa is a hard kill, and if we miss, you can be assured he will hunt us and kill us one by one. I want no part of killing Ranger Mesa."

Carlos is angry because of Juan's remarks but knows that the others present feel the same. "Do I have cowards working with me? Must I do everything myself?"

"Carlos," Antonio says, "we are not afraid of Dan Mesa, but why ask for trouble we don't need? You said yourself, you want to present a much cleaner and more positive image. Killing Mesa will work against everything you want to accomplish."

"Okay, Antonio, we'll table that for now. Just kill or kidnap Ranson. Call your contact at ranger headquarters and find out for sure what route they are taking back to Tucson.

In Tucson, a call is put through to Colonel Grant's office and his secretary answers.

"Ranger headquarters, Maria speaking."

"Maria, this is Antonio, and I need to know the route Ranger Mesa is taking to bring Ranson back to Tucson."

"Antonio, I can't give you that information! If they find out I told you, they would send me to jail. I have already done too much. I am afraid all the time now. I can't do what you ask."

"Listen to me, Maria, either you tell me what I want to know or I will fix it so your boss will find out everything. Señorita, what will it be?"

"Antonio, I thought you cared about me, but all you want is information. This is the last time I do anything for you. Your threats will not scare me anymore. Ranger Mesa is leaving Virginia via I-85. He will connect to I-64 and then to I-40. That is all I know. Don't ever call me again."

Antonio smiles to himself and thinks, *It really doesn't matter, because it is time for me to find a new job. Carlos is becoming overly ambitious, and it could spell his doom.*

In Wheeling, West Virginia, the group stops for food and to stretch.

Dan Mesa turns to Ransom and says, "You are safe traveling with us as long as you remember someone has already tried to kill you and your best bet is to do as I say so you can live to become an old man. I will not hesitate to shoot you if you try to escape or if you attempt to harm or put my friends in danger. Do you understand me?"

Ranson knows Mesa will do exactly as he has said and nods his head in agreement. "Ranger, I have no desire to die," he says. "Believe me, I will follow your orders to the letter."

They stopped at the Cracker Barrel Restaurant. Now they go inside to eat. As always, Ranger Mesa is alert and ready, because he knows it only takes one minute of carelessness to get killed. He is consciously observing every person he sees—man, woman, or child. He asks for a table for five away from the window. He knows all eyes are on him because he is armed and wearing a badge. They are an interesting lot—one white male, a Hispanic male, a black female, and two black males. Dan sits so he can observe every approach.

Scott Ortiz is watching Mesa's every move and smiles to himself, thinking, he hasn't changed one bit. If anything, he is more watchful and alert. I know why they sent him; he is the right person for this job. He is a dying breed, and that is a shame. The world needs more people like him. I only wish I could bring happiness to my old friend's life. He deserves to be happy after all he has done for this country and its people.

The waitress approaches and asks for their order. Nadia orders a chef's salad, and Jonathan orders the fried chicken dinner. Ranson orders a steak, and Scott orders a burger. Dan orders soup, a cheese sandwich, and iced tea. The conversation between everyone is is lively and slowly everyone returns to their meal.

As is always the situation, though, someone has to start something.

"Hey you over there, what kind of lawman are you?" Mesa turns slowly and looks at the man with eyes that burn like fire. The man suddenly realizes he is facing someone who could be very dangerous, so he changes his tactic and says, "Mister, I don't mean any harm; it's just that I haven't seen a Texas ranger up close before."

"Mister, I am not from Texas. I'm from Arizona, and I'm an Arizona ranger. Texas rangers wear a silver star and we wear a gold star."

Mesa turns around and continues his conversation at the table.

Jonathan asks, "Son, do things like that happen to you often? It seems as if you attract trouble wherever you go."

Agent Ortiz has known Dan Mesa longer than anyone at the table and knows how sensitive Mesa can be when he is questioned in such a manner. He responds in a friendly off-hand way, saying, "Oh, he has been like that since the first time I met him. We have known each other for more than thirty years. He is like a lightning rod when it comes to trouble. Dan walks in to a bar and every tough guy in the place wants to try him. I guess that is why he doesn't go to bars very often, unless he is with a lady. I do believe women soften him up. Garnett was always able to soften him up and calm him down."

Mesa smiles and drinks his coffee quietly. He excuses himself to go to the restroom.

When he leaves, Nadia says, "I have known Dan for twenty years, and I realize I really don't know him at all. Before he became a ranger, he smiled more, and now I only see him smile when he is with Devlin. He is too serious. But being a ranger is really what he is all about. It suits his personality to a T. I only wish he could find happiness with someone. He and Garnett belong together, and I know he loves her dearly and she loves him, although she doesn't want to admit it. Scotty, you have known Dan longer than Jonathan and I. Can you tell us what makes him tick?"

"Mrs. Williamson, Dan Mesa is an enigma. I love him like a brother, and yet he only allows me to get so close. He is the best friend I've ever had. He'd walk through hell for a friend and never complain. When we were younger and thought we owned the world, we fought our way out of a lot of bad places. As he got older, he changed into the responsible and dependable person you see now. He was never reckless though. I don't know what drove him and Garnett apart, although I suspect it was due to his love of the West. I do know she hates the West, and he hates the East."

Dan returns and sits down and their meals are served. After the meal, he pays the bill, and all depart. Mesa's sixth sense kicks in;

he gets that old familiar feeling. He knows someone is watching them.

He turns to Jonathan and says, "Dad, we are being watched. Let's hurry and depart."

"Son, I have that same feeling. It is as if I am back in Korea. I always knew when an attack was coming, and I feel it now. We will be hit before long. Scotty, look under your seat and you'll find an old Thompson machine gun and three magazines of ammo."

Ranson looks at each one of them and shakes his head and says, "Meana is crazy if he attacks you people. I wouldn't attack you for all the money in the world. Carlos was always a little crazy. He only attacks if he is sure he can win. Someone has told him something that makes him believe he has the upper hand. However, don't ever underestimate Carlos Meana. He is a very treacherous and dangerous man."

Nadia looks at Jonathan and smiles.

"I love you, honey, so don't let anything happen to you or me."

The group continues down I-64, finally reaching Saint Louis, Missouri, and connecting with Highway 67 south to take them through southern Missouri and northern Arkansas and into Little Rock. There they will change to I-40.

It has been three days since they left Richmond, and they have had no trouble yet. Everyone is becoming edgy, because they know it is coming. It is only a matter of time. Dan sees a rest stop and decides to stop. He pulls into the rest stop and turns the wheel over to Jonathan.

"They are behind us," he said, "so we'd better face them here."

Mesa and Scotty go outside to meet the trouble. Scotty carries the Thompson, and Mesa carries two side arms, a 9-mm, and a .357 magnum. Two cars pull in and immediately stop, assessing the situation. Slowly, they ease forward, and Mesa and Scott step out to meet them.

The shooting starts, and when the smoke clears, one car is on fire and the other is shot full of holes. Neither Ortiz nor Mesa is scratched. They walk ahead and stop to examine each man. After close examination, they find that no one is dead, but all of the men are banged up severely.

"Who is in charge of this group? You'd better speak up now."

A tall lanky gentleman says, "I am Peter Whitfield, and I am in charge. What do you want?"

"I am Ranger Dan Mesa of the Arizona rangers, and you just committed a felony by attacking and trying to kill a law enforcement officer. However, you are not the ones I want. I want the crowd in Washington, DC, and the ones in Tucson. I suggest you go back to whoever hired you and tell them you weren't up to the job. If I see you again, I will shoot you on sight. There isn't anything this side of hell that will stop me. Now turn this hunk of junk around and get out of here."

As the assassins turn to leave, one tries his hand and reaches for a gun, suddenly the calm is shattered by gunfire again. Mesa walks into the melee steadily shooting, killing one, and seriously injuring another.

"Is there another of you who'd like to try his hand at killing me?"

An Oriental fellow steps out and says, "I don't believe you are as tough as they say you are, and I intend to prove it. Let's see how tough you really are."

He takes a karate stance. Mesa tosses his weapons to Scott, loosens his tie, and takes it off. They circle each other, and his opponent tries a roundhouse kick. Mesa steps in and blocks the kick. He grabs his opponent's ankle and twists hard, breaking the ankle. In one motion, he kicks the man in the testicles and smashes his knee with short, sharp, breaking kick. He drops the man's leg and steps away, reaching for his gun and strapping it on. He turns and walks away.

He and Scott load into the motor home and drive away. No one says a word. As Jonathan drives, slowly everyone relaxes. Nadia makes coffee and pours brandy into Dan's coffee. She turns toward him, and he notices a tear in her eye. He gets up and takes the steering wheel, telling Jonathan to look after Nadia.

He drives down the highway as solemn as a church mouse.

Scott turns to Dan and says, "You really are hell on wheels. When did you learn karate?"

"Scotty, I never learned it. What I know, I picked up from watching you and observing others. I hate fighting, but when I have to fight, I fight to win, and I won't be merciful. This is being forced upon me; I will do what is necessary to accomplish my job."

"Dan, I have known you for over thirty years, and as I said to Mr. Williamson, I really don't know anything about you."

Dan turns toward Scott and smiles meekly.

"Okay, buddy," he says, "what you want to know?"

Scott looks at him and smiles, saying, "Go to hell."

Suddenly, the tension eases.

"Dan," Nadia says, "at that rest stop when they attacked, weren't you afraid? I watched you, and every move you made was as if you had rehearsed everything ahead of time. Son, you are not ten feet tall and bulletproof. You've been shot once, and from what you told me, there is a lady in Yuma who was shot and almost killed in your presence. How do you do what you do? Has life made you so hard? I love you like you are my son, and Jonathan feels the same, but we find that we don't know you at all."

Jonathan is watching Mesa as Nadia speaks and sees how each word is like a lightning bolt to his soul. He knows the pain Dan Mesa is feeling. He knows it quite well, having been there himself, but that is another story.

"Mom, I am a ranger. That is who I am and what I am. I am good at what I do, and I like what I do. I don't intentionally make myself a target. I want to live to be an old man and to see Devlin have children. I love that boy dearly, and I don't plan to get myself killed. You and Dad are my responsibility, and I won't let anyone hurt you. Ranson is my responsibility, and I plan to get him to Tucson in one piece. Speaking of Tucson, I should call Captain Johnson and let him know what happened."

The phone rings at ranger headquarters in Nogales.

"Ranger Headquarters, Sergeant Savalas speaking."

"Savalas, Mesa here. May I speak to the captain?"

Savalas sticks his head in at the captain's door and says, "Sir, Sergeant Mesa is on the phone and wants to speak to you."

Captain Johnson takes the phone and says, "Dan, how are things and where are you?"

"Sir, we are heading west on I-40 in Texarkana, Arkansas. We stopped at a rest stop and were attacked by what I assume to be assassins sent by Carlos Meana. We are unhurt, but there is a traitor in the rangers either there in Nogales or at the colonel's office in Tucson. How else would they know what direction we are going and what highway we are taking? I am afraid I had to use some deadly force on the attackers. One was killed; the others are only banged up."

"Sergeant, do whatever you have to do to protect the prisoner and yourself. I will notify the colonel, and he can notify the Arkansas state police. I know we ask a lot of you, Sergeant Mesa, and this one is above and beyond. I want you to know that it is appreciated. Oh yes, the colonel sent down a commendation for the work you did in apprehending Jackson. Call me at home later on tonight and tell me what route you are taking."

"Thanks, captain," Mesa says. "Sir, have you heard anything from Sonia?"

"No, Dan, nothing of late."

"Thanks, sir."

When Dan terminates the call, he turns to Jonathan and says, "Dad, when we get to Dallas, we are going to change directions. We will take I-35 south to San Antonio and then take I-10 west to Tucson."

"Son, about this traitor in your organization, do you have any idea who it may be?"

"Dad, I know everyone in Nogales; I don't believe the leak is there. I believe it is in Tucson at the colonel's office. The person who is leaking the information has to have access to everything we do. I will call Captain Johnson tonight and bounce it off of him."

In Amado, Sonia is preparing for work when the phone rings. It is Captain Johnson.

"Hello, Miss Perdenales, this is Captain Johnson of the rangers calling. How are you doing?"

"Captain, I am well, and I hope all is well with you. Has something happened to Dan?"

"No, Dan is okay. He is on assignment to Virginia and should be returning within a few days. He asked me if I had heard from you. He still cares about you, you know."

Sonia works to regain her composure and says, "I know he does. Please tell him I care about him."

"Is that all you want me to tell him? I thought that surely you wanted me to tell him you love him."

"Captain, I am still trying to fit Dan into my life. I don't want to lie to him and make promises I can't keep. He deserves better than that from me. As you know, he has been through a lot. I know I am putting him through a lot now, but at least he knows I am not leading him on."

"Sonia, I guess that is why I am concerned about seeing the two of you together. He needs you, and believe it or not, you need him. It is up to you if you want to make it a couple. Take care. I will be checking on you again soon."

They hang up the phone. Sonia hurriedly gets dressed and prepares to leave for work. She notices a black Chevy Camaro following her at a distance. Being a cautious person, she speeds up and calls ahead to the Cow Palace and tells them she is being followed. She arrives at the Cow Palace, and the Camaro continues down the road.

The driver of the Camaro turns around and drives back to the Cow Palace, stopping briefly, possibly to records Sonia's license number. Sonia watches from inside and makes a note to call Captain Johnson of the rangers.

She turns to Sylvia Animas and says, "Sylvia, I believe someone is following me. That black car stopped, and the driver took down my tag numbers. What should I do?"

"If I were you I would call that ranger fellow and tell him," Sylvia says. "He will know what to do. He could be a stalker or a serial killer. Sonia, you have to call the police, because this is serious business."

"Sylvia, maybe you are right. I am going to call Captain Johnson right now."

The phone rings at ranger headquarters.

"Sergeant Savalas, may I help you?"

"Sergeant, I am Sonia Perdenales, a friend of Dan Mesa. If possible, I'd like to speak with Captain Johnson."

"Yes, ma'am, I will get him for you." Savalas walks toward the Captain's office.

"Captain, Sonia Perdenales, Dan Mesa's friend is on the line for you."

"Captain Johnson here, what can I do for you Sonia?"

"Captain, today when I left for work, a black Chevy Camaro followed me all the way to work and then turned around and stopped at the Cow Palace to take down my license number. Then it went on. I'm frightened and not sure what to do."

"Sonia, did you by chance get the license number of the Camaro?"

"Yes, I did. It was one of those personalized plates with the word *HAMMER* on it. It was an Arizona plate."

"Okay, I don't want you to go home tonight. Do you have a friend you can spend the night with? If so, go there, and don't drive your car. Leave it parked, and we will come and get it. I will have the plates run to find out to whom the Camaro belongs. I will call you back in about an hour with whatever I find out."

"Thanks, Captain Johnson, I really appreciate this. Could this have anything to do with Dan?"

"Sonia, why do you ask that?"

"I am asking, because I just have this intuition that he is in danger and that someone has tied us together. I am frightened for myself and for him. I do love him, and I want to protect him the same as he would protect me. I just can't be a part of his life right now. He is a wonderful man, but he is dangerous and leads a most dangerous life."

"I understand, Sonia. I will be in touch."

Captain Johnson hangs up the phone, turns to Bonefacio, who has just entered, and asks him to run the license number. They wait, and the information appears on the screen with the name Antonio Blackbear, Carlos Meana's man.

Captain Johnson turns around slowly with a frown on his face.

"Sergeant, do you suppose Antonio is trying to kidnap Sonia?" he asks. "I have a feeling he is thinking that, by kidnapping Sonia, he can force Sergeant Mesa to give up Ranson for Sonia. He is making the worst mistake of his life. If anything happens to that lady, I wouldn't give five cents for his life expectancy. If she is hurt or killed, Sergeant Daniel Mesa will declare World War III. He will make that last situation with Jackson look like a Sunday picnic."

Captain Johnson straps on his weapon and takes charge of the situation, something he hasn't done for a long time. He has a feeling all hell is about to break a loose.

CHAPTER FOUR

In Amado, at the Cow Palace, Sonia is working the evening shift. When she goes to her car to get a pen, she is suddenly struck from behind and passes out. A man very gently carries her to his car and speeds off.

Sylvia sees the car and runs inside to call the police. Before the police arrive, Captain Johnson and the rangers arrive. Sylvia is hysterical and tries to tell them what happened. Finally, she settles down and tells the rangers about Sonia's kidnapping.

The captain swears softly and says, to no one in particular, "Dan Mesa is going to declare war on Carlos and Antonio. There will be dead bodies everywhere you look."

"Sergeant Savalas, contact Sergeant Mesa and tell him what has happened. Then I am going to Tucson to talk with the colonel."

In an RV on I-35 heading south to San Antonio, Sergeant Mesa and Agent Ortiz are reminiscing about old times when the phone rings. Dan checks his phone and sees that it's Savalas.

"Sergeant Mesa here."

"This is Sergeant Savalas."

"Hello, Savalas. How are things in Nogales?"

"Dan, I have some bad news for you. Antonio Blackbear, one of Carlos's men, kidnapped Sonia. The captain thinks Carlos had her kidnapped as a way of forcing you to hand over Ranson. We know that Antonio is driving a black Camaro with tags that read *HAMMER*. He will probably send someone to contact you and to demand Ranson's release. I know you care a lot about Sonia, but you can't give up Ranson for Sonia."

"Savalas, I haven't lost a prisoner yet, and I won't lose one now. Carlos has signed his death warrant; I will see him dead if he harms one hair on her head. We will drive straight through until we get to Tucson. I am sure he will attempt to contact us before we get there. Tell the captain he can be assured that Ranson will arrive on time. Sonia doesn't deserve this. She paid her dues when her husband was killed in the line of duty. I will be in touch soon."

Jonathan watches in silence as Mesa lays the phone down. He notices a sudden change in Mesa's entire disposition. Dan Mesa has suddenly become very deadly. Jonathan realizes that Dan is the right person to do the job that needs doing. The man has a heavy responsibility. He understands Garnett's reasoning for not wanting Dan to be a policeman. He is constantly in harm's way. Devlin needs a father who will be there. Yet he understands Mesa's decision to be a ranger. Someone has to do what he does. Someone has to care and protect those who can't protect themselves.

Scotty looks at Dan and says, "Dan, what is happening in Arizona that you aren't telling us?"

"Scotty, my friend Sonia has been kidnapped by one of Carlos's men, Antonio Blackbear. The captain believes it was done in an attempt to force me to turn Ranson over to Carlos. Both Carlos and Antonio have signed their own death warrants. I will not rest until I send them both to hell," Mesa says. "Sonia was married to a policeman in Denver, and he was killed in the line of duty. It took her some time to get over it. Then she ran into me, and we became friends. One night a few months ago, we went to dinner and dancing. We were leaving this club when a man and a woman tried to kill me. He wasn't fast enough. I killed him, and the lady knew enough about life to give it up. In the past few months, I have had to use this gun more than I ever did in Vietnam or the Persian Gulf. I have killed six men in less than twelve months. I am not proud of it, but it was either them or me. Now I plan to kill two more men, and I don't feel any regret or remorse. They started this; now I will end it. Sonia deserves better from life. After seeing me kill that man, she turned on me and said she couldn't handle it, and we parted. She is the second friend to suffer because of me. Maybe Garnett was right to just distance herself from me.

"Daniel Mesa, I have known you for twenty years, and there isn't a more decent person in the whole world than you," Nadia says. "Don't you go feeling sorry for yourself. You do what you have to do, and we will support you. We are passing through San Antonio now, and we will be in Tucson in a couple of days at the speed we are traveling. When we get there, you and your people try to get that lady back unhurt. I will say a prayer for her."

Back in Tucson, word has gotten to Carlos that Antonio has kidnapped Sonia Perdenales. Suddenly Carlos is deathly afraid. He calls Antonio and demands that he come and see him. Carlos's tone is such that Antonio dreads seeing him.

He arrives at Carlos's hacienda and walks in.

"Antonio, who told you to kidnap Mesa's friend?" Carlos asks. "Just what the hell do you think you are doing? You have just screwed up any chance I had of becoming legitimate. Now where is she? She had better be safe and unhurt. If you hurt one hair on her head, I will kill you myself. We have been friends for a long time, but this time, you went too far."

"Boss, I was only trying to help. We have her, and the ranger will have to give up Ranson for her. She is his friend. They are very close, so he will have to give up Ranson."

"Antonio, you don't know Mesa as I do. He will not give up Ranson for anyone. Now he will come after you and me. He will never give up. Our only choice is to get across the border. Let's see what is on the news about her kidnapping."

Carlos turns on the television.

"This is Fiona Bacuss, reporting from Amado where a lady named Sonia Perdenales was kidnapped by Antonio Blackbear, a known accomplice of Carlos Meana. The reason for the kidnapping is unknown. Ranger Captain Johnson of Nogales is on the scene and has told this reporter that the rangers will take every possible step to find Miss Perdenales. I have learned from other sources that Sonia Perdenales is a personal friend of Arizona ranger Sergeant Dan

Mesa. The question is, does this have anything to with the sergeant? This is Fiona Bacuss reporting from Amado."

Carlos turns toward Antonio and says, "I am sure the border is sealed and they are looking for us. Where do you have this lady stashed?"

"I have her at your house in Patagonia. She is a nice lady. I can see why Mesa likes her."

"Antonio, if you want to stay among the living, you will leave her alone. If you hurt her or cause her to hurt herself, I will personally shoot you. Do you understand me? Dan Mesa already has it in for me for killing his friend about ten years ago. Now you have added one more reason for him to kill me. If I die, so will you. I told you I was working on an idea so that we could turn an illegal business into a legal business. Because of your actions, all that has gone up in smoke. We will be lucky to survive until next month. You don't know the rangers like I do. They will track you to hell and back. They are all tough men, and Captain Johnson and Dan Mesa are the toughest. Johnson is an old Lobo, and he taught Mesa. If both of them come after us, we are dead. So you had better keep her safe and sound."

In Yuma, it is a cool October morning. Alana is preparing for work when she hears of the kidnapping. She yells to her mom.

"Mom, come quick!"

"What is it, child?" Matilda asks.

"Mom, do you remember the lady Dan told us about in Amado? Well, Carlos Meana and his men have kidnapped her. The Santa Cruz guys are sealing the border and hunting Carlos and Antonio. If I know Dan Mesa, he is headed toward Tucson. I would hate to be Carlos and Antonio. Mom before this is over, a lot of blood will be spilled and people will die."

"Alana, how is it that a man like Daniel Mesa winds up with so much trouble in his life? He can't seem to get a break. Everyone he becomes involved with seems to either get hurt or they hurt him. I pray that he find happiness during his lifetime. He is too good of a man to go to waste. So my darling daughter, think about what I am saying. The two of you could do great things together."

Alana looks at her mom and smiles.

"Mom, one thing at a time. I have to get comfortable with my new situation in life. What if he doesn't want me anymore? I treated him very badly. As you said, he is too good of a man to let go. I do love him dearly, and when this is over, I plan to tell him."

On the road somewhere approaching El Paso, Dan is driving, and they are listening to Marty Robins on the radio. Oddly enough, the song is about an Arizona ranger and is entitled "Big Iron."

Scotty turns to Jonathan and says, "Mr. Williamson, doesn't that song remind you of someone you know?"

"Yes, it does, son. I first heard that song when I visited Garnett and Dan when they lived in San Antonio. They had been married about a year when we went for that visit. I had been stationed at Williams Air Force Base during World War II but didn't know much about the west. When I met then-Lieutenant Daniel Mesa for the first time, I thought he was a joke. But he wasn't then, and nor is he now. He took me horseback riding, and I watched him handle a horse. I knew at that moment that he was just what he appeared to be. He flew home with Garnett to ask for her hand. When he walked through that terminal door, he looked like he had just stepped out of a western novel." He pauses, then adds, "He doesn't fit in the East. I know why he prefers to live here in the West. He is a part of it, just as surely as the cactus and the roadrunners. He would die if he had to live any other place. That song 'Big Iron' should have been written for him. He is that ranger."

The song ends and another begins—"From Whence Came the Cowboy" by the Sons of the San Joaquin. Dan drives on seemingly with one thing on his mind, and that is to rescue Sonia and then make Carlos and Antonio pay dearly.

As it approaches dinnertime, Nadia asks, "Where are going to eat tonight? Honey, why not stop at a roadside park, and we can fix supper in the RV. It will be good for all of us. Dan, what are your thoughts on the subject?"

"Mom I like the idea of a cook out. I hope there are steaks. I believe I could eat a horse."

"Dan, I see a roadside park ahead. Maybe we can stop there and cook supper. It will be great to just sit for a while and enjoy the sunset. You need to relax for a while. Why don't you take out that smug pot you call a pipe and smoke it and relax? Jonathan and I will fix dinner."

Dan pulls into the parking area, and everyone unloads. Jonathan and Nadia prepare dinner. Scotty, Ranson, and Mesa sit and talk.

In Patagonia, Arizona, it is raining. It is one of those sudden electrical storms that happens in Arizona and is sometimes deadly. Suddenly, lightning strikes a transformer, and a fast-burning fire begins that spreads to Carlos's house, which is immediately engulfed in flames. By the time the fire department arrives, the house is too far gone to save. After the firemen rush in, they discover a body.

Jim Killian, a rookie fireman, discovers the body. He finds a slightly melted driver's license and discovers the identity. He calls the fire chief, Captain Orlando Garcia.

"Tell me what we have, Jim."

"Sir, I discovered a body that appears to be that of Sonia Perdenales, that friend of Ranger Mesa that was kidnapped."

Captain Garcia turns around slowly and says, "Oh my God. This is going to tear Dan apart. He was really crazy about her. We'd better call Captain Johnson at the rangers and notify the local police. Hell is about to burst wide open."

The phone rings at ranger headquarters in Nogales.

"Arizona rangers, Sergeant Savalas speaking."

"Sergeant Savalas, this is Captain Garcia from the fire department. I need to speak to your captain. It is an emergency."

"I will get him right away, sir." Savalas rushes into Captain Johnson's office saying; "Sir, Captain Garcia from the Fire Department is on the line for you."

"Thanks Sergeant."

"Hello Orlando, what's up?"

"Sam, I have bad news. It is as bad as it gets. We responded to a fire at a home in Patagonia. By the time we drove from Nogales, the house was a smoldering ruin. When going through the rubble, we found the body of a female."

"Orlando, I believe I get the picture. You found Sonia's body?"

"Sam, I've had to do some terrible things as a fireman, but this is the worst I've had to deal with. I knew her, and I know Dan Mesa. Sam, what will he do now? You and I have known him a long time, and I am afraid he will go crazy first and then there will be dead people all over southern Arizona."

Captain Johnson clears his throat and slowly says, "Old friend, I don't even want to think about what he will do. Whose house was it that burned? Please don't tell me it belonged to Carlos Meana."

"Yes, it was Meana's house, but there were no signs of him having been there. Sam, when we found her, her hands were tied with some type of cord that survived the fire. She didn't have a chance. It makes my blood boil. I will tell you this: If I could get my hands on Meana or Blackbear, I would kill them myself."

"Thanks, Orlando, for calling. I need to call the colonel and let him know what has happened. The FBI will have to be told also. It is now a federal case, involving kidnapping and manslaughter or maybe even murder. The coroner will have to tell us the story. I will talk with you later."

When Captain Johnson turns around, he see the rangers waiting at the door He knows he has to tell them what has happened, and he suddenly feels very nervous. \

"Guys, that was Captain Garcia of the fire department. They answered a fire alarm at a house in Patagonia. The house had burned, and they found Sonia's body inside. Her hands were tied. The house belonged to Carlos Meana. I have to call Colonel Grant first, and then I have the task of telling Sergeant Mesa. That is one task I am not up to."

Sergeant Savalas remembers how much in love with Sonia Dan was. He also knows that all hell is about to break open.

"Captain, this isn't good at all. Dan Mesa has paid a heavy price these last few years. This one could break him. How do we handle this? How can we help Dan? I know him well, and someone is going to pay for what happened to Sonia. I hate Meana, but even he doesn't deserve what is going to happen to him and Antonio."

A private phone rings at Colonel Grant's home. When the red phone rings, Grant knows something bad has happened. The number is that of Santa Cruz Company, Sam Johnson.

"Hello, Sam. I know that, whatever it is, it is bad. So, tell me the bad news."

"Sir, you are right. The fire department here answered a fire, and they found the body of Sonia Perdenales in the ruins. Her hands were tied. We don't know the cause of her death, but it appears to be asphyxiation due to the fire. The coroner will know the actual cause of death by tomorrow. We have kept it quiet from the reporters until I could talk with you. Sir, you know all hell is about to break open when I tell Sergeant Mesa about this. I can't let him hear about it from the television or radio news."

"Sam, do what you think is best. I will notify the FBI, and I'll call you later on tonight."

In the coroner's office, Dr. Jaime Hernandez is working on the body and reaches his conclusion. He calls Captain Johnson.

"Sam, Jaime here. I just finished the autopsy on Sonia. The cause of death is smoke inhalation. She also had a small gash at the back of her head as if she had been hit there. If she had not been bound and restrained, she could have gotten out before it got bad. It is my opinion that this was intentional. You should go to the district attorney and ask for a charge of murder. Someone should pay dearly for her death."

"Thanks, Jaime, I will be in touch."

Supper has been completed, and Nadia is playing the guitar as Dan sings a wayfarer's song about the sea. Dan's cellular phone rings.

"Sergeant Mesa here," he answers.

"Dan, Captain Johnson here. Dan, I don't know any other way to say this, so I am just going to tell you. There was a fire in Patagonia, and the Nogales Fire Department responded. It was a bad one. By the time they got there, the house had burned. When going through the rubble, they found a body. It was Sonia. According to Captain Garcia, her hands were bound. The coroner, Dr. Hernandez, said the cause of death was smoke inhalation. I wish there was something I could say or do to make it better. Get back here as soon as you can. There is a lot we need to do. Dan, I know you well, and I know how your mind works. Please, don't go off half-cocked. Promise me you'll come in and talk before you do anything."

"Captain, I'll see you soon."

He shuts the phone off and walks away stiffly.

Ranson breaks the silence when he says, "Who died? I can tell from the look on your face that someone has died."

Dan spins around with his gun in hand, walks up to Ranson, shoves the barrel in his mouth, and cocks the hammer. Ranson's eyes are as big as saucers.

Nadia cautiously walks over and puts her hand on Dan's arm.

"Son, you don't want to do that," she says. "That's not the way."

Mesa becomes aware of his actions and relaxes his grip on the gun. He sits down and slowly tells them what happened. Scotty walks over and pats his friend on the back and walks away. He remembers a time when he too felt the loss of someone special.

Ranson stands up and apologizes to Mesa for his words. Mesa just walks away without saying anything. Jonathan loads up the RV, and they drive into the night.

In Tucson, the television, radio, and newspaper news agencies have been notified, and there is a continual news broadcast. Carlos has learned of the fire and knows he has to kill Dan Mesa before Dan kills him. He calls his friends in Dallas, and a contract is put on Ranger Daniel Mesa for two hundred thousand dollars—dead.

As is always the case, word drifts back to Tucson, and the rangers are alerted.

In the meantime, Carlos and Antonio are running for their lives. Twice, they have tried crossing the border, but due to constant identity checks, they know they can't risk it.

Mesa arrives in Tucson and turns Ranson over to Captain Johnson. He is extremely irritable and stays away from everyone.

Captain Johnson calls Mesa into his office and says, "Sergeant, I don't know what to say to you to make things better, so I won't try. Colonel Grant and I are working hard to find those responsible. Let us do our job, please."

Mesa looks at the captain for a few seconds and says, "Sir, she didn't have to die. Someone has to pay for her death. I need to get Jonathan and Nadia to my place. I have my friend Scott Ortiz of the FBI with me as well. I will be in touch."

Mesa drives to his ranch and gets Jonathan and Nadia settled in. He turns to Ortiz, says thanks, and walks away. He climbs into his truck and slowly drives away.

Twenty-four hours after Sonia's death, no one has seen Dan Mesa. The investigation into Sonia's death continues. The FBI has taken over the case along with the rangers. Carlos's and Antonio's photos have been circulated with warrants for their arrests. So far, though, no one has seen or heard from them.

Scotty and Jonathan have been searching everywhere for Dan. It has now been thirty-six hours, and they've found nothing. Scotty, Jonathan, and Nadia have been living at Dan's place. Captain Johnson comes by for a visit.

"Jonathan," he says, "have you heard anything from Dan since he arrived? He has never done anything like this before. He is hurting, and he is dangerous now."

"Dan will show up in a few hours," Agent Ortiz says. "I finally figured out where he is. He is preparing himself for the task at hand.

If I know him, he is getting into the mind of Carlos and Antonio. But he doesn't know there is a contract out on him."

In Yuma, Major McMasters is listening to the news when he hears about Sonia's death. He walks into Lieutenant Osborne's office, where she is watching the news as well.

"Alana, it seems as if trouble follows Sergeant Mesa wherever he goes. What do you say to a man who has faced as much as he has faced these last few months?"

"Sir, I wouldn't know what to say. I have been thinking about it, and no one could know what to say or do. I was thinking of that lady Sonia. He spoke of her once. I got the feeling there were a lot of unspoken things there. It is hard to get him to talk about himself, but I do know he cared a lot about her. She was the one who ended the relationship because of the nature of work he does. Her husband was a policeman who was killed in the line of duty, and apparently, she never got over it. Major, Dan Mesa is going to go nuts over this. You saw what happened when he and Jackson met. That was child's play in comparison to what will happen now."

"Lieutenant, please call Captain Johnson and ask if there is anything we can do to assist them. Also inquire about Sergeant Mesa."

The phone rings at ranger headquarters, and Sergeant Savalas answers the phone.

"Arizona rangers, Sergeant Savalas speaking."

"Sergeant Savalas, this is Lieutenant Osborne from Yuma. How are you?"

"Ma'am, I am well. What can I do for you?"

"Sergeant is the captain in? If so, may I speak to him?"

"One moment, ma'am."

"Captain Johnson, I have Lieutenant Osborne from Yuma on the line. She wants to speak with you."

"Put her through please," Johnson says. Then he picks up his phone. "Lieutenant Osborne, how are you and what can I do for you?"

"Sir, I am recovering and doing better each day. The reason I am calling is because of what happened to Sonia. The major wants to know if there is anything that we can do to help and asked that I inquire about Sergeant Mesa. He is well liked here, and everyone is concerned about him."

"Lieutenant, Sergeant Mesa is missing. No one knows where he is, but we suspect he is out in the desert getting ready for his confrontation with Carlos and Antonio. But what he doesn't know is that a contract has been put on him."

"Sir, what can we do to help him? He is very special to me. I can't let anything else happen to him. If you hear from him, please call us right away. Thanks, sir."

Captain Johnson hangs up the phone but is very worried. He knows his friend's life is at stake.

CHAPTER FIVE

In Tucson, the colonel is watching the news and bangs his fist on the desk, rattling the whole room.

His secretary rushes in and asks, "Colonel, what is wrong?"

"Maria, you are fired. You are lucky that I am not pressing charges against you. You told Carlos and his group about Ranger Mesa. If he gets hurt, I will hold you responsible. I want you out of this building in ten minutes, or I will have you arrested. If I ever see you again, I will arrest you."

"Colonel Grant, I didn't have a choice. I didn't know what to do. I know I should have told you, but I was afraid you wouldn't help me! I am sorry for letting you down."

"Lady, I don't want your sorrow or anything else. One of my best rangers has lost a lady he cared about because of you and your friends. GET OUT OF MY SIGHT!"

Maria leaves broken and crying. Colonel Hiram H. Grant is a man with few illusions about himself and life. He too has smelled the acrid smell of gunpowder and the stench of death in Vietnam and as a ranger. He knows what the rangers in the field go through, which is why he is so angry with Maria. She has possibly helped in the death of Sonia Perdenales.

Traveling south on I-19 is a dusty bronze Toyota 4Runner being driven by a man who is small in stature but big in heart and courage. At this moment when no one can see him, tears are streaming down his face, and his heart is as heavy as a brick. Sergeant Dan Mesa of the Arizona rangers is heading back home to begin a journey that will end in the deaths of several men and maybe justice for Sonia Perdenales.

When Dan arrives in Nogales, he reports in to Captain Johnson.

"Hello, Captain," he says. "Is there anything new on Sonia's murder?"

"Sergeant, where in the name of Hanna have you been? You've had all of us worried to death about you. There is a contract on you, and we suspect it was put out by Carlos or some of his cronies."

"Captain, I had to get away from here for a day or two," Mesa says. "I need to contact Sonia's parents and see about funeral arrangements for her. I've never spoken to them, but I know she was close to them. I keep asking myself if she suffered because of me. It doesn't make any sense. She wasn't a threat to anyone. She was just a nice woman who shouldn't have been involved in this. Someone will pay for her death. Sir, do you have any leads on the contract taken out on me?"

"Sergeant Mesa, do I need to remove you from this case? I know it is personal, and I know there isn't anything anyone can do to make it hurt less, but I can't have you going off half-cocked. Take a few days off and mourn her death. Come back ready to make those bastards pay dearly for her death."

"Captain, I have it under control. I don't need time off. I can do my job."

"Sergeant, this is not a request; it is an order. Take time off or turn in your badge. Dan, look, you need some time off, if only a couple of days. You are at the end of your rope. I know you, and I know you are capable of killing someone with the least provocation. I just want to make sure you kill the right person under the right circumstances. Now, will you do as I ask?"

"Yes, sir. I'll take a couple of days off, but after that and the funeral, I will cry havoc and let loose the dogs of war. Someone is going to pay for her death. Captain, have the FBI check Vermenti Pellegrinni and see if they can determine whether he put out the contract. Carlos and Pellegrinni have a history together. Better yet, I'll ask Scott to look into it for us."

With those remarks, Mesa leaves the Captain's office.

Captain Johnson calls in Ranger Bonefacio Hernandez.

"Bonnie, I want you to shadow Sergeant Mesa without him knowing it."

"Captain, you know I will do anything you want me to do, but Dan is one of us. I can't and won't do that."

"Bonnie, Dan is not in trouble. I want you to shadow him to keep him from killing someone. He is angry and on the edge. Just keep him out of trouble. He is my friend; I don't want anything to happen to him. Someone has put a contract out on him, and he is going to try to find out who did it. I just want someone covering his back."

"Captain, that is something I can and will do. I like Mesa, and so do most of us. He is a hard case but fair and honest, and if he is your friend, he is the best friend you'll ever have. But if he is your enemy, then God have mercy on your soul."

"Bonnie, keep me posted and watch you back too."

In El Paso, Sonia's parents and family are planning the funeral when the phone rings.

"Hello, this is the Cortez residence."

"Hello, I am Sergeant Daniel Mesa of the Arizona rangers and a friend of Sonia's. I must apologize for disturbing you, but I have to ask about the funeral arrangements and if there is anything I or the rangers can do to help."

"Ranger, I am Sonia's mother, Ophelia. She spoke of you often. She cared for you a great deal. I know she'd want you here. The funeral is scheduled for Saturday at Saint Paul's Cathedral at eleven a.m. Will you be there?"

"Yes, ma'am, I will be there. I will arrive tomorrow. I just want you to know I . . ." For the first time in his life, Dan Mesa breaks down.

"Ranger Mesa, will you be okay? You are welcome here anytime. It is a hard thing for all of us to understand. She said you are a special person, and she wanted me to meet you. We'll talk when you arrive."

"Thank you, Mrs. Cortez. I don't know if I will ever be okay again. This is something I feel responsible for. I will see you tomorrow."

Napal Cortez, Sonia's father, walks into the room and asks, "Honey, who was it on the phone?"

"Napal, it was that ranger whom Sonia often spoke of. He must be something special for her to have cared as she did. He almost broke down over the phone. I could tell by the way his voice shook. Unless I miss my guess, that man is not someone to tangle with. The anger in him and the hurt is tearing him apart. Whoever killed our little girl will regret it something terrible. He will arrive tomorrow."

"Ophelia, how will we know him? Does he want us to meet him at the airport?"

"No, dear, but I will know him anywhere. According to Sonia, he is about five feet five inches tall and weighs around one hundred fifty pounds. He is African American but not black. He has brown skin and a face that seldom smiles He always wears a gray western hat, boots, jeans, and a western tie. You'll know him without a doubt."

In Nogales at Mesa's ranch, Dan and Agent Ortiz are in conversation.

"Scott, could you check with your people and find out if Pellegrinni has put out a contract on me or if he has done anything out of the ordinary these last few days?" Mesa asks. "According to my captain, there is a contract out on me. I am not afraid, but it does make it difficult for me to do what needs to be done if I have to watch my back constantly."

"Dan, I will call right now. Someone should be there in the office."

When the phone is answered at the bureau in Washington, DC, Ortiz hears, "This is the FBI, Agent Schmidt speaking. May I help you?"

"Dave, Scott Ortiz here. Do me a favor and check and see if Vermenti Pellegrinni has taken out a contract on anyone lately. I am primarily concerned about an Arizona ranger named Daniel Mesa. I'm in Nogales, Arizona, and you can reach me at five two zero nine zero eight two three four seven. Dan Mesa is my best friend, and I would appreciate anything you can find out. There was a kidnapping here, that ended in the murder of a very special lady. Dave, all hell is about to break loose down here, and unless I miss my guess, the world will be minus several criminals before this is over. I don't want him to go off half-cocked and kill the wrong person."

"Scott, isn't he that ranger who was involved in that shoot-out in Albuquerque a few months ago?"

"Yes, he is the one. The lady who was kidnapped and killed was his lady, someone he valued highly. Dan Mesa doesn't get involved easily. She must have been a great person. Call me as soon as you know anything."

"Scotty, wait a minute," Schmidt says. "The information is coming in now. According to our info, there is a contract on Dan Mesa of Nogales, Arizona. The amount is five hundred thousand dollars. Damn, someone wants his hide bad. Tell your friend to watch his back. Our sources say the contract is being financed by Pellegrinni."

"Dave, I owe you one. Just name it, and I'll be there. Thanks."

Scott slowly cradles the phone and turns around.

He looks at Mesa and says, "Dan, there is a contract for five hundred thousand dollars on you head. Pellegrinni is financing it. That is a considerable sum of money, and every would-be assassin will be after you. What are your plans?"

"I plan to carry on with what I am doing but have eyes in the back of my head. I will wear a vest, and I will be very cautious. I plan to stay alive. I have a little fellow who needs me," Mesa says. "I have to prepare for the funeral."

Dan leaves the room to prepare for the trip to El Paso.

In the air aboard Southwest Airlines flight 3655, Ranger Dan Mesa is sitting with his eyes closed when the pilot announces, "Ladies and gentlemen, we are approaching El Paso airport, and the weather is mild and dry. The temperature is seventy-five degrees with a slight overcast sky. So sit back, and we will land shortly. I hope your trip to El Paso is an enjoyable one."

When Sergeant Mesa reaches the baggage claim area, he recognizes Sonia's mother because she is a slightly older version of Sonia. Mrs. Cortez seems to recognize him immediately and walks toward him.

"You must be Ranger Mesa," she says. "Your appearance is exactly as Sonia described. She really liked you a lot. I miss her so much. We were more than mother and daughter; she was my friend also."

Dan immediately turns away to prevent her seeing the tears in his eyes. Mrs. Cortez pats him on the back, and they walk toward the baggage area to retrieve his luggage.

In the car headed toward home, Mrs. Cortez looks at Dan and asks, "Ranger Mesa, what will you and the rangers do about Sonia's murder?"

"Mrs. Cortez, we know who did it, and we will get them one way or another. The main person responsible for her death is Carlos Meana, but he didn't kidnap her. Antonio Blackbear, a crony of Carlos, kidnapped her. They have disappeared, but I will find them, and they will pay. Another associate of Carlos has put a contract out on me for five hundred thousand dollars. I will settle with each one of them. The law wants them, and the law will have them. That I promise."

Mrs. Cortez looks deep into his eyes and possibly into his soul and sees the torment the ranger is dealing with. She wonders how he is able to continue doing what he does. They arrive at the Cortez residence and are greeted by Mr. Cortez and Sonia's two sisters.

Mrs. Cortez says, "This is Sergeant Dan Mesa of the Arizona rangers, a friend of Sonia's. Dan, these are my daughters, Mardi and Amelia, and my husband and Sonia's father, Napal."

"Hello, everyone. It saddens me to meet you under these circumstances. Sonia wanted me to meet all of you under friendlier circumstances. She was very special to me, and I am so sorry about what has happened. My commander, Captain Johnson, sends his condolences, and so does the entire ranger detachment. She was well liked by them."

Napal Cortez thinks, *I like this fellow. He reminds me of myself sometime back. He has character and he cares about people but there is something driving him.* "Sergeant Mesa, I know you've had a long trip," he says out loud, "so we'll get you settled and then we'll talk some."

The house is a large adobe structure with massive rooms and beautiful tapestries hanging on the wall. There are several old pictures on the wall that tells the story of an old family. Mesa spots a picture of a dark-skinned man almost his double and stops to stare for a moment. Napal walks back and smiles, saying, "I thought that would get your attention. That is a picture of you at a rodeo I participated in in Houston about thirty years ago. The horse you road that day was one of the toughest horses I have ever seen. Man, you should have gotten a higher score. Your ride was one of the best I have ever seen in my life."

Dan Mesa smiles a sad smile and says, "Thank you, sir. It was a tough ride. That horse almost made me give up rodeos."

After Dan unpacks his bags, he changes into jeans and a shirt. He takes off his gun and suddenly feels quite naked without it. He walks into the kitchen, and Mrs. Cortez hands him a cup of coffee and pours in brandy.

"Dan," she says, "this is my own prescription. I know you don't drink much, but you need this. It will settle you down some. I can tell just by looking at you that you are on edge, so drink the coffee and have some cake. I baked it myself."

He samples the coffee and has to agree it is good and so is the cake. Mesa is remembering how he and Sonia met and it brings tears to his eyes. He suddenly realizes Mr. Cortez is speaking to him.

"Sir, I am sorry. I was thinking about Sonia. What was your question?"

"No need to apologize. I asked what had been learned about Sonia's death."

"We know that Antonio Blackbear is an employee of Carlos Meana, one of our local crime bosses. They kidnapped Sonia. I was sent to Richmond, Virginia, to escort a William Ranson back to Tucson to testify against Carlos. Carlos hired a hit man to kill Ranson and, I guess, to kill me. It didn't turn out the way he wanted. One hit man was killed, and the other got away. Blackbear kidnapped Sonia as a way of putting pressure on me to release Ranson. I don't know if Carlos ordered it or not. He is still guilty in my book. He has posted a five hundred thousand-dollar bounty on me dead. I am sure someone will try to collect it; however, they will discover that I won't die easily. There is an all-points bulletin out for both Carlos and Antonio, and we will capture them. It is only a matter of time. What they did to her was unconscionable. They kidnapped her and left her in a house with her hands and feet tied. Lightning struck the house, and it caught on fire with her in there with no way to escape. I promise you they will pay, one way or another. She was one in a million, and I loved her dearly."

Suddenly, Mesa rises and leaves the room almost running. He feels himself ready to explode.

All are quiet. Ophelia turns to her husband, and he follows Mesa out to the barn. Napal walks up and stands next to Mesa, who is quietly smoking his pipe, deep in thought. He hears Napal's approaching feet and spins around with his hand poised and ready to draw. Then he must realize where he is, and he relaxes. His expression is pure animal anger. He reminds Napal of a cornered wolf he trapped once.

"Ranger Mesa—Dan, I should say—it wasn't your fault. Those two men are the reasons my daughter is dead, not you. I am going to tell you something I have only told one other person and that is Ophelia. In my younger days, I was a Texas ranger and a darned good one. I was engaged to marry a young white girl from around Kingsville, Texas. The local whites didn't like it, and the Klan got involved. They kidnapped her, and she was brutally raped and murdered. It almost drove me crazy. I hunted each one of them down and used the law to execute each one of them. Then I resigned from the rangers and became a simple rancher.

"I know what you are going through. Meeting Ophelia is what saved me from losing my mind. I couldn't imagine life without Angela. That was her name. It took me five years to get over what happened. I still have dreams about it, but not as often as I did. Dan, I can't promise you you'll ever get over what happened, and I can't promise you that you'll get past your feelings for Sonia, but it will get better with time. You have got to let go sometime, because if you don't you will die inside. I am a good judge of men, and you are a good man. Someday, some lady will be happy that you are a part of her life. Keep Sonia in here," he says, pointing to his heart.

The two men continue talking while walking toward the horses.

Ophelia and the sisters watch their father comfort a man who should be a stranger but isn't.

Mardi turns to her mother and asks, "Mom, why is it that Ranger Mesa, a stranger in our home, seems like he belongs here?"

"You know, it feels the same way with me," Amelia says. "It's as if Sonia was here with him and introducing him to us as her fiancé or something."

"Girls, I can only say that your sister and you girls are special people. God blessed us with the three of you. You were like triplets. I only wish she were here. Girls, go into the hallway and look at the picture in the frame at the bottom."

They go into the hallway, and Amelia drops her coffee cup.

"Mom, that's the Ranger. How did you get this picture?"

"That picture was taken about thirty years ago when he was very young at a rodeo in Houston. Your father was a participant, and he and Sonia took that photo. She was going to show it to Dan when she brought him here to meet us. Your father said that the horse Dan is riding in that photo was the toughest and meanest horse he had ever seen. He said Dan should have won the competition but didn't because of his race. In the early seventies, black people weren't accepted in the rodeo profession."

Mardi looks at the picture and sees the date as June 1970.

"Mom, where has he been all this time? Has he been a ranger all these years?"

"As I recall, Sonia said he spent twenty years in the air force and retired a few years ago as a captain. His wife left him, and he joined the rangers and the rest is history. He has apparently made several enemies. Do you remember the news articles they had about the ranger who was involved in that shoot-out in Albuquerque a few months ago? Well, that ranger was Sergeant Daniel Mesa. He and Sonia had some problems about a shooting he was involved in in Tucson, where he had to kill a man who was sent to kill him. There was another shooting in a bar in which he was involved. Anyway, Sonia had problems dealing with it because of her husband having been killed. She was adjusting and was so in love with Dan; she would have found a way to make it work."

CHAPTER SIX

Meanwhile back in Nogales, Captain Johnson has made a discovery.

"Sergeant Savalas, we have been notified that Carlos Meana and Antonio Blackbear have been spotted in Douglas by the local police. Go to Douglas and find out what is going on there. Stay under cover, because there are rumors that some of the police are on the take. Contact me as soon as you get there, and get an assessment of the situation. Sergeant, stay alive."

In Douglas, Arizona, Carlos is trying to get across the border into Mexico. He believes he has connections but is having a problem due to what he has done. He is in the office of the chief of immigration services.

"Carlos, you are in trouble with the rangers, the kind of trouble I don't need. It will cost you more money than you can afford, plus I know the commander of the rangers in Nogales, and he is not a person I want as an enemy. I recommend you find someone else. I won't put myself in jeopardy for you or anyone."

"Roberto, I need your help. I have to get to Mexico. Now either you help me or you'll regret it."

Roberto Gonzales, a tall slender man and one slow to anger, turns slowly to look at Carlos.

"Old fellow, you'd best get yourself together and get out of here before I forget we are cousins."

Carlos leaves the office of immigration, swearing to himself. He knows he will get even with Roberto one way or another. He calls Vermenti on his cellular phone.

"Mr. Pellegrinni, this is Carlos Meana. Sir, have you taken care of that matter in Arizona?"

"Carlos, my boy, you problem is being taken care of, unless our people aren't up to it. We are spending five hundred thousand dollars to take care of the situation. You will owe me, and I will collect."

"Thank you, sir. I won't forget."

Carlos knows he can relax a little now. Sergeant Dan Mesa of the Arizona rangers will soon be history.

At Mesa's place in Nogales, Jonathan and Nadia are exploring the ranch. They are walking along a trail, hand in hand. Jonathan is concentrating on the problems Mesa in facing and turns to Nadia.

"Honey, what will become of Dan? He is like our son, and I am worried about him. There is a price on his head, and he is acting as if it is nothing to worry about, but I know he is worried. That man has more bad luck than anyone I know or have ever met."

"Jonathan, I love you because you are the best man I know. You care about people, and you love me dearly. Sweetheart, I don't know the answers to the questions you ask, but I do believe God has his hand on the situation. I heard Dan praying the other night. He asked God just to see him through all this and help him find peace and happiness before he dies. You know that is my prayer for him too. Devlin needs him, and he needs that boy. I believe he would have fallen apart a long time ago if it had not been for Devlin. He told me that when he and Garnett first separated, it took all he had to just stay sane. He loves our daughter deeply. Isn't it a shame they can't find a way to make things work?" Jonathan stops and just holds his wife for a long moment. Finally, he says, "I am so blessed to have you in my life, Nadia. I couldn't make it without you." She smiles, and they continue walking.

In El Paso, the day is reaching an end, and plans are being finalized for the funeral. Friends and family members have been dropping by all day.

Ranger Mesa decides to go horseback riding on the Cortez ranch. He chooses an Appaloosa gelding to ride. As he rides, he thinks, *I have come a long way over the years, and yet, I haven't gone very far at all. I am far passed thirty, and what do I have to show for it? A broken heart and an almost broken spirit. Sonia, I wish you were here. The little time I spent with you was so beautiful. I just can't believe you are gone. You were so full of spirit and love. It seems something bad happens to everyone I care about.* He hunches his back against the wind and gallops down the trail, a lonely man with the weight of the world on his shoulders.

Mesa rounds a bend in the trail and suddenly sees light reflected off something. He leaves the saddle as a bullet glances off the saddle horn. He hits the ground and rolls behind a tree, gun in hand, looking for the shooter. He sees movement and fires two shots fast, and then runs to another tree. He fires a third shot and hears a groan. He knows he has scored a hit. He runs to the spot and sees blood and a high powered rifle, a 30/30. He knows the contract is for real.

He takes his handkerchief and uses it to place the gun in the coiled rope on the saddle. He climbs back up and rides for home.

When he reaches the ranch, Amelia is waiting. She sees the bullet mark and the rifle and immediately asks what happened. Dan tells her the short version. They walk inside and call the police to report what has happened. The El Paso police in turn call the Texas rangers and report the situation. Sergeant Thomas Ryan, a ten-year veteran ranger, arrives at the Cortez ranch. He is a tall, lean man of about forty-years-old, with a friendly smile.

"Hello, I am Sergeant Ryan of the Texas rangers, and you must be Sergeant Mesa of the Arizona rangers. Man, it is good to meet you. I've been following your actions for the past two years."

Dan Mesa smiles and shakes hands with the Texas ranger. The two men stand talking and Napal takes pictures of the event. Ryan says good-bye to the Cortezes and shakes hands again with Ranger Mesa.

Ophelia and Mardi walk out together smiling. Mardi walks over to Dan and gives him a hug, saying, "This is for Sonia. She would have gotten a kick out of seeing you two rangers together. But on a serious note, you should be careful. There is a price on your head, and apparently, someone is taking it very seriously. We want you to stay alive and healthy."

Mesa smiles.

"I plan to stay alive too," he says, "but I can't hide from these characters. Someone has to stop them, and that is what I get paid to do. But this time, it is personal. Someone is going to pay dearly for what has been done. I don't make promises often, but I promise each of you that the person responsible for Sonia's death will pay a heavy price before this is over."

Ophelia knows she has to lighten the moment and food seems to do the trick. She smiles at Dan and understands his pain and suffering.

She walks toward the house, turns saying; "Okay, let's go inside for supper. I've cooked baked chicken with asparagus, scalloped potatoes, brazed carrots, and corn. We are having lemon coconut pie for dessert. Dan, I expect you to eat heartily. I am a great cook."

Ophelia turns around and walks arm in arm with Napal into the house with Dan and the sisters following.

Saturday morning brings rain, something seldom seen in El Paso, Texas. The limousine arrives, and the family leaves for the funeral. Mesa drives one of the family cars following the hearse. The funeral is sad. Everyone who knew Sonia seemed to like her. The chapel is filled. All eyes are on the dark-skinned gentleman in the black suit with a star on his chest as he walks in and takes a seat behind the family.

The service lasts ninety minutes. Ophelia cries softly, and so do Mardi and Amelia. Napal's face is drawn tight, and his eyes are red. Mesa's face is like stone, and there is a pronounced grinding of his teeth. When he suddenly realizes he is grinding his teeth, he stops.

When the service ends, they all leave for the Cortez ranch. Family and friends arrive at the family ranch. Mesa wanders out to the corral where the horses are. His face is wet with tears, something no one will ever see again. His shoulders are slumped, and his fists are clenched.

Unknown to him, Mardi and Napal are watching from a distance. They slowly turn and walk away, not wanting to intrude.

Inside, the people are lively, remembering Sonia's zest for life. Ophelia likes the light-heartedness of the crowd but wonders where Mesa has gone. Napal and Mardi explain what they have witnessed. Ophelia walks outside and stands next to the lonely figure lost in grief. He suddenly becomes aware that he is not alone, wipes away the tears, and regains his composure, apologizing for his weakness.

Ophelia says, "You don't have anything to apologize for. She was my child, but she was more. She was my friend and companion, and she is still here with me in spirit. Daniel, keep her safe in your heart, and never forget what she meant to you."

She walks away softly, leaving Dan to gather himself together. Then Mesa turns around and follows her inside.

Mesa knows he has to return and start searching for Carlos. He says good-bye to Sonia's family when he arrives at the airport.

When Mesa arrives in Tucson at the airport on Sunday, Captain Johnson meets him.

"Sergeant, the Texas rangers contacted me about what happened in El Paso. Are you okay? How did the funeral go?"

Mesa says, "Yes, sir, I am okay. The funeral was done in a tasteful manner, and her family was great. She was a well-loved person. I hope, when it is my time to die, someone will weep for me."

"Dan, take a few days off and go visit friends. Come back to work on Thursday. In the meantime, I will contact all the local police departments to see if they have anything on Carlos or Antonio. When you return, you have my permission to do what you do so well. This is not a suggestion; it is an order, sergeant."

"Yes, sir. I will take a few days off, but when I return, someone will pay dearly for what happened to Sonia. Captain Johnson, I want that person dead, and I want to be the one to pull the trigger and watch him die."

Captain Johnson is watching Ranger Mesa as he speaks. He is aware that Mesa's actions are classic Mesa, said without any outward emotions with the exception of obvious anger. Johnson is worried about Mesa and wonders what he will do.

Captain Johnson turns on the TV to channel 23; KBOT news is broadcasting.

"Good evening, I am Eric Sandoval of the editorial department of KBOT. I want to talk to you about something I believe to be a blot on the law enforcement officers of Arizona. I am talking about one of the Arizona Rangers, a Sergeant Daniel Mesa of the Santa Cruz rangers. It seems that another person has died because of Sergeant Mesa's actions. My sources tell me that Sonia Perdenales, a close friend of Mesa's, was kidnapped and murdered because of him. Granted, Sergeant Mesa did not pull the trigger. But because of his reputation and actions, people are afraid of him, and they take actions that often times result in the death or injury of innocent people. It is time a dinosaur such as Ranger Mesa becomes extinct. It is time he enters into the twenty-first century or disappears. The number of shootings he has been involved in is amazing. It is doubtful he remembers. A check of the records says he has killed or shot fifteen people in the last ten years. Sergeant Mesa, it is time for you to go away. Maybe it is time for the rangers to go away. This is Eric Sandoval for channel twenty-three news and good night."

Captain Johnson's fist crashes on the desk, and the walls rattle.

The phone rings, and he answers, "Captain Johnson here."

"Sam, did you see the new editorial about Dan Mesa? That son-of-bitch Sandoval needs to have his goobers caught in a vice and squeezed until he passes out from the pain. I guess under the circumstances the less said and done about it the better. We will let the governor's office handle everything. Where is Sergeant Mesa?"

"Sir, Sergeant Mesa is taking a few days of well-deserved leave on my orders. He fought it, but he knew I was not joking, so he reluctantly took leave. When he returns, I plan to turn him loose and let him do what he does best."

"Sam, it seems as if he really can't get a break. This state and country owe him a lot, but we don't realize it. Let me know when he returns. Take care, Sam; it could be worse."

In Douglas, Arizona, Carlos and Antonio are discussing their future and trying to stay ahead of the law.

"Carlos, maybe we should consider leaving Arizona and moving to Texas, or New Mexico, or maybe even Colorado? There we can hide out for a long time. It would be nice to just get away from this life for a while," Antonio says.

Carlos is far ahead of Antonio.

"You know something? You are right," he says. "I will sell my sedan and buy a pickup truck. I want a Dodge with a camper and four-wheel drive. I think a used truck will bring less attention."

"Boss, we should probably change our appearances. I will grow my hair longer and grow a moustache. You should grow a beard and a moustache."

They arrive at a dealership, and Carlos trades his '99 Lincoln town car for a '98 Dodge extended cab truck with a camper thrown in.

"Antonio," he says, "I have always wanted to buy a truck and drive across the country, but living in the city didn't allow for such. Now is the time to branch out and try new things. So let us go forward and seek new adventures."

"Boss, that ranger is not going to stop hunting us. He is hell on wheels when he gets angry. I know we have a contract on him, but we haven't heard anything from anyone, so he is still alive. I believe I could take him out myself. I don't think he is all that tough. People are always talking about him and how tough he is. I believe I can take him."

"Antonio, you are a fool. I should just let him kill you, but since you are the only friend I have right now, I will have to protect you. Together, we may be able to take him, but alone, neither one of us is capable. I know Ranger Mesa well. He took Jose, and he was tougher than either one of us. Dan Mesa is angry now, and he is extremely dangerous. He never allows his feelings to overrule his thinking, and a thinking man is dangerous. You and I are responsible for that woman's death, and he knows it. He plans to kill both of us; that is something I am sure of. Why in the hell did you have to do something so stupid as kidnap his girlfriend?"

"Boss, I thought that was what you wanted. I figured if we had her we could have made a deal for Ranson."

"Antonio, you don't make deals with the likes of Daniel Mesa. He would have shot you. The plain truth is you and I have a serious problem by the name of Ranger Dan Mesa. I hope the contract is carried out, because I am not going to jail, even if I have to kill myself."

In the maroon Dodge truck four-by-four with extended cab and camper that Carlos purchased. They proceed toward San Antonio. Carlos knows that he can get help in San Antonio to take Ranger Mesa out of this life.

In Yuma, Alana is watching the news when Matilda walks in. She sees the affect the news broadcast has on Alana, and she walks over and shuts off the TV.

"Honey, that newscast isn't worth watching. He is a blooming idiot, and anyone who pays attention to what he has to say has a serious judgment problem. Eric Sandoval made his name in the industry off the pain and suffering of others. He is the type of news reporter who would stick a microphone in your face right after you lost your husband in an auto accident. He feeds off others' misery, and he take things out of context and changes them to fit his latest crusade. He is on a mission to discredit the rangers just because they are there. He wants to discredit Dan Mesa, because Dan is a target and because Ranger Mesa is something he can never be. Dan Mesa is an honest-to-God man, and he stands for something."

"Mom, it really gets my temper up when someone attacks Dan for no reason. He deserves better. I remember how I treated him, and it still bothers me. Sandoval advocates doing away with the rangers. I feel like going over to the TV station and punching him in his face. But that would only give him something more to talk about and cause a lawsuit for the rangers."

"Alana, when this is over, what do you plan to do about Dan? He will never be the same again. I know his type; he will always blame himself for her death. Wherever he is at this moment, he is in torment. I can sense it. He reminds me of your father. Those two men are replicas of each other. It's almost like he is a reincarnation of your father." Matilda turns and walks away, remembering her husband and her feelings for Dan Mesa. *He belongs to Alana.*

Ranger Bonefacio Hernandez has put on a beard and moustache and is following Ranger Mesa. He knows where Mesa is headed. He is going to Sierra Vista.

"Captain, this in Hernandez," he says when he calls to report. "I am following Dan, and he is going to Sierra Vista. What is in Sierra Vista?"

"It isn't what. It is *who* is in Sierra Vista, and the who is an old friend of his who helped him find his life when his wife left him. I will tell you about it later. Stay on him, but don't let him see you."

Dan Mesa arrives in Sierra Vista and parks in front of the Chardon Blieu. He notices a beige Lexus with Maryland tags and two men changing the tire. They don't fit with the locals. Something in the back of his mind sounds a warning. He walks over to them.

"Gentlemen, I know why you are here. Believe me, you aren't men enough for one, and you aren't smart enough for the other. Take some free advice and go back to Maryland or Washington and tell Vermenti you aren't up to it. If I see you again, I will shoot first and ask questions later. Do you understand what I am saying to you?"

The younger man makes a move toward Ranger Mesa and immediately regrets it. He is suddenly staring down the barrel of the biggest pistol he has ever seen, a 44 magnum. He starts to sweat and his mouth is extremely dry.

Dan turns to the older gentleman and politely says, "Sir, if this man is your friend, I suggest you have a long talk with him about life and death. It would be a shame to shorten his life at his young age. Please pay attention to what I have told you. May you have a blessed day."

Mesa turns and walks away.

Unknown to Mesa, Ranger Bonefacio Hernandez has witnessed the entire incident and passes it on to Captain Johnson.

The older would be assassin looks toward the younger one and says, "Lorenzo, you have a lot to learn about people. That man is dangerous. Had I been him, I would have killed you. The only reason he didn't kill you was because he wears a badge. I saw something in his eyes, and believe me when I tell you do not be fooled by his politeness. He was only inches away from killing you. Next time, he will kill you and make no mistake about it."

"Johnnie, you are too old and too careful. I will kill him next time. Watch and see."

Johnnie "the Butcher" Martin, short for Johnnie Martinelli, looks at Lorenzo Balducci and shakes his head in a sad way.

"Good evening, sir, are you here for dinner and do you want smoking or nonsmoking?"

"Yes, one for dinner and in the nonsmoking area, please."

Charley takes note of the man, who seems to be in his early forties and is physically fit and not handsome but has a presence that speaks of courage and a hint of sadness in his eyes.

"Ma'am, is Ms. Olivetti working this evening?" he asks. "If she is, will you please tell her that an old friend would like to see her?"

"Who shall I say is asking for her?"

"Just tell her Daniel Mesa is asking for her. Thank you, Ma'am."

Charley walks away hurriedly and tells the waitress to go to the stranger's table.

The waitress approaches, saying, "What would you like to drink, sir?"

"I would like a glass of iced tea, please, with lemon, and a glass of White Zinfandel for my guest, who will be here shortly."

Dan's mind returns to Sonia. *Sonia, I wish I had been there for you. This shouldn't have happened to you. I promise you they will pay for what was done to you. I shall have to live with this for the rest of my life. I will get everyone who was a part this. I will make them pay!*

In the meantime, Charley knocks on Janie's office door.

"Come in, Charley. You look worried. What's wrong?"

"Ms. Olivetti, there is a rather handsome black man wearing western gear and a badge asking for you. He looks familiar, but yet I don't know him. What shall I do?"

"Charley, he is an Arizona ranger named Dan Mesa and a very, very dear friend. He is the one I let get away. Where is he seated?" she asks. "Oh, I bet I can tell you. He is seated so he has a complete view of the room with his back to the wall, right?"

"Yes, but how do you know that?"

"I know Ranger Daniel Mesa better than most. He is one in a million, and I mean exactly that. Show me where he is sitting."

Dan sees her coming and breaks out in a sweat. He rises as she approaches.

"Hello, Janie," he says, "it is good to see you again. I . . . I . . . well, what I mean is you are lovely."

"Why, Daniel Mesa, I do believe you are blushing! You really are happy to see me, aren't you?"

"Janie, I am always glad to see you. Every time I see you, you take my breath away. I guess I still have you under my skin. Please, have a seat. I ordered a glass of wine for you. If I remember correctly it is White Zinfandel?"

"Dan, I heard about Sonia, and I am so sorry. I heard she was a friend of yours. Have you caught those responsible for it?"

"No, I haven't, but I will. I can promise you that. It seems that the culprits are Carlos Meana and Antonio Blackbear of Tucson. They kidnapped her and took her to a house and left her there. The house was struck by lightning, and she burned to death. They tied her to a chair, and she was gagged. Every time I think about it, I just want to kill them slowly and let them suffer as she did. I keep having these nightmares . . . I can hear her screaming my name. I should have been there."

Janie is watching his face and sees the pain and hurt he is going through. Before she knows it, she is crying softly.

Mesa regains his composure and looks up to see her tears. He immediately apologizes.

"Janie, I am sorry for bothering you with this. I told you I would be back to spend some time with you after I finished that Jackson affair. I didn't think it would be under these circumstances. Captain Johnson told me—no, he ordered me—to take a few days off. I do believe he is worried about me."

Mesa smiles a crooked half smile, and his face suddenly lights up for a second.

"Dan, why don't you follow me home, and I will prepare a meal for you? It has been a long time since I cooked for a man."

"Okay," Dan says, "but I must warn you, there is a price on my head for five hundred thousand dollars. I met one of the assassins a few minutes ago. They were changing a tire across from the restaurant. I warned them that, the next time I see them, I will shoot first and ask questions later. Just in case they don't hear well or understand English, maybe I should park my truck in your garage until I leave Sierra Vista."

"Dan Mesa, how is it that you manage to stay in so much trouble?" Janie asks. "Well, I love you, and I will take you any way I can get you, so follow me."

Janie lives in an exclusive section of Sierra Vista in the foothills in an old refurbished ranch house with stables and horses. It seems that her past profession paid high dividends. Dan Mesa, a friend from years back, has never mentioned her past profession. He just likes her as a friend, and there are unspoken feelings that he dare not go into. He parks his truck in back of the house in the barn under the Breezeway. They walk inside. Janie turns around and smiles at him.

"Dan, do you mind if I change into something more comfortable than this gown? Follow me upstairs, sir."

Dan smiles to himself, remembering how she looks in a nightgown. He knows that, for a few minutes, he can just be Daniel Mesa, a man with a beautiful woman who loves him and demands nothing.

I guess I am a fortunate man who has some very good friends. Janie has always been there for me, but I have been there for her as well. Why can't we settle down together? Mesa is contemplating these things when Janie walks in wearing a lavender gown that takes his breath away. He stands there with his hat in his hand, smiling like a kid in a candy store.

"Daniel Mesa, you look as if you are seeing me for the first time. What is wrong? Don't you like me?" She smiles, knowing that she looks absolutely gorgeous.

"Janie, I just want to say . . . well, what I meant to say is . . ."

Suddenly, he finds himself in her arms, and her lips meet his. The whole world seems to be right for once in his life. A sea of warmth and contentment envelops them, and no one else matters for a while. Afterward, Mesa falls asleep and sleeps fretfully. He awakens to find that Janie is standing there watching him. He smiles.

"Janie, why can't we fall in love get married and just enjoy being with each other? I have been in love with you since we first met, and that has been more years than either of us wants to remember."

"Dan, I love you as well and always have. The problem is that I have been around the track a few times. There have been several men in my life, and you know that. Can you take me as I am and love me regardless of what I have been?"

"Janie, all I want is for you to be happy and for me to be happy. It doesn't matter what you once were or did. What matters is what you are now and plan to be in the future. I love you, and that is all that matters."

She smiles at him and walks toward the window to look out.

"Dan, you have issues and things you must deal with. Sonia's death is one you have to deal with. While you slept, I watched you. I heard you call her name, and I saw you crying. It tore at my heart to see you in such pain. I cannot and will not put you through pain again. I hurt you once, and I will never hurt you again. The only way I can ensure that I don't hurt you is by not getting too involved in a relationship with you. I do love you more than you can imagine. When all this is over and you've gotten over Sonia, please ask me again; I promise you won't have to ask twice, okay?"

"Janie, I plan to hold you to that promise. I promise you I won't ever try to change you. I want you just the way you are. I also love you dearly. Now what shall we do for an encore?"

"Dan, I want you to just relax and enjoy this time we have. You don't have to try to please me. I am your friend now and always. I promise I won't run away and won't object to what you do for a living either."

Meanwhile back in Patagonia, the fire department is still investigating the fire that killed Sonia Perdenales.

"Chief, look at what I found. I found this gas can laying in the weeds on the side over there. Chief, I don't think this was a total lightning strike. I believe this was arson and the lightning just happened to strike too. This is straight-out murder."

"Bill, have the lab boys from Tucson checked this place with a fine-tooth comb. I want these sons of bitches to pay dearly for what they have done. I want the evidence handled with care and no contamination. This has to be done by the book. This one is for Dan Mesa. He deserves to know the truth, and I'd hate to be the one responsible for this. He is already angry, and this will push him over the edge. I'd better call Sam."

The phone rings at the ranger station in Nogales. "Arizona rangers, Corporal Garcia speaking. Hello Pop, what can I do for you?" his son answers.

"Son, is Sam in his office? I have some more bad news for him."

"I will get him for you."

"Hello, Orlando," Captain Johnson says when he picks up, "what do you have for me?"

"Sam, we were finishing up our investigation of the fire in Patagonia, and we found something that makes this more than a lightning strike. Sam, that house was drenched in gas and set on fire. The lightning struck the house just by coincidence. This is capital murder. Sam, what will you tell Sergeant Mesa?"

"Orlando, this is one time I wish I was a dogcatcher instead of a ranger. I will just have to tell him the truth. Orlando, let's meet after work. I need a drink or maybe two."

"Old friend, I'll meet you at the bar at five thirty p.m. Take care. We'd better keep an eye on Dan. What is the latest on Carlos and Antonio?"

"Well, we know he bought a maroon Dodge pickup in Douglas. It has a camper on it, and they are supposed to be heading toward San Antonio. I have notified the Texas rangers to keep an eye out for them. Sergeant Savalas is shadowing Sergeant Mesa. Let me know if anything else turns up."

Janie and Dan are watching an old Bogart movie when the phone rings.

"Hello?" Janie says. "Oh hello, Captain Johnson. Yes, Dan is here."

"Dan, Captain Johnson wants to talk to you. He sounds strange. I wonder what is going on."

Mesa takes the phone, wondering to himself what else can go wrong?

"Hello, sir, what can I do for you?"

"Dan, I just got off the phone with Chief Garcia, and he told me that the house fire that killed Sonia was not due to lightning. Someone drenched that house with gas. It is a clear case of murder." The phone is silent for a few seconds.

"Dan, are you still there?"

Dan's voice is hard and bitter as he answers, "Yes, sir, I am still here. I will return immediately. I want to get started looking for those two. I'll see you in a few hours." After Dan hangs up, he turns to Janie. She sees the change in his face and knows he will be leaving. She waits for him to speak.

"Janie, I have to return to Nogales. They found that it was not a lightning strike that started the fire. It was arson and a clear case of murder. The house was drenched with gas. The lightning was just coincidence." He turns around quickly so she won't see the anger in his eyes.

Janie walks around and looks into his eyes. What she sees frightens her and she backs away quickly.

"Dan, sometimes you frighten even me. I know you better than most people, and what I see in your eyes is death. Promise me you will be careful and only kill if you absolutely have to."

"I can't promise you that. They killed her, and I plan to kill them—today, tomorrow, or next year. It may take me a year, but I will catch them."

He hugs her and then turns and walks away with his bags. As he gets into his truck, a bullet spits dirt and glass and shatters the right window of the 4Runner. Mesa dives for cover and comes up shooting at the sound. A second shot is fired, putting a hole in the brim of Mesa's hat. Mesa dives under the truck and comes out with an M16 and two grenades. He throws one and waits as it explodes.

A voice rings out saying, "Hold it. We give up! Ranger, please don't shoot. We give up."

"Throw out those guns and walk this way. I know one of you is hurt, so drag him out, and if you move one muscle I will kill you like the dogs you are."

Two men emerge, and one is missing his right hand, and the other one is bleeding. Mesa walks up to them and strikes one with all his force and turns and kicks the other in the groin and walks away. Seeing what is happening, Sergeant Savalas rushes up to stop Mesa. Mesa turns around swiftly so that the rifle is pointed at Savalas; he is consumed with anger.

"Dan, it's me Savalas. Don't shoot. I am under orders to follow you, so don't shoot."

Mesa relaxes his grip.

"Okay, Savalas. You'd better call the police and notify headquarters."

Dan rushes toward Janie as she comes running.

"Dan, I saw them and yelled, but you didn't hear me. Are you all right? Are you injured?"

"Honey, I am fine. I was lucky this time. Now you go back in, because I don't want you involved in this at all. I love you, and now I am going away, and you won't see or hear from me for a while. Just know I love you. Good-bye."

The Sierra Vista police arrive with Captain Heath, who remembers Ranger Mesa from the Jackson affair.

"Hello, ranger," he says. "How are you? What happened here?"

"Captain, these two gentlemen opened fire on me as I got into my truck. If you check, you will find that they are on the payroll of Vermenti Pellegrinni of Washington, DC, and Baltimore. He is the local crime boss. They were paid to kill me to keep me from finding Carlos Meana and Antonio Blackbear. They are the ones responsible for the fire in Patagonia that killed my friend."

"Sergeant Mesa, wherever you are, there is definitely action. Your captain asked me to be on the watch for you. We'll take your statement, and then you can go. Captain Johnson said to tell you to return to Nogales immediately and that they have new information."

The ride back to Nogales is uneventful, but Mesa arrives at ranger headquarters with his temper beyond dangerous. He rushes into the captain's office, where Captain Johnson is waiting as Mesa storms in.

"Sergeant, sit down and shut your mouth and listen," Johnson says. "I sent Savalas to shadow you, because we knew there were men sent to get you. I was trying to save your life."

"I know you were, and I appreciate it, but I have to find these men and make them pay for what was done to Sonia. I ran into two of their hired guns who were—"

"Sergeant Mesa, I want you to listen to what I have to say. I can't have you going off half-cocked and killing everyone you believe to be mixed up in this situation. You are my friend, but I will have your guts for garters if you screw up. So far, we know Carlos is headed toward New Mexico and possibly Texas. He bought a truck, and it has the On Star system, and we can track him using it until he realizes what we are doing. Right now, he is on I-10 headed east. Dan, sign out one of the ranger vehicles; that old truck of yours has taken a serious beating, and you need something more dependable."

"Okay, sir, I will. I won't let you down. Captain, have you heard from Lieutenant Osborne lately?"

"No, sergeant, I haven't, but they are probably busy with that prison break they had last week. Two of the individuals who escaped were friends of Blackbear. You had best be careful, because I believe Carlos and Pellegrinni planned that prison break. Those two are skilled at killing and mugging people. The Yuma police captured them about five years ago. Sergeant, when was the last time you qualified on the weapons you are carrying?"

"Sir, it has been a year or so, and yes sir, I am due. I will take care of it today. I believe Savalas needs to qualify also. I'll grab him, and we'll head to the range."

Mesa reports to the firing ranger to qualify, and after several rounds of firing, Dan emerges with a score of 298 hits of 300 shots. Savalas qualifies with 290 of 300.

He and Mesa are walking toward their vehicles when Mesa's truck suddenly erupts in flames. Mesa is blown across the parking lot. The 4Runner is totaled. It is now a broken link with his past. He has owned it since it was new in 1989.

People are rushing from everywhere. Captain Johnson arrives at the scene and sees Ranger Mesa on a stretcher bloody and bruised. He is unconscious, and there is a bad bruise on his head. Sergeant Savalas isn't so lucky; he is dead.

The ambulance attendant is checking Mesa's vital signs when Mesa goes into cardiac arrest. They apply the electrodes and bring him back, and the ambulance departs immediately for the hospital running code red all the way. Captain Johnson stays behind until Savalas's body is removed to the coroner's office. Then he leaves for the hospital. He goes immediately to the emergency room.

"I am Captain Johnson of the Arizona rangers, and one of my men was just admitted," he says to the nurse at the desk. "He is Ranger Daniel Mesa, a victim of an explosion. Can you please tell me about his condition?"

"Ranger, I am Nurse Helen Garza, and I admitted him. His doctor is Doctor Raymond Burke, one of our best surgeons. All I can tell you right now is that he is in serious condition with internal bleeding. Does he have close relatives here? If so, you may want to call them."

"He is divorced and hasn't any family close by," Captain Johnson replies. "His mom lives in Louisiana. I am his boss and friend, so if there is anything he needs, you tell me."

"Ranger, why don't you have a cup of coffee, and I will see what I can find out about him. Isn't he that ranger who killed that Jackson fella and whose girlfriend was kidnapped?"

"Yes ma'am, he is and also a damned good friend. He has a son who would surely miss his father if anything happened to him."

Nurse Garza departs, and Captain Johnson takes a seat and waits.

In the operating room, Dr. Burke is working frantically to save Daniel Mesa's life.

"Clamps please. He has started hemorrhaging again. How is his blood pressure, nurse?"

"It's steadily dropping. He is fighting, doctor. He has a will to live like nothing I have ever seen. Who is this guy?"

"Nurse, I was told he is one of the Arizona rangers and was caught in an explosion where one ranger was killed. I have stopped the bleeding and repaired the tear in his heart. Now, let's check that head wound. Doctor Wilson, how bad is his head wound?"

"Ray, he has sustained a bad blow to the head, and I suspect a concussion. If we can stop the swelling, he has a chance—a small one, but a chance. Look at his blood pressure. It has leveled off, and his breathing is normal. I have a feeling he is going to be okay. This guy is a fighter. If he is as tough on his job as he is in this operating room, I'd hate to face him."

Dr. Burke looks at Mesa and says, "Ranger Mesa, I have done all I can. Now it is up to you to recover. I hope someone somewhere is praying for you."

As the doctors leave the emergency room, Nurse Garza approaches Dr. Burke and asks how Ranger Mesa is doing.

"The ranger is holding on, but it is still touch and go. Please notify his next of kin just in case."

"Doctor, his boss is in the waiting room waiting for a report on the ranger. What should I tell him? He doesn't have any next of kin here. He is alone. He is that ranger who captured that Jackson fella a few months ago. He is also the one whose girlfriend was kidnapped and killed a few days ago. I get the feeling this guy is something else."

Dr. Burke walks into the waiting room and sees Captain Johnson and says: "Ranger, I'm Doctor Burke. We have stabilized the ranger, and so far so good. He stands a good chance of recovery, if we can reduce the swelling in his head. He has a concussion, and he is in a coma. We will just have to wait and see. He is a fighter, and that is good. Captain, tell me about this Mesa fellow."

"Doctor, Dan Mesa is one in a million. I have known him for a few years. He is a good guy, the best friend you can have, and probably the worst enemy you could have if you cross him. He is one tough little guy who has had some really bad luck of late but managed to survive it all. He was shot about six months ago, and he recovered fast. He just lost a friend he cared for deeply, and I suspect the same people carried out this attempt on his life. I am going to place a Ranger on his door until he is conscious again. If he needs anything, just let me know. I don't want any information released about him unless it is okayed by me. I want a blackout on this case. They could try again. This is the third attempt in less than two weeks."

"Captain, can I assume that he was under a lot of pressure and that he was determined to catch the person responsible for his lady's death? I ask that because it seems to be the reason he is so determined to live. Medicine can only do so much. The rest depends on the individual. Thank you for telling me about him."

"No, thank you and your staff for caring for him. He was lucky, but Ranger Savalas wasn't so lucky. If Dan Mesa recovers from this, there will be hell to pay by whoever is responsible for this."

In Tucson, it is the news hour at six p.m., and the news reporter says, "Good evening, I am Laura Denton, and we have breaking news of an explosion in Nogales at the ranger's station. We will now go to the reporter on scene, Chuck Garrison. Chuck, are you there?"

"Yes, Laura. We are in Nogales at the ranger detachment for Santa Cruz County, where someone planted a bomb in one of the rangers' personal vehicles. One ranger was killed instantly, and the other one is in serious condition at the local hospital here. They are keeping the name of the deceased ranger quiet until his next of kin has been told. The injured ranger is the same one who was responsible for the capture of Jose Guittierrez-Jackson. He is also the same Ranger whose girlfriend was killed a few days ago. Ranger Dan Mesa is well known in the ranger circles and well respected. However, it is apparent that someone has a grudge against him and is trying to kill him. Live in Nogales at the ranger station, this is Chuck Garrison of Channel 12 News."

"There you have it," Laura says. "It seems that, once again, Ranger Mesa is the center of attention in the law enforcement arena. This is Laura Denton reporting."

In Yuma, Arizona both Alana and her mother, Adelaide are listening to the news and so is Major McMasters.

A telephone rings in Washington, DC, at Vermenti Pellegrinni's house. The answering machine turns on, and the caller leaves a message. "The target in Arizona has been hit, although not a center hit but just as deadly." The machine cuts off. A figure listens and smiles.

In an office at FBI headquarters, Agent Scott Ortiz is listening to the recording courtesy of wiretapping. He is puzzled about the term *target*. His first thoughts are of Dan Mesa, his friend and brother. He picks up the phone and calls Captain Johnson in Nogales, Arizona.

When the phone rings at ranger headquarters in Nogales, a ranger answers, "Arizona rangers, Sergeant Jones speaking. May I help you?"

"Sergeant, I am Agent Ortiz of the FBI calling from DC. May I speak to Captain Johnson?"

"Sir, if you'll hold I will get him for you."

"This is Captain Johnson," "How are you, Agent Ortiz? I know why you are calling. There was an explosion, and Dan was seriously injured. We don't know how bad it is yet."

"Captain, I suspect it was spearheaded by Vermenti Pellegrinni but requested by Carlos Meana. If Meana and Pellegrinni had anything to do with this, they will seriously regret it. If Dan dies or is permanently disabled, there is not a rock they can hide under. If you need anything, just give me a call."

"Thanks, Agent Ortiz. Dan is a good friend of mine too. I will keep you posted on his condition. Since you are there in the area, will you please tell his ex-wife and in-laws? He is in the Tucson Medical Center with an around-the-clock guard. The explosion killed one of our rangers, Sergeant Savalas. As you are aware, when a cop is killed, it becomes open season on criminals. Carlos and Antonio Blackbear are moving targets now. Take care, and I will be in touch."

Scott hangs up the phone and suddenly realizes what he has to do. He walks into his secretary's office and prepares to sign out.

"Annette, I will be out for a couple of days. Do you remember that ranger who came to see me about a few weeks ago?"

"Yes, sir, I do. He was a handsome fellow in a cowboy sort of way."

"He has been my friend for almost thirty years. Today, he was almost killed in an explosion arranged by someone here in Washington, DC, or Baltimore. I have to go and visit his son and ex-wife and tell them what has happened. This I don't like doing. Send an e-mail to the director and let him know I can be reached on my cellular phone or at Jonathan Horatio Williams's in Baltimore as four zero nine five five five three eight two seven."

The drive to Baltimore is uneventful, and he arrives in an hour. Jonathan opens the door and seems surprised to see Scotty.

"Scotty, what brings you to Baltimore?" he asks.

"Sir, I have some bad news. There was an explosion in Nogales, and Dan was injured badly. Someone placed explosives under his truck. Dan wasn't in the truck at the time, but he was approaching it when it exploded. He received internal injuries, and they don't know how severe they are. He has a concussion and is in a coma. I have and agent who was keeping watch over Dan and he told me what happened. I also spoke with his Captain."

"Scotty, come into the den. Would you like a drink? I think I need one now."

At that moment, Nadia and Garnett walk in. Immediately, they seem aware that something is wrong.

Garnett speaks say; "What has happened to Dan? Don't tell me he is dead?"

Jonathan moves to her side, saying, "Honey, he has been injured, but he is still alive. According to Scotty, someone placed a bomb under his truck, but he wasn't in it. He was walking toward it when the bomb exploded. He has internal injuries, a concussion, and he is in a coma."

Garnett rushes out of the room followed by Scotty.

"Jonathan, I have always dreaded this day. He is as close as we will ever get to having a son. He's like my own child. I pray that God will keep him safe."

"Honey, he will be okay. Dan is a tough fellow; he will make it through this. He made it through Vietnam and the Persian Gulf, and he will come through this too. We will say a prayer together for him. I don't believe this is sitting well with Garnett. This very thing is one of the reasons she left him. All of her fears have come to be a reality."

In the backyard, Scotty is trying to comfort Garnett.

"Garnett, he isn't dead. He is only wounded, and I know he will recover. Dan Mesa is too damned mean to give up and die. He has Devlin to live for, and he loves you still."

"I have always been afraid something like this would happen, and now it has come to pass. He could have a job doing anything he wants to do, but no, he had to be a bloody Arizona ranger, and now he could die. What do I tell Devlin? How do I explain what has happened? Devlin looks on him as his hero. That boy would die if some happened to his father."

"Hey, he is going to be okay. Just wait and see. I have to leave and return to Washington and take care of some things, but I will be in touch."

"Scotty, do the rangers know who did this to Dan?"

"They have a good idea, but I know exactly who did it, and I will take care of them in a most appropriate way, using the law."

"Scotty, I have known you as long as I have known Dan. Don't you do anything that will get you into trouble. Dan wouldn't want that, and neither would I."

"I promise you that whoever did it will pay, and that is all I promise. I love you, kid. I will talk to you soon. Oh, he is in the Tucson Medical Center, and you can call anytime to check on him."

After Agent Ortiz gets into his car and leaves, Garnett stands there not wanting to cry. Yet somewhere deep inside, she knows she still has feelings for that stupid bullheaded man. Suddenly overcome with emotion, she breaks down crying. At that moment, Devlin arrives from school. Nadia and Garnett try to explain to Devlin what has happened to his father.

"Devlin, Dad was injured in an accident. Someone blew up his truck, and he was injured. He is in the hospital in Arizona and may have to stay there for a while. I want you to say a special prayer for Daddy every day until he is well. God listens to our prayers, especially those of young children."

As they walk into the house the child looks at his mom and grandmother, and tears begin to flow down his cheek. Nadia and Garnett are also crying. Devlin turns to his grandfather.

"Granddad, we need to go and see Dad. He needs us, and I need him."

Later that night, a child's prayer is sent up to heaven with the hope that God will answer his prayer. Other prayers are also sent toward heaven.

Meanwhile, back in Washington, DC, a dark-clad figure enters a palatial home. No alarms go off, and no dog barks. A closer look reveals that the dog is dead and the wires to the alarm system have been cut. The dark figure moves stealthily from room to room as if searching for something or someone. He moves on the ball of each foot like a ballet dancer. He approaches the master bedroom, pauses, and enters, moving quietly, and pounces on his victim. The figure plunges a dagger into the heart of the man lying in the bed. The man stiffens, kicks his feet violently, and dies. The dark-clad figure leaves in the same manner he arrived without anyone noticing.

Chapter Seven

The butler discovers Vermenti Pellegrinni's body early the next morning, and the police are summoned to the residence. Detective Sergeant Francine Miller arrives to conduct the investigation. Sergeant Miller is a seasoned policewoman with ten years of military service as a criminal investigator and five years in the Washington, DC, police department as an investigator. She is a crack shot and skilled in the martial arts.

"Okay, fellas what do we have here?" she asks.

Sergeant John Pierce of the DC police says, "Detective, it appears that someone killed the family pet, a German shepherd, and disconnected the alarm system. I can tell you one thing for sure—whoever this person was, he or she is a professional. We have dusted and found no fingerprints, no footprints, nothing! I believe this was a mob hit. This was done too perfectly. Most likely Mr. Pellegrinni pissed off the wrong people or, as the expression goes, "He left the door open, and the wrong dog came home."

Sergeant Miller walks the perimeter looking for signs. Suddenly, she stops and looks at an impression on the grass.

"John, come and look at this," she says. "It is a footprint, but the imprint is so light, as if he was floating. I have seen this before, but it was in South Korea. This individual is skilled in the martial arts, and I'd say he was an import from someplace overseas. I agree it was a mob hit; whoever is paying the bill paid a tidy sum for this person. I'd bet a hundred-dollar-bill this person is no longer in this country."

The coroner takes the body away. That day, the Washington Post headlines read "Noted Mob Boss Vermenti Pellegrinni Murdered in

His Bed." The article goes on to say, "The police believe it was a professional job possibly carried out by other mob bosses."

The black-clad figure removes his clothing, burns it, and takes a bath. He removes all traces of the fire from his fireplace. He fixes his breakfast and makes a toast to his friend.

Dr. Garnett William-Mesa reads about the execution of Pellegrinni and immediately knows who the killer is. She says a prayer and goes off to work. She has a strange feeling that the hand of destiny has taken control and wonders where it will end. From work, she calls the Tucson Medical Center.

"Hello, I am Dr. Garnett Williamson-Mesa, and I am calling to inquire about the condition of Sergeant Daniel Mesa of the Arizona rangers. I am his ex-wife. I know you can't release information without the approval of Captain Johnson, so please call him for approval. I will hold while you do so."

"Dr. William-Mesa, I am Nurse Garza," the woman on the line says, "and Captain Johnson said you'd probably call. I have to ask some questions to ensure you are who you say you are. The first question is what was Ranger Mesa's last job in the air force when he was on active duty?"

"His last job was that of base commander at Ankara Air Station Turkey."

"That is correct. The next question is what is your son's name?"

Surprised, she answers, "His name is Devlin Jonathan Williamson-Mesa."

"Your answers are correct. Now what can I do for you?"

Garnett's voice cracks a little as she speaks, "I want to know Dan's condition and what his chances of survival are."

"Dr. Williamson-Mesa, the ranger's condition is serious, but once he is out of the coma, we will know more. He has been in a coma for thirty-six hours. There is some swelling of the brain due to bruising caused by a blow to the head. He has a concussion, but being in a coma allows the brain to heal itself. Tell Devlin that, if there is any way possible, we will save his father."

With a trembling voice, Garnett thanks Nurse Garza and hangs up the phone.

Dr. Burke is passing by as Nurse Garza hangs up the phone.

"Dr. Burke," she says, "that was the ranger's ex-wife on the phone. They may be divorced, but that woman loves that man dearly. I am a good judge of people. I don't know what their problems were, but she still loves him. Her voice was breaking the entire time she was on the line. He is a lucky man. Let's try to save that man. According to his wife he has a little boy who thinks his father is a hero."

"Nurse, I am on my way to check on him now. Walk with me for a bit," the doctor says.

They enter Mesa's room. His breathing is easy, and his color is good. Dr. Burke opens Dan's eye and shines a light into it.

"I am not dead yet," Mesa whispers, "although, I feel like I have been ridden hard and put up wet."

Dr. Burke jumps back and smiles, saying, "Welcome back, ranger. It is good to know that you are still with us. Nurse, let's check his blood pressure and reflexes."

His blood pressure readings are approaching normal, although his right leg shows no reflex at all.

"Ranger, we have a problem with your right leg. It shows no reflex at all. Now don't panic; it could be due to the trauma to your head. Your brain is bruised badly, and your heart was torn. We repaired the injury, but you are not out of the woods yet."

Almost immediately, Dan begins to shake, and his eyes roll back in his head. A code blue is signaled, and a team instantly assembles. Dr. Burke explains that the shaking and rolling eyes were due to the blunt trauma to his brain, and that there is a possibility of him being unconscious for a while.

When Captain Johnson checks in, he is told that Mesa's condition is still serious and is told of his momentary conscious state.

In San Antonio, Carlos learns of Pellegrinni's death during the evening news at Carlos's brother's house.

"Good evening," the news anchor says, "I am Donald Ramos, and this is the CBS Evening News. We begin the news with the death of the notorious crime boss Vermenti Pellegrinni. His butler found his body earlier today. The authorities say his death was an execution. It is the opinion of the police that his death was a professional hit. We will go to John Ackers on the scene in Washington, DC."

"Good evening, Donald. We are on the scene at Mr. Pellegrinni's home in Washington, DC. It is apparent that the killer knew what he was doing. The family pet was killed and the alarm system disconnected. He was killed with a dagger to the heart in such a way that it led the authorities to believe it was the work of Oriental assassins. Apparently, Pellegrinni was moving into the territories of some of the other bosses and was taken out because of that. The police are looking for an assassin from the Orient and are working with Interpol to find out if they are aware of any person fitting such a description. Back to you, Donald."

"Thanks, John, and now on to the rest of the news. The president is still considering going to war in the Middle East . . . ."

Carlos turns the TV off and is shaken. Antonio's face is drawn and he is afraid.

"Boss, who killed Señor Pellegrinni? Was he moving into another boss' territory as the news said?"

"Antonio, someone killed Vermenti, but it wasn't because of that. If Mesa wasn't in the hospital, I'd say he did it, but he couldn't have. Someone is onto us and our connection with Pellegrinni. We'd better lay low."

Back in Nogales, Captain Johnson is on the phone with Colonel Grant.

"Sam, how is Sergeant Mesa doing? Has he regained consciousness?" the colonel asks. "I found myself actually saying a prayer for him. I am not much of a religious man, but this time I figured it was out of my hands and someone much more powerful than me is in control. I am angry, and I want to kill someone, but whom?"

Sam replies, "Sir, Sergeant Mesa did regain consciousness for a few minutes, but something happened, and he went into spasms and convulsions. By the time the doctor got him settled, he had gone back into a coma. According to his doctor, Doctor Burke, it was an expected reaction and it is good, because as long as he is unconscious, the brain heals better. I want to go see him, but I just don't know what to say or do for him. I also want to kill those responsible, and they are Carlos Meana and Antonio Blackbear. They have gone undercover, and right now, we don't know exactly where they are. We do know they are in San Antonio, but where?"

"Captain, have we missed something in this case? I want you and your people to pull out everything you have on Carlos and Antonio. Examine all information—I don't care how trivial it may seem. Talk to everyone who may have had an association with them. Talk to the FBI and the drug enforcement people. Oh yes, also talk to immigrations and the border patrol. They have been watching Carlos and his people for years. Let me know what you find out. I'll talk with you soon."

Captain Johnson hangs up the phone and ponders want to do next. He decides to calls in all the rangers to hold a big meeting. The Arizona state police are alerted and the local Detachment sends Captain Francesco Benadetti. Major McMasters of the Yuma ranger detachment sends Lieutenant Alana Osborne.

The meeting is held in Nogales with Captain Johnson in charge. The media has been notified and several prominent news correspondence are present. The meeting is called to order.

"Ladies and gentlemen, the reason I called this meeting is because Colonel Grant wants an all-out search for anyone who may have had dealings with Carlos Meana and Antonio Blackbear. They have gone undercover, and we haven't been able to find them. We know they were in San Antonio, but where we don't know. We want to coordinate with the border patrol, immigrations and naturalizations and the Drug Enforcement Agency. Carlos was dealing in drugs and in Illegal aliens. We are happy to have Captain Benadetti of the state police and Lieutenant Osborne of the Yuma ranger detachment working with us. I personally thank you for coming on board. We can really use your help. Are there questions?"

In one voice, everyone asks about Sergeant Mesa's condition. Lieutenant Osborne is quiet, but then she asks, "Captain, have the doctors said whether Dan—I mean the sergeant—will pull through this?"

"I spoke to Doctor Burke, Dan's doctor, and he told me he just didn't know. Dan's heart had to be sewn due to a tear in it, and then there is the internal bleeding and his brain is swollen. He did regain consciousness for a few minutes. Then he went into spasms and back into a coma. I notified his brother, Sergeant David Mesa of the Ruston, Louisiana, police department, as well as his ex-wife, Doctor Garnett Williamson-Mesa of Baltimore. At this point in time, that is all I can tell you. If you know of some good prayers, I ask you to say them for Sergeant Mesa with the hope he recovers and comes back to us. I want you to check with your informants, and don't let anything slip by you no matter how unimportant it may seem. Let's get rolling. Keep me informed of what you find. Lieutenant Osborne, can I see you for a minute?"

The group departs, and Lieutenant Osborne remains.

"Alana, how are you holding up under the strain? How are you personally?"

She smiles a pained smile and says, "Captain, I'm okay physically, but mentally, I feel like this is my fault somehow. The last time I spoke to him, it was not very pleasant, and I am not sure how he felt about me when he left. Then Sonia's death and now this! He has been through a lot over the years and never complained; he just kept on doing his job. I just don't know what to do." The lieutenant turns her back to the captain to prevent him from seeing the tears in her eyes. Captain Johnson waits quietly until she regains her composure. Slowly, she turns around and continues, "I just don't know what to do. I want to go see him, but what do I say."

"Lieutenant, go see him. Maybe if you just talk to him, the sound of your voice may help bring him back."

In the medical center in Tucson, a vigil is in process. Sitting in the waiting room are Janie Olivetti, Dan's goddaughter Sierra Montoya and her mother, and a fellow unknown to anyone. He is of Hispanic origin and is wearing a white suit, expensive tan shoes, and a black silk shirt. Osborne is watching his every move. She alerts the guard on duty at Sergeant Mesa's door, who calls for backup asking for a plain-clothes person.

A Sergeant from the Tucson Police department arrives and walks over to Lieutenant Osborne and says, "Hello, Alana, how's our boy doing?"

Lieutenant Osborne recognizes what is happening and plays along, "He is the same—no change. Look, I could use some coffee. Let's go to the cafeteria." She winks at Sergeant Burke, and they make it look as if they are leaving, but they only go around the corner.

"I am Sergeant Burke, and I must apologize for my actions, but I figured that, by appearing to be a friend, no one would catch on. I saw a gentleman in a white suit. Would that be the person in question?"

"Yes, sergeant, it is, and I believe he is a hit man sent here to finish the job on Sergeant Mesa. He has a certain look about him, and I know I'm right!"

Sergeant Burke smiles and says, "Lieutenant, you have a keen eye. That man is a killer, and if he was sent to kill your ranger, then someone is paying out a lot of money. He is a professional, and there he goes out the door. He has several aliases so we don't know his name, but according to Interpol, he has killed several people in Europe and even in the Soviet Union. We suspect he is from Portugal. He speaks Spanish, English, French, and Russian, and maybe even some of the Chines languages. You and I know him, but he doesn't know who we are, and that gives us an advantage. We will pass around pictures of him to our police department and also to the rangers and the border patrol. Let's make sure that whoever is guarding the sergeant is familiar with his face."

Captain Johnson has taken over the investigation and has the forensic team double-checking everything about the explosion.

"Fellows, I want you to start here at the point of impact and work yourselves outward to about one hundred yards and see what you find. If you don't find anything, then work your way out to two hundred yards. Whatever you find, bag it and bring it in. Next, I want to know what kind of explosive was used and what type of fuse was used and where was it placed on the vehicle. Check our files and those of Interpol to find out if they have anything on an assassin that uses this particular method of operation. There is one other thing. Do you remember those two prisoners who escaped from the Yuma prison? Find out their names, because they are friends of Carlos, and they may have been the ones responsible for planting that bomb. Also find out where Jose Guittierrez-Jackson's family members are, because they may have a score to settle with Dan Mesa."

Pictures of Armanti Sandoval, the gentleman in the white suit, are sent to every police department in the Southwest and also to immigrations, border patrol, customs, port of entry, and the FBI.

Sandoval, who is now going by the name of Saul Rodriguez, has a room at the Marriott about five blocks from the hospital. He is watching the news when he sees his photograph appear on the evening news. He knows he has to leave town immediately. He gets up, packs his bag, and does a sweep of the room to ensure he hasn't left any incriminating evidence. After a close inspection, he leaves the key on his bed and goes down the back stairs quietly. He stops and does a close inspection of the parking garage to see if anyone is watching. He gets into his rental car and departs the garage. Unknown to him, he is being watched by Sergeant Burke.

"Police three to headquarters, over."

"Headquarters receiving. Go ahead Police three."

"This is Sergeant Burke, and I am tailing Armanti Sandoval. He is heading west on Nineteenth Street driving a bronze Cadillac Catera. License plate number is Arizona TLR three four five. I am following but at a distance. I need backup. Send someone quickly. He has spotted me and is increasing his speed. He has turned left on Mesa Verde, heading for the interstate."

"Police Three, just follow him, but don't get into a speeding contest with him. We have notified Sergeant White and the Eye in the Sky is moving."

Sergeant Burke continues following Sandoval as he takes I-10 and heads west. She is running reds and traveling at seventy miles per hour, the posted speed limit. Burke is thinking, *Where is he headed? There isn't any place to escape to. He is increasing his speed. Where the heck is the Helicopter?*

"Police three, this is your Eye in the Sky. I have Mr. Sandoval, and I'll follow him and keep you posted."

The chase continues with Sandoval to increasing his speed. Suddenly, his car skids into another car, causing a five-car pileup. His car flips over and bursts into flame. Instantly, Sergeant Burke is on the scene, and the fire department and ambulance are notified. Traffic is backing up on the interstate as Burke approaches the burning car. Suddenly, it explodes and an inferno is created. The fire department eventually extinguishes the fire but finds no body.

"How did he escape?" Burke asks the deputy fire chief. "The fire had to reach a temperature of three hundred degrees. How did he escape?"

Deputy Fire Chief Gonzales shakes his head, saying, "Sergeant, it is impossible for anyone to have escaped that fire; I can't explain it."

The chaotic situation is cleared up, and traffic order is restored.

Sergeant Burke reports to headquarters and is still trying to figure out how Sandoval escaped from a burning car. She reports to her supervisor saying; "Lieutenant Hyatt, when the smoke cleared, there wasn't a body or anything to show that Sandoval was ever there. It is as if he just vanished. I can't explain it, and neither can the fire department. The only conclusion is that he was wearing some type of fire retardant clothing that allowed him to escape without being injured. He is a master of disguise, and he knows how to escape and evade capture."

Lieutenant Hyatt considers the situation and says; "Sergeant Burke, I want the TV stations to plaster his face on every screen, and I want his face in every post office and police station. I want Sandoval in prison."

Sandoval arrives in Baltimore and sends a telegram to Carlos Meana, informing him of what has taken place. Carlos reads the telegram and slams his fist on the table.

"He is still alive. How can one man be so damned lucky?"

"Boss, he isn't so lucky," Antonio says. "Look at what has happened to him. He had to kill his best friend, Jose Jackson in that shootout in Albuquerque and his lady friend is dead, and he has been injured. I don't think that is lucky at all. I would not want to be Ranger Mesa. He has a destiny with death. I plan to kill him myself. I am tired of his face and of his reputation. When he gets back on his feet, I will hunt him down and kill him."

As Carlos listens to Antonio, he knows his friend has the desire to kill Dan Mesa, but he wonders if he has the ability. Killing Mesa is a monumental feat, and so far the score is Mesa five and his opponents zero.

The days change to weeks, and Mesa lingers between death and oblivion. Garnett visits the hospital and takes Devlin. He looks at his father and kneels and says a prayer while holding his father's hand. He turns to his mother and smiles.

"Mom, Dad will be okay," he says. "He gripped my hand when I touched his. He knows I am here."

Garnett looks at her son and is startled with his revelation.

"Devlin, how do you know that?" she asks. "The doctors say Dad is very sick and he may never recover."

"Oh Mom, Dad will be with us for a long time. I have it on good authority. God has told me so."

Devlin walks away smiling, leaving his mother to wonder about her son.

In Nogales, Captain Johnson is talking with the father of Sergeant Savalas.

"Mr. Savalas, the rangers will take care of everything for the funeral. There isn't a need for you to worry about anything. I only wish I could bring him back. He was a good ranger. I can promise you that we will find the ones responsible for it. You know Sergeant Mesa would be here if it were possible. But he is still in a coma."

"Captain Johnson, will Dan pull through this? He and my son were such good friends. I will miss the two of them playing their crazy pranks on each other."

Captain Johnson looks surprised.

"Mr. Savalas, are you telling me that Dan Mesa has a sense of humor?" he asks. "I haven't ever seen or heard him tell a joke. I didn't know he had it in him. He is always serious and never smiles. However, Sonia did make him smile. Just the mention of her name brought a smile to his face. I don't know if he will pull through this one. He has been lucky in the past, but this time, I just don't know."

Sergeant Savalas's funeral is held at the Catholic church in Nogales with the whole city attending. The rangers are the pallbearers, and they provide the police escort. Savalas is laid to rest in the Veteran's Memorial Cemetery.

Mesa has been in a coma for three months and there are no signs of Carlos, Antonio, or Sandoval. Captain Johnson rants and raves about how they have vanished. The Rangers and the State Police are searching everywhere for them but so far no success. The hours, days and weeks continue to pass and Mesa hangs on.

In Tucson, Dr. Burke is making his round and stops to check on Ranger Mesa. As he enters, Mesa is trying to sit up.

"Well, ranger, welcome back to the land of the living. It has been three months since your injuries. Now take it easy, because we have to administer all sorts of test. How do you feel?"

Mesa needs a shave, and he looks somewhat confused. He has a full beard, something Mesa would never wear under normal circumstances. He sees his reflection in the mirror, and in a hoarse voice, he says, "Doctor, may I have a razor to shave?"

Doctor Burke smiles and says, "Ranger, you have been in a coma for three months and the first thing you ask for is a razor to shave? You ex-wife was here, and she said that was what you'd do. She knows you quite well, and she is a very nice lady. Okay, I will get you a razor, but first we have some tests to conduct."

Over the next several hours, Dan Mesa is examined and re-examined. Finally, after four hours, Dr. Burke comes in total amazement.

"Ranger Mesa, after every possible exam, we find nothing wrong with you. You are totally healed. The tear in your heart has healed, and the brain swelling no longer exists. The only thing left is to see if you can walk. I will send in an orderly to help."

"Thank you, Doctor Burke. I shall be in your debt forever. I need to call my mother and brother and let them know that I am okay. My mother is probably worried. Has either Lieutenant Osborne or a Miss Janie Olivetti been in?"

"Yes, both were here several times. They may even be here now. I will check and see. It is good to see you feeling better. I was not sure you'd recover so well. You have a lot of scars on your body. You have paid one hell of a price to do what you do. I, for one, owe you a debt of gratitude. I could never do what you do and have done."

Doctor Burke walks down the hall to the waiting room and sees Lieutenant Osborne and Captain Johnson.

"I have some good news for both of you. The ranger is conscious and talking. We have done every test possible, and he seems to be totally recovered. I am worried about his ability to walk. That is the next thing to check, but other than that, he is definitely okay. He asked for a razor to shave. Apparently, he hates wearing a beard."

Captain Johnson smiles and says, "He does hate a beard. Doctor, may we see him for a few minutes?"

"Yes, that will be good for him. He seems a little confused, but that is normal under the circumstances. He asked if the lieutenant had been in."

Dr. Burke leaves and Captain Johnson turns toward Lieutenant Osborne and says, "Alana, you go in first. He needs to see your face, and you need to see him conscious and be alone for a few minutes. I will come in after about fifteen minutes."

"Thank you, captain."

She walks to the door, knocks, and walks in. As she walks in, she sees his face and smiles at the beard.

"Dan, it is good to see you up and around," she says. "I was worried about you."

Dan smiles and says, "It is good to see you, Alana. You must excuse my appearance. I haven't had a chance to shave or clean up. I did manage to brush my teeth. I found that I can still walk without falling." He gives her a small smile.

She walks over to him and hugs him, noticing how he backs away a little before he hugs her. Slowly, he relaxes a little.

"Dan, I thought I had lost you this time. You have got to be more careful because I . . . ." She breaks down crying.

Dan walks over and is holding her hand when Captain Johnson walks in.

"Sergeant, you look well, and I am happy that you will be with us for a while longer. You gave us quite a scare." The Captain walks over and shakes his hand, smiling. "Dan, it is good to have you back. I have to give you some bad news. Sergeant Savalas was killed in the explosion that injured you. We uncovered evidence that leads us to believe it was a professional job. A professional hit man named Sandoval was hired to do the job, and we lost him on the freeway, but we will find him again."

"Captain, give me two weeks, and I will be back at work," Dan says. "I will find Carlos, Antonio, Sandoval, and everyone associated with this. I will tie it all to Pellegrinni."

"Dan, you don't have to worry about Pellegrinni. He is dead. Someone killed him the same day you were injured. The DC police believe it was one of the families who feared he was taking over their territory. He was executed in the Oriental fashion."

Upon hearing of the Oriental-style execution, Dan Mesa knows who killed Pellegrinni. He smiles and says a prayer for his friend.

The captain leaves, and the room is empty except for Alana and Dan Mesa.

Alana finds herself alone with Dan Mesa, a man of mystery, a man of extreme kindness, and yet a complete savage when the need arises. She has seen those sides of the man, and yet she knows nothing about him.

"Dan, you have been through a lot, but looking at you now, it seems as if nothing has happened to you. You recovered so quickly. How do you do the things you do? I find that you always surprise me. You have to start being a little more careful. You aren't ten feet tall and bulletproof. There are those of us who worry about you. I met Janie Olivetti, and I met Dr. Garnett Williamson-Mesa and a little fellow name Devlin Mesa. They all seem to have great feelings for you. That little fellow is something special. I see why you talk about him so much."

Ranger Mesa has a surprised look on his face and a smile.

"I know that some people care about me, especially Devlin. He is what keeps me going when I want to quit. I haven't been there for him as I'd like to be, but I guess that can't be helped. You said Garnett was here as well? That is a surprise. I didn't think she'd come."

"Dan Mesa, that lady still cares about you although she may never take you back. Always remain friends with her. I like her and the person she is. She said to tell you that her dad and mom send their love."

"I have always done things my way and lived life my way. It prevents anyone else from getting hurt because of me. Had it not been for me, Sonia would still be alive. I will make Carlos and Antonio pay dearly for what they have done. Is there still a bounty on me?"

"Yes, there is, and we don't know for sure who put up the bounty, but we do know that there are people waiting to kill you for it. So what do you plan to do about it?"

"I plan to get on with my life and train for complete recovery. Then I'm going after whoever is responsible for all of this."

At that point, Dr. Burke walks in and says, "Ranger, you need rest, so get into bed, and if you are a good fellow, I just may let you go home tomorrow under the condition that you take it easy for a few days. You have to have someone stay with you, just in case you have fainting spells. You took a healthy blow to your head. You will have headaches for a few days, but don't worry, they will go away. Who can stay with you for a few days?"

"Doctor, I live alone, and I don't have any family that lives close by," Dan says. "I guess I will have to stay here a bit longer."

"Doctor, I will stay with him until he gets on his feet. I am down here on temporary duty assignment, and it will work to my advantage to stay with him and save me considerable money as well."

Dan Mesa smiles one of his rare smiles as he turns toward Dr. Burke.

"Sir, I guess I will be leaving this hospital after all. Please express my appreciation to all the doctors, nurses, and staff for taking such good care of me. I owe them a debt of thanks."

They arrive at Dan's ranch in Nogales. He notices that the horses have been fed and that the place is clean. He is walking toward the kitchen to prepare coffee as Alana walks in. He smiles at her.

"Alana, how is your mom doing? I should call her."

"She is fine. Dan, why are you so nervous around me? I am still the same person I was six months ago. I realize I may have said things when I had amnesia, but I am back to being me, and I care a great deal about you. So now, tell me what you are feeling and experiencing."

"Alana, it seems as if everyone I love pays a heavy price for loving me, and I don't know why it happens. It is not safe for you to be around me. You have been shot and Sonia kidnapped and killed. Ranger Savalas, a close friend was killed as well. Jose is dead, and I am running out of friends. I don't have many friends left."

Mesa slams his fist on the table saying; "I' m going to make coffee. Would you like some?"

"Yes, coffee would be great if you have cream for it."

Mesa continues toward the kitchen and suddenly straightens up and collapses. Alana rushes to his side, but he is unconscious. She calls 911, and an ambulance is sent. She makes a second call to Captain Johnson of the rangers to tell him what happened and then follows the ambulance to the hospital. Mesa is admitted, and the waiting begins. After two hours, Dr. Burke comes in.

"Lieutenant Osborne, Sergeant Mesa is resting well. There really isn't anything to worry about. This was expected. He apparently overexerted himself and just passed out. It probably will not happen again, but I want to keep him here for a few more days."

"Doctor, can I see him for a few minutes?"

"Okay, but just for a few minutes. He isn't fully recovered yet, and it will take another week before he will be one hundred percent. I will drop in to see him in an hour."

She walks into the room, and Mesa is sleeping but fitfully. She knows he is having a nightmare again. She lightly taps him on the arm, and he awakens with a start. He looks at her for a moment, totally confused.

"Where am I, and how did I get here?

"Dan, you collapsed and I brought you back to the hospital. Dr. Burke says you will be okay. You overdid it a bit. He wants you to stay for a couple of days. I am going to report into Captain Johnson and Major McMasters and then I will be back. You go to sleep and rest."

Alana leans over kisses Mesa on the lips and says; "Here is a present just in case." She place a gun in his hand. He says thanks and he smiles a sleepy smile and drifts off to sleep.

Mesa is having a nightmare and suddenly awakens, knowing someone is in his room. His hand closes around the handle of his pistol, and he rolls to the floor. The dark figure opens fire on the bed, and Dan Mesa returns fire, wounding the assassin in the chest. Security rushes to the room as Mesa struggles to get up from the floor. Sergeant Dan Mesa has a grazed head and a bullet burn on his arm.

The police arrive along with the rangers while Dr. Burke is treating Mesa's head wound. Captain Johnson walks in with Sergeant Burke.

Johnson looks at Dan and says, "Sergeant Mesa, are you all right? It appears that someone still wants you dead. I think you should go into protective custody.'

"Captain, I have always fought my own battles, and I am not about to turn tail and run from these characters. I will meet them head-on. They started this, and I am going to end it. They killed Sonia and Savalas, and they have tried to kill me several times. Now it is my turn, and I plan to make everyone associated with this pay the ultimate price."

"Sergeant, I will not have you or any of the rangers involved in personal vendettas while wearing that ranger badge. Do you understand me?"

For the first time in his life as a ranger, Dan Mesa pulls the star off his chest and hands it to Captain Johnson.

"Sir, I quit, because I will never give up hunting those who did this to Sonia and Savalas. I love being a ranger, but I will leave the rangers before I give up my quest."

Captain Johnson realizes he is about to lose one of the best rangers he has. Suddenly, he realizes that the best way to keep track of Mesa is to keep him active as a ranger, because left to his own devices, Sergeant Daniel Mesa could be a force to reckon with.

"Sergeant Mesa, no one leaves the rangers. You are a ranger until you die. Just keep me posted on what you are doing. Now, tell me what happened."

Mesa relates what happened to the captain. In the meantime, the suspect is being treated in the emergency room. He asks to speak to Dan Mesa.

"Doctor, please, I must speak to Ranger Mesa. Please I don't have much time left."

When Dan Mesa arrives in the emergency room, he says, "Yes, what do you want from me and who the hell are you?"

"Ranger, I was sent by Carlos to kill you. He has also put a contract on your family, your ex-wife and son. I am sorry."

He gasps and dies on the operating table, never telling them who he is.

Mesa telephones Garnett. The phone rings in her office at Johns Hopkins.

"John Hopkins Hospital, how may I help you?" someone answers.

"I am Sergeant Daniel Mesa of the Arizona rangers, and this is an emergency. I need to speak with Doctor Garnett Williamson-Mesa."

"One moment please."

Mesa waits for what seems like and hour but is only a few minutes.

A voice answers saying; "Daniel, this is Garnett. What is wrong?"

"Garnett, pick up Devlin immediately and stay in the hospital until you hear from me. There is a contract out on you and Devlin. My captain is in the process of notifying the local police. But don't you trust anyone until I get there. I will be there in a matter of hours, and Scotty will be there too. I am sorry I got you into this. It seems as if someone wants me dead and doesn't care who has to die for that to happen. I will notify Scotty now, and he will escort you."

"Daniel, what is all this about?"

"Well, I had a fainting spell and went back to the hospital for a day. It wasn't anything serious and I am okay. While I was here, someone tried to kill me, but I got him. He told me about the contract before he died. Now, I promise all will be all right. You and Devlin will be okay."

"Dan, I am holding you to your promise. I know this isn't your doing, but I still get angry with you because of your job. Why can't you just give it up and do something else?"

"Garnett, if I did give up my job as a ranger, would you come back to me?"

There is a silence on the other end and then a deep breath.

"No, Dan, I will not return to you. It isn't that I don't love you. It's because too much time has elapsed, and we are different people now and can't go back."

"I see. I will make sure things are safe for you and Devlin. Give him a hug for me. Take care and don't take anything for granted. Good-bye."

At FBI headquarters, the phone rings in Agent Ortiz's office.

"This is Agent Ortiz," he answers. "How can I help you?"

"Scotty, this is Dan Mesa, and I need your help. Garnett and Devlin's lives are at risk. In attempt to get to me, someone has put out a contract on them. I need you and your people to provide protection for them."

"Dan, I will see to it personally. I understand they tried to kill you too. Take care of yourself, because I can't afford to lose my best friend. I don't do well at funerals."

"Thanks, Scotty. I owe you one, and I will repay it. Garnett and Devlin mean a lot to me, and I don't want anything to happen to them."

"Dan, I will protect them with my life. The only way they will get them is through me, and that won't happen. They are going to disappear until this is over. No one—not even you—will know where they are until this is over. So go and do what you do so well."

Mesa hangs up the phone and rushes to the airport for a flight to Baltimore. When Mesa arrives, he is escorted to the air reserves headquarters.

"Hello, Captain Mesa. I am Colonel Williamson, Garnett's first cousin, and I have been tasked to fly you to Baltimore the fastest way possible. Agent Ortiz will meet us at the airport. Take care of my cousin. She is one in a million, but you already know that."

"Thanks, colonel, and I will do everything in my power to protect them. Scotty will take care of them while I put this whole situation to rest. It has gone on long enough, and too many people have suffered because of it. Now I am going to make some very bad people pay with their lives."

"Captain Mesa or Ranger Mesa, I am glad you are one of the good guys, because you would make one hell of a bad guy. These fellows you are after, do they deserve what you are about to do to them?"

"Yes, sir, they deserve it and more besides. They killed a lady friend of mine and a fellow ranger, and they have tried killing me three times. The second time, they almost succeeded, but the third time I was ready for them, and the assassin paid with his life. Now I am going on the hunt. There will be a lot of dead people before this is over."

When they arrive in Baltimore, they are met at the airport by the FBI. Mesa proceeds with Scotty to Johns Hopkins Hospital. Garnett has Devlin with her when Mesa arrives. The entire nursing staff has been alerted that the rangers have arrived. Mesa walks in with his traditional jeans, western shirt, badge, and white hat. Only today he is carrying a hidden gun, a 9 mm. Mesa's features are drawn and tight, and he is wearing his death face.

As they step outside the hospital, two individuals open fire. Mesa pushes Garnett and Devlin to the ground and opens fire, emptying the revolver into the first assassin. With his left hand, he draws the 9 mm and opens fire. He puts four bullets into the second individual as she opens fire on him.

"Dan, stop. You will be killed," Garnett yells, but Mesa keeps running toward the lady, firing. She switches from the revolver to an automatic and continues firing until she drops, mortally wounded.

As suddenly as it started, it is over. Dan Mesa has two bullet holes in his hat, a bullet hole in his sleeve, and a bullet burn on his arm. He calmly holsters his weapons and rushes to his ex-wife and son. Both are unharmed. Garnett is visibly shaken, and Devlin is crying. Mesa picks his son up and comforts him. He puts his other arm around Garnett and holds her for a few minutes.

Agent Ortiz takes over searching the woman and man for ID, but he finds none. The ambulance arrives, and the bodies are taken away to the coroner's office. Slowly, order is restored, and Mesa takes Garnett and Devlin to her father's home. Scotty accompanies them.

Jonathan and Nadia are waiting when they arrive. Nadia sees a difference in Dan. She notices the drawn lines around his mouth and a smoldering fire in his eyes. She sees a man carrying more burdens than anyone man should carry.

"Mom, Dad, I am sorry all this happened. It seems that I am always apologizing these days. This attempt on Garnett and Devlin is related to the situation in Arizona, and I didn't know it would go this far. I will terminate this entire situation when I get back."

"Son, sometimes you just can't control some situations. Jonathan and I know that you didn't intentionally cause all this. Remember that we were there for some of the action. You just do what you have to do, and you will be in our prayers."

"Thanks, Mom," Dan says, "I needed to hear you say those things. I believe Garnett faults me for what has happened. I would never do anything to harm her or Devlin. They are most important to me. I guess it is time for me to move on before she really gets angry with me."

Garnett walks into the room and looks at Daniel Mesa with eyes as cold as ice. She turns away and then says, "Dan Mesa, if you ever endanger our lives again, you will never see me or Devlin again. What happened today was your fault. Don't ever bring your problems around us again."

Devlin comes into the room, and Dan picks him up and hugs him.

"Son, I love you dearly, and I would never intentionally hurt you or Mom. What happened today was because bad people wanted to hurt me because I am going to arrest them. They hurt two of my friends, and now they have tried to hurt Mommy and you. Always remember and know that I love you more than anything in this world."

Mesa turns slowly and walks out the door with stiff shoulders and a heavy heart. He gets into the rental car and drives away.

Inside her parents' home, Garnett is as silent as a mouse. All eyes are on her.

"Garnett, I can't believe you said that to him," Scotty says. "I have known both of you for more than twenty years, and I love you both, but never have I seen you treat anyone like that, most of all someone like Daniel Mesa. He would gladly give his life for anyone in this room. They don't come any better than him. You have just destroyed a very good man."

With those words, Scott walks out the door.

Chapter Eight

On a flight back to Arizona, Mesa is deep in thought when he suddenly realizes someone is speaking to him.

"I must apologize for my behavior," he says. "I didn't realize you were speaking to me."

The flight attendant smiles and says, "I was asking if you'd like a beverage of some type."

"Yes, a cup of coffee would be great . . . with cream and sugar."

She looks at him, deciding whether she likes him or not. She thinks, *He looks so alone, as if he is carrying the world on his shoulders.* She hands him the coffee and asks, "What do you do for a living?"

"I'm an Arizona ranger from Nogales, Arizona."

"I didn't know Arizona had rangers. I thought only Texas had rangers." She smiles at him, and he smiles back. "So, ranger, by what name are you called? I am Monica Saint Jacque from New Orleans, Louisiana."

He looks at her with eyes that never blink and says, "I'm Daniel Mesa, a sergeant in the rangers."

"Sergeant Mesa, it is my pleasure to meet you and the Arizona rangers. Well, I must complete my work, but I hope I see you again very soon."

She walks away smiling with a walk that tugs at his memory. She reminds him so much of Sonia, it's as though Sonia has been reincarnated. Suddenly, he feels very lonely.

The pilot announces that they are approaching Tucson, so Mesa prepares to depart the plane. Suddenly, Monica is standing there.

"Ranger, this is my turn around point from New Orleans to here. Maybe someday when you aren't busy chasing the bad guys, we could have dinner?"

Mesa is surprised and stammers, "Yes, I'd like that. Here is my card. It has my duty phone on it and my cellular phone."

She hands him her number and smiles, saying, "Don't forget to use it sometime." She smiles again. "She must have been some lady." Then she turns and walks away.

Dan Mesa is perplexed. He thinks, *There is something wrong here. This is a replay of Sonia. How did she know I was thinking about Sonia?*

Alana meets him in the airport, and she greets with a smile and a kiss.

"Cowboy, it is good to see you. I will be the first to say that I really missed you a lot. Have you eaten? You are very thin. I am worried about you. Captain Johnson told me about what happened in Baltimore, and I am sorry it happened again. One of these days, we will find peace and happiness."

"Alana, I missed you too. What have you done to yourself? There is something different about you. What I mean is, you have always been beautiful, but today you are exceptionally so."

"Dan, you haven't seen me for a few days, and you just missed me. Now, are you hungry? Because I am. I found a Greek restaurant on Fifth and Main named Odysseus. The food is absolutely great, especially the stuffed grape leaves, olive salad, and the lamb chops."

"Okay, Lieutenant Osborne, lead on. I am hungry."

They arrive at the restaurant, and the meal is excellent by Mesa's standards.

He looks at Alana and says, "Something strange happened on the plane. One of the flight attendants approached me and started a conversation, asking me what kind of work I did. I told her I was a ranger. She continued talking, and when she left, she said, 'She must have been some lady.' She smiled, handed me her address, and walked away. The strange part is how she knew I was thinking about Sonia, and the address she gave me is the same as Sonia's. Am I crazy or is something strange about this? Her name is Monica Saint Jacque."

"Dan, I know you are not crazy, and yes, there is something strange about what happened. Can you describe her?"

"Yes, she was about five feet six inches and weighed about one hundred twenty pounds. She has long, wavy brown hair and hazel eyes. She is possibly of African American descent and probably French—the same as I am. That isn't much to go on, but that's all I can tell you. We can call the airline and ask them about her."

Once they get to ranger headquarters, Captain Johnson is briefed, and he puts through a telephone call to Delta airlines in Dallas.

"Captain, there was a flight attendant by that name who worked for us about ten years ago and she was killed in a crash ago. She was the best in every way. Why do you ask?"

"Ma'am, this is going to sound crazy," Johnson says, "but one of my rangers was on Delta flight seven three two today from Baltimore to Tucson. He says he met someone by that name, and she was a flight attendant on that flight." Johnson describes her to the lady on the phone. He hears her take a deep breath.

Then she says, "Captain, your ranger described her to the finest detail, and yes, that was Monica. I can't explain it either."

"Thanks, ma'am, for all of your help. I will keep you posted on what we turn up."

The captain turns to Mesa and Osborne with a ghostly white face.

"Guys," he says, "the lady you described was killed in a crash about ten years ago; she did work for the airline. This is crazy. I need a drink. Now we are dealing with ghost. Sergeant, do me a favor and close this case as soon as possible."

Sergeant Dan Mesa turns around and walks out without saying a word. Mesa goes to the Ford dealership and buys a one-year-old Ford F150 4x4 with a V8 engine and off-road tires. The truck is midnight blue with an extended cab, shiny mag wheels, a wench, and running lights. It has duel exhaust and a distinctive exhaust sound.

Mesa then goes to his ranch and assembles an arsenal consisting of one M16 with one hundred rounds, one twelve-gauge shotgun with buckshot and one hundred rounds, one 30-30 Winchester with two hundred rounds, a .357 magnum with three hundred rounds, and ten hand grenades. It is September, so he takes five pairs of jeans, shirts, underwear, and hiking boots as well as several MREs (meals ready to eat) and a sleeping bag with a first aid kit.

Finally Dan returns to ranger headquarters and reports to Captain Johnson.

"Sergeant," the captain says, "the last we heard from Carlos and Antonio, they were in San Antonio. The Texas rangers have been keeping an eye on them for us. When you get to San Antonio, report to Major Boca Huerta, and he will bring you up to date. Oh, yes, you are now a temporary agent for the FBI. This will allow you to follow them anywhere they go. Sergeant, please be careful. These guys are playing for keeps. Now, go and do what you do so well, but stay alive and don't kill anyone unless you have to."

"Thanks, sir," Mesa says. "I will be careful. Please tell the colonel thanks as well."

Dan Mesa drives eastward on I-10 toward New Mexico and Texas. He covers nearly five hundred miles, and the Ford covers the miles effortlessly, but still it's not the 4Runner.

"I miss that truck, and I miss Savalas. I will make someone pay for your death, old friend."

In the meantime another plot unfolds in the home of Carlos's brother in San Antonio. They are celebrating Mexico's independence from Spain, when Carlos speaks.

"I still have a problem in my life known as Ranger Daniel Mesa," he says. "That hombre is driving me mad. I can feel his presence. He is either in San Antonio or he is headed in this direction. He knows I was involved in the señora's death, and he knows I tried to kill him and his friend, Ranger Savalas. He also knows I put a contract on his ex-wife and his son. I will have to kill him, or he will kill Antonio and me. He will never give up, and so I must stop him. If someone did to me what I have done to him, I would kill not only him but his entire family. I don't know what he will do, but I can tell you he is one angry, dangerous man. On a good day, he is one mean son-of-a-bitch, but when he is angry, he is ten times meaner."

Francisco Meana, Carlos's brother, is somewhat different in that he is trying to become respectable. He is a petty criminal with convictions for theft and trafficking in women after dark.

"Carlos," he says, "you are my brother, but I will not have you bringing your troubles to my home. If I were you, I'd try contacting Jackson's family and asking them to help you get rid of Mesa. I hear they'd love a chance to get even with the good ranger. I just happen to have a number where you can reach that female cousin of theirs, Mandy. She is a looker but tough as any guy who ever drew a gun. She hates Mesa with a passion. It seems he scorned her advances some time ago, and she hasn't forgotten that. Plus, Mesa killed Jackson."

"Francisco, you know you just saved the day. I owe you one for this," Carlos says. "Brother, do you see that police car cruising by? I am getting the feeling he is looking for me. I am going to slip away. Take care, and maybe I will see you when this is over."

With those words Carlos and Antonio leave south San Antonio, and using back roads, they start making their way back toward Arizona, hoping to make it to Yuma before the police realize what they are doing.

Dan Mesa arrives in San Antonio and reports to Major Huerta. As he enters the building for the Department of Public Safety, he notices a familiar face, or he thinks he does, and Dan Mesa never allows a warning to go unchallenged. He makes a note in his ranger daybook. Then he walks in and speaks to the receptionist.

"Good afternoon," he says. "I'm Sergeant Daniel Mesa of the Arizona rangers, and I'd like to speak to Major Huerta. Here are my credentials."

"I am Morgana Blake, Ranger Mesa," she says. "The major is expecting you. Your Captain Johnson called and told us you were coming. Carlotta will take you to the major. Welcome to San Antonio."

Carlotta is young and somewhat provocative. Mesa is familiar with the type and keeps a very business-like demeanor.

"Ranger Mesa, have you been to San Antonio before?" she asks. "Oh, here we are. The major's office is here. If you need someone to show you around, I am available."

Mesa opens the door and steps in. In the room is Major Boca Huerta, a military veteran and a veteran of many Ranger fight. In the room are several rangers who are looking at various reports. As Mesa walks in all talking stops.

Mesa speaks, "Sir, Sergeant Mesa of the Arizona rangers, reporting."

"Welcome to San Antonio and to our headquarters. Captain Johnson told me why you are here. Now how can we help you?"

"Sir, I need your help in locating a Carlos Meana and Antonio Blackbear. These are the latest photos we have of them. However, rumor has it that Carlos has grown a beard and Antonio is sporting a mustache and longer hair. I believe I saw Carlos and Antonio as I was entering the building. He was driving a Dodge truck, maroon in color, a four by four with a camper on back and Arizona tags."

"Ranger Mesa, if you were Meana, what would you do? Where would you go?"

"Sir, I would go to a place where I could see anyone coming after me. He came here to get help from his family. He has a brother named Francisco Meana, a petty criminal. Are you familiar with him? If I couldn't get help from my brother, I would try to find someone who had a grudge against the rangers and talk them into helping me. There is one family he would go to, and that would be the family of Jose Guittierrez-Jackson, the family of the man I killed a while back. They'd help him. I would probably hide out someplace in the southwest, close to the border. The Big Bend country or the Davis Mountains would be appropriate. Sir, I recommend an all-points bulletin along I-10 west and Highway 90 west. If possible, have your sketch artist put together pictures of Meana with a beard and Antonio with a mustache and pass it along to all state police and rangers along that route. I will notify the Arizona rangers in Yuma and Tucson to watch for the Guittierrez family leaving and heading east. May I use a phone to call my captain?"

Major Huerta buzzes Carlotta saying; "Carlotta, will you come in please? Carlotta opens the door and walk in saying, "Yes Sir?

Yes, Carlotta will you show Ranger Mesa to a phone."

"Ranger, please follow me."

Mesa follows Carlotta, who once again makes it known she is available. Mesa say "Thank you but I never mix business and pleasure." He smiles politely and continues with his business. The telephone rings at Santa Cruz Headquarters.

"Santa Cruz headquarters, Ranger Hernandez speaking."

"Bonnie, this is Dan Mesa. Is the captain in?"

"Yeah, Dan, hold on a minute."

"Mesa, how are things in San Antonio?" The captain asks when he picks up.

"Sir, things are good here," Dan says. "Captain, while talking with Major Huerta, we came to the conclusion that Carlos and Antonio are probably heading toward the Big Bend country and into the Davis Mountains. Once they get deep into those mountains, we will never catch them. Also, I believe Carlos has contacted Jose's family, in particular Mandy. They'll probably join forces to fight us. Captain, I believe we should contact Major McMasters and ask him to put a watch on the family members to determine if they are heading in this direction."

"That's a good idea, Dan," the captain says. "I will put Alana on it immediately. Have you spotted Carlos?"

"Yes, sir. I saw him as I was entering the building this morning. He has a beard, and Antonio has a mustache. They were traveling in a maroon Dodge truck with an extended cab and a camper on back. It is the same one they purchased in Douglas. They don't know I'm here. Maybe we will finally have a break."

"Dan, take care of yourself and remember that Jackson's family hates your guts. They would love to kill themselves a ranger, in particular one Daniel Mesa."

Mesa nods his head and says, "Major I plan to be very careful but thanks for caring."

Sergeant just remember that your aren't bullet proof. Now let me speak with Major Huerta."

Mesa hands the phone to Major Huerta saying, "Sir Major Johnson wants to speak with you. Captain Johnson here. Sir, thanks for your help. Are you familiar with this case we are working on?"

"Yes, I am. How can we help you?"

"Sergeant Mesa is deeply involved in this case, and I would appreciate it if you and the fellows could keep an eye on him. He is a damn good ranger, and this case is personal for him. He is the only person I have who can bring a conclusion to it. He has a temporary appointment as an FBI agent, but Texas is your domain, and I would prefer it be a Texas and Arizona joint effort to capture Carlos and Antonio."

"Captain Johnson, we are more than happy to work with you and Sergeant Mesa. I have kept a close watch on this case, and I'd love to see Carlos and his entire family locked up. I believe the Sergeant is correct in his assessment of the situation. If I were Carlos and Antonio, I'd head for the closest route to the border. There are smuggler routes into Mexico through those mountains that we aren't aware of. The sooner we get into place in those mountains, the better off we are. There are a few places in southwest San Antonio where we may be able to get some information. Let's stay in touch, okay?"

"Major, I really appreciate this. If I can ever return the favor, just call."

In a small café in Toronto, Canada, Satan—in the form of Armanti Sandovaldecides to lend a hand. He is reading the *Dallas Morning World* where he reads an account of the case involving Carlos Meana and Antonio Blackbear.

> Carlos Meana and Antonio Blackbear, two underworld figures, are sought by the Arizona and Texas rangers for their involvement in the kidnapping and death of a lady in Amado, Arizona. They are also sought in the bombing death of Arizona ranger Sergeant Savalas. A fellow ranger, Sergeant Daniel Mesa, was injured but is recovering. The rangers are actively looking for any and

> all evidence leading to the whereabouts of Carlos Meana and Antonio Blackbear. They are wanted in the deaths of Sonia Perdenales and ranger Sergeant Savalas and for the injury of Sergeant Mesa.

Sandoval contemplates the situation and decides to place a call to his friends in Houston.

"Mark, this in Armanti Sandoval. Are you familiar with the situation in Arizona involving Carlos Meana?"

"Yes, I've kept up with it, because it interests me. I want to see how Carlos handles himself. He is always shooting off his mouth about how he can take care of business. I want to know if he is all mouth or what."

"I know he is a big mouth," Sandoval says, "but should we get involved in this situation? Someone took out Pellegrinni, and we know it wasn't one of our people. Is there another player in this game that we are not aware of?"

"Armanti, I honestly don't know, but I have been monitoring everything that has happened. I don't like any of it. I wish you could have ended it all, but apparently, that wasn't meant to be. You had best stay clear of this whole thing. Let me work it from our end. As it stands now, we have the Arizona ranger, the Texas rangers, and the FBI involved and possibly another party that neither one of us can identify. I don't like unknown factors. Stay where you are until you hear from me personally. Do you have all the comforts of home there?"

"Mark, I believe your decision is a wise one, and yes, I am very comfortable here."

Armanti Sandoval is a very careful man, and he never allows anyone to get too close. The women in his life are the pay-as-you-go type. Things weren't always this way. There was a time when he was a successful college professor, teaching philosophy. Then his wife was accidentally killed in a botched hit on a government witness posing as a teacher. After the funeral Sandoval mourned his wife, and then he extracted revenge. The rest is history. His hit list numbers twenty-two confirmed kills in five years. His path of death reaches all the way to the Soviet Union.

Mark Adams is a third generation Mafia family member and cherishes his Sicilian blood. He is careful in all he does. He knows he should just wait and watch, but he decides to contact his informant at Texas ranger headquarters in Austin. Sometimes it is good to cultivate relationships with various groups of people. He places a call to an office in ranger headquarters, and secret information is passed on to Mark Adams

In the meantime, Captain Johnson calls Major McMasters in Yuma.

"Major, Captain Johnson here. I have it on good authority that Carlos and Antonio are going to try to contact Jackson's family to ask them to join in the fight against Sergeant Mesa and the Texas rangers. If possible, could you check with your sources and find out what is cooking around there?"

"Sure, Sam, not a problem. I will send the lieutenant and some backup to a couple of places down on Yuma Avenue. Someone will talk. I will call with whatever we find out."

"Thanks, Major. I owe you a big one."

McMasters walks down the hall to Lieutenant Osborne's office. The Lieutenant is busy on the computer when he walks in.

"Good morning, sir. What can I do for you?"

"Alana, I want you to take three rangers and go down to Yuma Street. Visit the hangouts of Jackson's friends and family and see what you can find out about them, Carlos, and Antonio. Captain Johnson believes Carlos has contacted or will contact them to help him get rid of Sergeant Mesa once and forever. If I was in their place and Carlos offered me the opportunity, I would probably go, and so will they. Find out what you can, and let me know."

"Yes, sir. When do you want me to get started?"

"You should get going right away."

I always wanted to be in charge so I finally have the chance to prove just how good I am, Alana thinks. So I'm going to use the Dan Mesa approach and take a few big tough Rangers with me. I think probably Corporal Dixon, Sergeant Rice, and Sergeant Benavidez will make the ideal team.

"Gentlemen, we have a mission to try to find out if Jackson's family has been contacted by Carlos and Antonio. There are some bars on Yuma Street where we can get information. We are going there. I chose you because of your abilities to take care of yourselves. I want each of you in your vests and armed. Remember, don't take any chances. If we have to, we will fight, but that is not our primary objective. Let's move."

Yuma Street is the kind of place the world could do without. Every kind of deviant hangs out there. The first place belongs to Harvey Harlan. He is an ex-marine sergeant who just happens to love the rough life. He is a standup guy and a good friend to the Rangers.

"Hello, Harlan," Alan says. "How's business these days?"

"Alana, it is good to see you," he says. "I see you are loaded for bear. What's up?"

"Well, I am sure you know about that business with Jackson and his family. Jackson is dead, but the story continues. It seems as if another nasty customer by the name of Carlos Meana and his sidekick, Antonio Blackbear, may be trying to contact them for help to get rid of Ranger Dan Mesa and some of the Texas rangers. Carlos is hiding out in the Big Bend country in southwest Texas."

"Alana, I do know that Martha, Miguel, and Carlo have been seen around the area. They are still angry with Dan Mesa and all of you for what happened. They will do anything to get even with Mesa. Be careful down here. There are some strange people on the street. Something is in the air. Take my word for it."

"Thanks, Harlan. We are going to the Tin Bucket. I've heard that the family hangs out there. Keep your customers inside for a while. I have a feeling all hell will break a loose before this night is over."

As Alana and the rangers are leaving, she sees a car parked with someone inside watching them.

"Guys, we are being watched so be careful," Alana says. "Remember, if it feels bad, it is bad. Use your gut feelings."

They enter the Tin Bucket, and Alana says, "Good evening, Manny. I want to know if any of the Jackson family is in here. Don't bother lying to me. I will know if you lie. Guys, fan out and cover every exit."

A loudmouth yells, "Hey you! Yeah, I'm talking to you, Mama. Why are you bothering us when you and I could be making music together?"

Several people break out laughing. Then the entire room turns silent as a really big woman, about six feet tall, walks toward Alana. Alana knows that the woman is Martha Guittierrez, Jose's cousin, and one of the people involved in the shoot-out with Jose and the rangers.

The lady walks toward Alana and stops about two feet away to make her pitch.

"Well, look at the ranger bitch. Someone ought to slap that badge off you."

The scene unfolds as if in slow motion. The lieutenant suddenly moves with a swift kick to Martha's left knee. As Martha turns slightly, Alana lands a punch to her kidneys. Before anyone can move, Martha is on her knees with her head forced to the side and the lieutenant's hand is in claw-like form, digging into Martha's throat. Martha is gagging and gasping for air. Alana looks around the room and slaps the woman on the side of her head. She passes out. The entire place is silent.

Alana turns around and takes Martha's weapon, and all hell breaks loose. In less than ten minutes, two men are shot, and one female wishes she had kept her mouth shut. The police arrive and take them to jail.

Alana and the group move on down the street. Suddenly, someone fires a shot, but no one is hit. The rangers take cover. Alana fires, hitting one gunman in the chest. Just at that moment, two more shots ring out, and Corporal Dixon fires, hitting one of the assassins in the chest. As quickly as it began, it is over. The score is rangers two and assassins zero.

Major McMasters arrives on the scene. Alana knows she has to go through internal affairs. The major is a humane sort of fellow and knows what a shooting does to some people. Yet, he knows he has to question Lieutenant Osborne.

"Alana, how did all this get started?"

"Sir, it started in the Tin Bucket when Martha Guittierrez attacked me, and it just spread. I took her out and disarmed her. I left her lying on the floor. Arresting her will serve no purpose. We left the Tin Bucket, and suddenly, all hell broke loose. The shooters were professionals, as you can tell from their weapons. Someone is paying a lot of money to kill us. The question is whether all this is associated with Sergeant Mesa and Carlos Meana."

"Lieutenant, I have to assume it is all related in some manner. Jose's family is vindictive and very nasty, and they do hold grudges. Do not become careless, as you may wind up a statistic, and that is not good. Stay alert!"

"Major, what do you want me to do now?"

"I want you to stay with this and see where it ends. I don't feel comfortable with things the way they are. I just have a bad feeling about all of this. Keep me posted about everything. I don't care how small it is, tell me about it. Visit Jose's parents and see what you can get from them about the family's involvement in this affair."

Chapter Nine

In Tucson, another story is unfolding at the Bank of America on Main and Fifteenth Street. There are two Corvettes parked in front of the bank; one is white and the other is a bronze color. Inside the bank, four women dressed in business suits are robbing the bank.

"This is a robbery, and we would appreciate if all of you would lie down on the floor and stay there until we are finished. If all of you will do as we ask, no one will be hurt. This money isn't worth your deaths. We are armed, and we know how to use these weapons."

The bank robbers are smart and only rob the tellers. These women know what they are doing; today is payday and each teller's drawer is full of money. There are cameras, but these women don't seem to mind. The entire robbery takes less than ten minutes, and then they are gone.

Then the police and the rangers arrive on the scene. They find very little to go on. The cameras reveal faces but the faces are those of Jane Mansfield, Marilyn Monroe, Sophia Loren, and of all people, Susan Pleshette. The police are baffled, because they know they are imposters. So who are these female bank robbers? It is interesting to note that they never fired a shot, and they didn't even hit anyone or raise their voices. They were dressed in the finest of clothes and, according to eyewitnesses, drove the fastest of cars. It provides a disturbing scenario for the police.

Back in the Big Bend country around Fort Davis, the Texas rangers have set up headquarters at the Davis Ranch. Major Boca Huerta, Sergeant William Schmidt, Sergeant Valentino Dickinson, Corporal Alvin Hayes, and Arizona Ranger Dan Mesa make up the investigation team. They set up with telephones and computer terminals with access to police, Interpol, and FBI records. There is a direct line to FBI headquarters in Washington, DC.

Rancis Davis is a third generation rancher and a very good friend of Major Boca Huerta. Major Huerta is a story in himself. He is a Vietnam veteran with a Purple Heart and the scars to show for it. He is a widow who raised three daughters by himself after his wife died in childbirth. He did an excellent job. The oldest daughter is an assistant district attorney in Austin; the second daughter is a lieutenant with the state police assigned to the Houston area; and the youngest is a captain in the army intelligence corps assigned to Seoul, Korea. Boca is a third generation Texas ranger and a well-respected law enforcement officer throughout the state of Texas. He is also known in the FBI circles as a competent man who can get the job done but also as someone to be left alone. He is hell on wheels in any kind of fight.

The site is set up, and Sergeant Dickerson is monitoring the phones in the office with the major and the rest of the group hanging around. Dan Mesa, being his usual self, is standing on the front porch smoking a cigar and drinking a cup of coffee. He is watching all approaches. He sees a dust stream in the distance.

"Major, I see a car coming in the distance. Should we go into defensive mode?"

"Sergeant Mesa, stay where you are. We will scatter."

Mesa is standing poised for trouble as the truck pulls into the yard. The door opens, and out steps another Texas ranger in the person of Sergeant Thomas Ryan.

"Hello, Dan, how the heck are you? What are you doing here?"

"Hello, Thomas, it is good to see you. My captain sent me down to work with you guys. I am temporarily attached to the rangers here."

Major Huerta and the rangers walk out.

"Hello, Thomas, my boy," Huerta says. "I was hoping they'd send you. I see you know Mesa, and you already know the other guys. Dan, Thomas is my godson and the best son I could ask for."

Thomas smiles and gives his godfather a bear hug.

"Pop, it is good to be here," he says. "Say, I'm hungry. When do we eat?"

"Son, there is coffee inside and some bear claws on the table. They are homemade and darn good. Let's go inside."

Everyone stands around talking. Slowly, Mesa works his way outside toward the corral. He saddles a roan horse and rides around the corral. He walks the horse back to the bunkhouse. He goes inside and approaches the major.

"Major, how about letting me ride out to scout the area, just to make sure we aren't being watched. I have this feeling that someone is watching us."

"Okay, maybe you are right. Go ahead and scout the area. If you aren't back in three hours, we'll come looking for you. Be careful, because these characters don't like you."

Mesa straps on his revolver, takes his Winchester and one hundred rounds of ammunition, and rides out. He checks his canteen for water and moves out at a trot. The roan has staying power and is somewhat playful. He sidesteps his way along for a while and then straightens out. Mesa takes a trail that heads into the foothills in a westward direction. He skirts the foothills, staying in the shadows so as to never reveal himself. The roan is a surefooted horse that seems to know that he is on a scouting mission.

Mesa is ever alert, looking for anything out of the ordinary. Sure enough, he notices a broken branch that is still damp with sap. He stops and examines the ground, looking for tracks and traps. He notices ashes from a cigar, which he collects in a small plastic bag. He climbs back into the saddle and slowly rides on. After riding for a mile or so, he notices a small smoke trail. He sniffs the air and smells coffee and, faintly, a woman's perfume. He loosens the rifle and moves out slowly, constantly looking about. The aroma becomes stronger.

He stops the horse and climbs down, tying up the horse. He moves out on foot. This reminds him of the jungles of Vietnam and a different time. It is amazing how an individual takes on the trappings of his surroundings. Mesa feels at home when he is on the hunt or, as Sherlock said to Watson, "The game is afoot."

As he walks, Mesa thinks, *Whoever this person is, they know the woods quite well. There is something about the smell that is familiar to me. Now where have I run into that smell before?*

Suddenly, a chill runs through his entire body. He remembers where he has smelled that fragrance before. It was on the plane on his trip back from Baltimore. The flight attendant, Monica Saint Jacque, wore that fragrance. Mesa stops suddenly and hits the ground. At that moment, an arrow barely misses him. He lies very still for minutes, just listening and testing the air. For some unknown reason, he is not afraid. It seems as if this is what he has trained for all his life. After thirty minutes, he crawls slowly and checks the entire area, looking for whoever shot the arrow. He finds a trap that someone set. It was aimed about chest high. Whoever set the trap was familiar with his height and weight.

He finds the campfire and the smell of perfume is even stronger. As he turns to leave, his foot strikes a rock, and something white draws his attention. He stops and picks up a piece of paper. It is a note with very distinctive handwriting. It reads:

> They are looking for you, and they are here in the woods. Be careful and know that I am watching over you. Don't try to find me, because I am not ready for you to find me. You have much to do, and thinking about me will distract you. One day, I will find you again. Keep your eyes open and your head down.

It wasn't signed, but Mesa knows who wrote it. It is Monica's handwriting; he is sure of it. He walks back to the roan and climbs up. He knows he is being watched but by friendly eyes. He raises his hand in a farewell salute and rides away.

He is loping along when he sees riders approaching. It is the major and Ryan. When they see him, they slow down. He tells them what happened, and they look at him as if they have seen a ghost.

When they arrive at the bunkhouse, Mesa sits down and tells them the entire story.

Thomas looks at Dan and says, "If anyone else told me a story like that, I'd say he was crazy, but from you, it sounds truthful. How do you explain all this?"

"There are some things on this earth that you just accept as truth and don't question," Sergeant Schmidt says. "If the airline acknowledges that this woman existed and was killed, then some power greater than us is in control of the situation. Dan, it seems like you have your own personal angel looking over you."

"Yes, it does seem like someone or something is watching over me. I think I will get some air," Mesa says.

Mesa walks outside to the corral. He lights a cigar and stands watching the sunset.

Major Huerta walks to the door and looks at the shadowy figure standing at the corral. He sees a slight shiver in the frame of the man standing alone and knows what he is going through. He turns back to guys and says "That man is facing tough times and I don't ever want to go through what he is going through. This case is one of the strangest ones I have ever dealt with. Not only do we have criminals to deal with, now we have something unexplainable. Boy, I love this job" and he smiles.

Thomas walks out to the corral where Mesa is standing.

"Dan, are you okay?" he asks. "I don't mean to intrude, but you worry me sometimes. Seems like you could use a friend."

"Thomas, sometimes it seems like all this is a dream, and lately, it is getting awfully strange. Now you take this lady Monica Saint Jacque. Thomas, if I didn't know better, I'd say she was Sonia. Everything about her is a replica of Sonia. She knows things that passed between Sonia and I, and the only way she could know it is if she was there. You must think I'm nuts, but it is all true. I can't explain any of this. Read this note I found today. I didn't mention it to the major."

He hands the note to Ryan, who reads the note and sniffs the perfume. He turns toward Mesa with the strangest look on his face.

"Dan, when I was on my way here, I stopped at a store outside of El Paso, and there was a woman in there who wore the same perfume."

"Thomas, can you describe this woman you saw?"

"Well, she was probably part African American and maybe French or Hispanic. She was very beautiful. She said she had a friend who was an Arizona ranger. At the time, it didn't dawn on me that she was speaking of you. But now I know she was speaking of you. It seemed like she knew me, and the crazy part is it seemed like I knew her."

"Thomas, the woman you described is Monica Saint Jacque. She was killed in a plane crash about ten years ago. I talked to the office of personnel records for the airline and I sent them a drawing of her, and they confirmed that the picture was of Monica. I don't have a clue as to what is going on. Maybe I do have an angel watching over me, or maybe this whole thing is a trick."

The supper bell rings, and they walk back to the bunkhouse to eat. The food is simple ranch fare consisting of steak with potatoes and gravy, string beans, corn on the cob, and salad. The cook also made a delicious apple pie. Everyone, even the Davis family, joins in for supper. Mesa eats only a small amount but loads up on coffee and a large piece of pie. He excuses himself and makes a phone call to Yuma, where the phone rings at the home of Matilda Osborne.

"Hello, this is Matilda."

"Matilda, This is Dan."

"Oh, hello, Daniel. It is so good to hear your voice. Alana and I were just speaking of you. How is San Antonio?"

"It is absolutely great to hear your voice. San Antonio was great. I'm at a ranch in the Big Bend country. We set up headquarters here. We believe the people in question are here in the Davis Mountains. Matilda, did Alana tell you about Monica Saint Jacque?"

"Yes, she did, and I have to admit that it's hard to believe."

"Matilda, have Alana get on the phone as well. Earlier today, Monica showed up here." Dan tells them the story.

"Dan, this whole thing is starting to sound very weird. You be sure to watch your back. This could all be a trick to get you killed."

"Alana, do me a favor and called the lady in Dallas and find out if there is anything new in relation to Monica. And Alana, don't forget someone here cares about you."

Dan hangs the phone up and walks outside into the night air. The desert gets cold at night, even in the summer. Mesa puts on his jacket and checks his pistol. Then he walks into the night, moving very carefully. He walks softly and stops every hundred yards to listen. This procedure continues for an hour.

Suddenly, Mesa sees a light in the distance about a half mile away. He walks toward the light. As he approaches, he hears voices. He recognizes Mandy's voice and slows down. He moves to within yards of them. They have tents and sleeping bags. A fire is going, and someone is cooking meat.

"I'm tired of waiting," Mesa says. "I want to face Dan Mesa and get it over with. He killed Jose, and I want to make him pay for it. It is time to act, not just sit here drinking coffee."

"Mandy," Carlos says, "if you go into this situation without thinking or planning, I promise you that you will be dead within minutes. These people are rangers, and they will kill you. I know Mesa, and so do you. He will shoot you without any remorse. He wants me badly, because of his lady friend's death. I have no illusions about Dan Mesa—he will kill me if he gets the chance, and he will shoot you if you force him to. I don't like the man, but I do respect him. He is honest and probably the best friend you could ever ask for. I just don't want him for a friend."

There is laughter and another voice says "Boss, what about me? Dan Mesa knows what happened to that woman and his friend, Savalas. He has me pegged as the one who is responsible. He will never stop unless we stop him. I don't want someone telling me that Mesa is dead. I want to see it myself, even if I have to pull the trigger."

"Antonio, you aren't fast enough, nor are you smart enough to kill Mesa. It will take all of us working together to get the job done.

We will have to kill more than Mesa. We will have to kill some Texas rangers too."

Suddenly, it gets very quiet.

Then an unknown person says, "I don't know about this. Those Texas rangers make their own laws. They will follow you to hell and back if you kill one of them. Mesa is in good company. He belongs with them, because he thinks like they do. Killing Mesa is bad enough, but killing a Texas ranger is pushing your luck. I suggest you kill Mesa and leave the rangers alone."

"I want Mesa dead. *Dead,* do you hear me? I will kill him myself," Mandy rages. "I don't need you. I am going after him tomorrow, with or without your help. I promised Jose's parents I would make him pay, and I plan to keep my promise."

Everyone just stares at her and backs away, leaving her to sit and stew. Suddenly, she gets up, packs her belongings, and leaves in her Jeep. Mesa takes a pad from his pocket and writes down the tag number and color. Then he backs away slowly and heads back to the ranch.

"Where is Sergeant Mesa?" Major Huerta asks. "He was here, and then he was gone. That man is like a ghost. I would not want him following me. I have a feeling he would be a tough person to get away from."

As the Major finishes speaking, Mesa walks in. He relays what happened to the major and the others.

"Sergeant Mesa, can you lead us back to where you were?"

"Yes, sir, I can, but we need to leave immediately, because they will be moving to another location. I believe Mandy's behavior scared them all. They know she is a loose cannon. I may have to kill her, and that is something I don't want to do. We were close at one time, but she changed, and now there is no turning back."

They all mount up and head out. They arrive at the camp and find it abandoned. Each ranger takes a section of the camp and goes over it carefully, looking for a lead. They find cigarette butts and matches. Everything is bagged and labeled. Finally, Ranger Schmidt finds what looks like a map.

"Major, this looks like a map of this entire area. I do believe we may have gotten lucky. If this map is correct, we know where they are headed."

"Everyone, saddle up and head back to the ranch," Major Huerta says. "We'll collect the supplies we need and head out again."

The crew head back to the Ranch to pick up all supplies needed, including several hundred rounds of ammunition.

Dan Mesa selects a Winchester repeater and takes his .357 Magnum revolver. He stops and packs his derringer. He walks outside and selects a vest and then climbs up on the horse. He is alert to every sound, knowing that there is always the possibility of an ambush. Mesa is slowly reverting to the soldier he was in Vietnam. There are so many places to set up an ambush. He stops and puts on his vest. The major, who has been watching Mesa, calls a halt.

"Everyone, put on your vest. I know they are warm, but it could be the difference between life and death."

Mesa looks at the major, smiles, and rides on.

They slowly climb higher. The temperature cools down, and the guys all put on their dusters. The horses are straining a little harder with the climb. Suddenly, they top out on a mesa, and they notice tracks of a horse with unique oval-shaped shoes.

Mesa climbs down and scouts around. There is the scent of perfume in the air and the fragrance is Chanel No. 5. Mesa knows it is Sonia's favorite perfume. He slowly unfastens the strap on his pistol. A shot is fired. Mesa hits the ground, palms his weapon, and fires two shots as fast as he can. He hears a grunt but doesn't move. The major and the other rangers arrive as Mesa rises from the dust.

"Dan, we heard three shots. The first one was from a rifle and the last two were pistol. Are you hit?"

"No, sir, I'm okay, but I believe I got the person who shot at me. I heard them groan and fall. I hope it is not whom I think it is—Mandy, one of Jose's cousins who swore revenge against me."

They rush to the trees and there, lying on her back with a bullet wound to her chest, is Mandy Guittierrez. Mesa kneels at her side, and she immediately reaches for her pistol. He grabs her hand and takes the weapon.

"Mandy, you are hurt badly. We need to get you to the doctor. Now, lie quietly while I call for the helicopter."

"Dan Mesa, you shot me you son-of-a-bitch," Mandy says. "I regret I didn't kill you. I had you in my sights, and suddenly someone sprayed something in my face. It was perfume and there wasn't anyone around but me. There is something wrong with this place. It is haunted or something."

"Mandy, I didn't know it was you. Someone fired at me, and I returned fire. I normally hit what I aim at. You were trying to kill me, so what do you expect me to do? Now, lie quietly. I am going to search you for other weapons."

Mesa conducts a search and finds a twenty-five automatic, a handgun, a hand grenade, and a knife. He looks at her, shakes his head, and tosses them aside. As Mesa walks away, Mandy gets up and dives for the pistol. Major Huerta palms his pistol and shoots from the hip, hitting her in the face. She crumbles to the floor. Mesa turns to look at her and then walks away visibly shaken. He thanks God that he didn't kill her.

Major Huerta calls for a helicopter. The helicopter arrives, and the body is taken away.

Sergeant Ryan walks toward Mesa.

"Dan, have you noticed that perfume smell? It smells the same as what I smelled at that store. What's going on here?

"Thomas, I don't understand it, but that perfume smell is what saved my life when Mandy fired at me. As soon as I topped out on this mesa, I smelled that perfume, and I hit the ground, and that is what saved me. I know that fragrance too; it is the same one that Sonia wore."

Major Huerta is also perplexed by what just happened. The medical examiner and the assistant district attorney remain to ask questions about the shooting.

Major Huerta says, "Sergeant Mesa, you and Sergeant Ryan scout the area and see what you can find. I have a feeling we aren't alone here. I want everyone to travel in pairs. I don't want anyone out there alone."

Mesa and Ryan disappear into the trees. Watching eyes smile and move away from them. The smell of perfume is heavy in the trees, but no one says anything. Ryan and Mesa hit the ground, and shots ring out in all directions. Using combat tactics, they turn in opposite directions to give them 360 degrees of fire coverage. They begin returning fire. The bullets come fast and furious at first. Mesa an Ryan begin moving closer for the kill. They pick their targets and fire to kill.

Carlos and his crowd are being counterattacked. They saw Mandy take the lead and die. Already Antonio has a bad burn across his forehead, and two or three are dead.

"Antonio, tell the others it is time to pull out. We will wait for another time," Carlos says.

Slowly, they withdraw, and Mesa and Ryan move forward to find weapons, ammunition, two night vision scopes, and a global positioning system (GPS) and the bodies of the dead. Tucked away inside a log is a sheet of paper. Mesa examines the area looking for booby traps. He doesn't find any, so he removes the paper. It is a letter addressed to him. It reads:

> Dan, I am sorry I left you in the way I did. I never wanted to leave, but I guess it was my time. God has a plan for all of us. I guess his plan for me is to watch over you for now. I never got the chance to say how much I loved you. I guess too many things got involved. I loved you then, and I love you now. Don't give up on love; it is

> waiting for you. You will know her when she comes by, just don't rush into anything.
>
> Carlos and Antonio are planning another ambush, but this time, they plan to ambush you while you are sleeping. Keep your eyes open and your head down, ranger. Remember, I am watching over you.

The letter ends without a signature.

"Thomas," Dan says, "read this and tell me what you think."

He hands the letter over. Ryan reads the letter and turns to face Mesa.

"Dan, this is like *The Twilight Zone*. Let's get out of here and let the major look at it."

Mesa smiles and says, "We are not in danger. We have a guardian angel."

They secure the area, and the major and the rangers arrive. Mesa hands the major the letter. Huerta reads the letter and hands it back to Mesa. Major Huerta feels a chill move through him as if someone is watching. He turns to Mesa.

"Dan, do you get the feeling that someone or something is watching us?" he asks.

"Yes, sir, I have that same feeling, but whatever it is, it isn't going to harm us. Those eyes you feel watching you are those of the person who wrote that letter. Don't ask me how I know, I just know as I always do."

They gather all the weapons and equipment. The major decides to move down the trail about a mile before they set up camp. Then they secure the camp. Sentries are posted, and bedrolls are laid out, but no one gets in them. The men are posted in the trees, waiting. An hour passes by and then two hours, and all's quiet. Around four a.m., it suddenly becomes extremely quiet—not even a cricket is heard. The guys wait. They hear horses approaching, and they wait.

A rider moves forward and opens fire, it is Carlos. Others open fire. Suddenly, the night is alive with gunfire. Carlos takes a bullet in his shoulder and runs away. Major Huerta continues firing as the assassins withdraw.

"Hold your fire, they have departed. Now let's see how much damage we inflicted on them. Sergeant Mesa, I know I put a bullet in Carlo's shoulder. Antonio pulled him out of the way or I would have put a deadly bullet in his chest."

Sergeant Schmidt finds one individual hiding under a log.

"Come out from under that log with your hands raise. If you try anything, I will blow your guts out through your back. I won't tell you again, so move," he says.

From under a log, a small hand sticks out. "Okay, I'm coming out. Just give me a minute; it was a lot easier crawling under here than it is to crawl out."

Sergeant Ryan is watching as a beautiful lady slowly crawls out. Sergeant Schmidt is standing in awe, not sure what to do. He turns to Major Huerta with a surprised look on his face. Everyone is surprised with the exception of Dan Mesa. He looks at the lady and asks, "Who are you, and what are you doing here?"

"Oh yes, you must be Ranger Dan Mesa. I left you a note telling you about their plans. I do hope you found it. You did find it, didn't you?"

"Yes, I did find it, and I thank you, but the question remains. Who are you and what are you doing here?"

"Dan, you never change; you are always business. When do you relax and enjoy life? Don't you know life is too short to be so caught up? Okay, I was just camping out here when I stumbled upon those guys, and I heard their plans, so I decided to lend a hand."

In a quiet voice, Mesa asks, "Lady, I asked you a question, and you haven't answered it yet."

"You know, you need to control your anger," she says. "I wonder how she ever managed to get along with you."

Major Huerta has been watching and listening. He notices Mesa's hands reach for his gun. He rushes forward and smashes his gun's butt against Mesa's head, knocking him cold.

"Lady, you are lucky I got to him in time. He would have killed you. I don't know who you are, but you surely do know how to push the wrong button."

"Major Huerta, I know exactly what I am doing. I had to find out just how much he loved her. He wouldn't have killed me. He would have come to his senses before he did it. He is a driven man, and somehow or someway, you must get him to relax and let go. One day, he is going to crack under the pressure. He faults himself for her death. It wasn't his fault."

"I know that but he has to realize it himself."

She looks around for a minute and says, "They have left, and they are heading back to San Antonio and Tucson. When he awakens, tell him that Carlos is heading back to Tucson. Major, please have someone to drive my truck back to your headquarters. I'd like to ride one of your horses."

Mesa is still out, so he is loaded into the jeep with Ryan driving, and the group heads back to the Davis Ranch. Mesa suddenly sits up with his gun in hand.

He sees Ryan and asks, "Who hit me and why?"

"Take it easy, Dan. The major hit you, because he thought you were about to kill that lady. You know, it is weird, but that is the same lady I saw in El Paso. She seems to know everything about you. Who the hell is she?"

"Thomas, that was what I was trying to find out. She is everywhere. I don't believe she is associated with Carlos in any way. She has a way of making me angry though. It seems as if she is testing me. Where is she now?"

"She's riding one of the horses, and we are riding in her jeep."

Mesa searches the vehicle, but there aren't any papers or notes or anything. He has searching eyes, and he goes over the Jeep section by section but nothing. They arrive at the Davis Ranch and Rancis and the kids are standing outside as they approach. The horses are stripped, rubbed down, and fed. Finally, they all head in for a late breakfast.

Mesa turns to Major Huerta and asks, "Sir, where is the lady who was with us?"

"She was right behind me," he says. "What the hell is going on here? Sergeant Schmidt, did you see her leave?"

"Major, she was right in front of me, and I swear I don't remember seeing her leave. How can this be?"

Ranger Mesa smiles and says, "Don't worry, I know what happened. You won't see her again; she did her job, which was to protect us."

They all rush outside to see if the Jeep is there. It is still there with a note attached to the window. The note reads:

> Dan, the Jeep is yours. The papers are in the glove compartment. I am sorry about pushing you so far, but I had to see if you loved me as I thought you did. Now I know. You have a lot to give, so relax and smile sometime. We will meet again in a different world. I will always watch over you, but you won't see me again. I love you dearly and good-bye.
>
> Sonia.

Mesa turns and hands the letter to Major Huerta and walks away slowly. He climbs into the Jeep and drives away.

Major Huerta reads the letter, and the shock of it all appears on his face. He turns to the group.

"I have seen and done a lot in my lifetime," he says, "but this is the strangest case I have ever seen. I don't know if we are dealing with a ghost or what. Sonia Perdenales, the same woman who burned to death in that house in Arizona, signed this letter."

Chapter Ten

Back in Tucson, Captain Johnson is busy with the Glamour Girl robberies. His phone rings.

"Sam, this is Boca Huerta in San Antonio, and buddy, we have strange occurrences going on here. We found a lady hiding in the woods when we were chasing Carlos, and you won't believe this. She said in a letter to Dan Mesa that she was Sonia Perdenales. One minute she was there talking to us, and the next minute, she was gone. No one saw her go, but we were all watching her. I can't begin to explain any of this. This lady has been seen on a plane from DC to Tucson, at a service station in El Paso, and here in the Davis Mountains. Sam, tell me I am not crazy."

"Now, now, old buddy," Johnson says. "I know how you feel. How is Mesa handling all this?"

"Sam, that is the problem, we can't read him at all. He keeps everything bottled up inside. In the letter to him, she said he needed to relax. She also said she would see him again in a different world and signed it Sonia. He handed me the letter and rode away in the Jeep she left him. That was two days ago, and no one has seen him since. He left his truck here and some of his clothes. He took his weapons and gear. Let me know if you hear from him," Huerta says. "Oh, yes, she said Carlos was headed back to Tucson, so be on the watch for him and Antonio. Carlos was shot when he tried to ambush us. Mandy, Jose's cousin, was also shot and killed—not by Mesa but by me. I shot Carlos in the shoulder. I was aiming for his heart."

"Boca, thanks for all your help. I owe you one. You should come on down and we can go hunting for deer. The season just opened the first of November. There is a slight chill in the air, but it's just right for hunting."

"Sam, you have a date. I will be down for Thanksgiving, if that is okay?"

"Sounds good to me. See ya."

Johnson hangs up the phone and calls for Sergeant Bonefacio Hernandez.

"Yes, captain? What can I do for you?"

"Bonnie, Carlos and Antonio are headed back this way. Notify the state police and the FBI. Also, Mesa is missing, Contact the rangers in Yuma to see if they have seen him. Also call Sonia's parents to see if they have heard from him. He is running around loose, and that isn't good. Find him, even if you have to put out an arrest warrant for him. No, don't do that. Just try to find him. There is one other person to call. Call Janie, that friend of his in Sierra Vista. She owns a restaurant and club there named Chardon Blieu."

The Rangers call Mesa's friends, but no one has seen or heard from him. They call El Paso to Napal and Ophelia Cortez, Sonia's parents.

"Mrs. Cortez, this is Captain Johnson of the Arizona rangers. Have you heard from Sergeant Mesa within the last thirty-six hours? He is missing, and no one seems to know what has happened to him."

"No, Captain Johnson, we haven't heard from him in over two weeks. Something must have happened to cause him to disappear without a trace. Can you tell me about it?"

"Mrs. Cortez, what I am about to tell you will sound unbelievable, but it is true," Captain Johnson begins. He tells her of the entire story involving the lady on the plane down to the most recent incident. "Mrs. Cortez, I swear to you everything I have said is true, and there are people who can attest to the truth of it."

"Captain Johnson, I don't doubt anything that you've said, because we have had some similar things happen here at the ranch. I thought I was losing my mind. I can't explain any of it. I understand why Daniel has reacted the way he has. I almost lost my mind when the apparition first appeared. It was as if she was still alive. A day or so later, when I was making breakfast, I turned around, and she was just standing there. She said, 'Mom, don't panic. I won't hurt you. I am here for you, Dad, and Dan.' She just smiled and disappeared. She has been back several times to talk to me. She says she has to protect Dan Mesa and make sure he doesn't do something he will regret."

"Mrs. Cortez, this whole situation is strange and different. It will be something to tell your children about. If Dan shows up there, please call me, and no one but me. He is my friend, and I am worried about him."

As Captain Johnson puts down the phone, it rings again.

"Captain Johnson here," he answers.

Captain Johnson, Lieutenant Osborne here on this end. Sir, have you heard from Sergeant Mesa in the past few days? The reason I'm asking is that I am worried about him. I got a letter from someone, and I don't know who. It simply said, 'Please watch over him for me, because I will be leaving in a few days, and I can't say good-bye.' There wasn't a signature or address, and I don't know where it came from. There was a fragrance present—something pleasant and different. Captain, you may think I am crazy, but I believe I saw the ghost of Sonia. I must be losing my mind."

"Alana, you are not crazy. Quite a number of people have seen her lately. She has visited people all the way to San Antonio. Major Huerta of the Texas rangers saw her and talked with her, and so did several of the men who were there. I can't explain it. Even her mother has seen her. It is apparent she is worried about Mesa and what he will do once he catches up with Carlos and his crowd. Lieutenant, I am worried about him too. We all are. I know him quite well, though, and he will call in eventually. This whole thing has been an ordeal for him. He had to hunt down his best friend and kill him and then his lady's death . . . it is a lot for any person to take, even Dan Mesa. He is a hard man, or so you'd think. But I have a feeling there is a heart there somewhere. If I hear anything from him, I will call you. Take care." He hangs the phone up.

Bonnie rushes into the captain's office.

"Sir, Colonel Grant is on the line for you, and he wants to know how we are doing on the robbery case."

"Okay, Bonnie, I will take it. The Major picks up the phone and says, "Hello Colonel, how are you?"

"Sam, where are you on that robbery case? Have we heard anything since their last robbery?"

"No, sir. No one has seen hide or hair of them. It is as if they just disappeared, but they haven't. They will show up again. They are too sure of themselves. They will strike again, and then we will be on them. We've contacted all local police and the state police. The problem is that we don't have a description of them. All we have is women dressed to look like Jane Mansfield, Marilyn Monroe, Sophia Lauren, and Susan Pleshette. How do we publicize that?"

"Yes, I know Sam. Does it ever end? It seems like every time we solve one problem another pops up. But if it weren't for the bad guys, we wouldn't have a job. But you know, I would give up my job if it would bring about peace. Keep me posted if anything changes," he says. "Sam, I got your report on the Meana situation and this ghost lady. This is all we need—female bank robbers and a female ghost. Sam, has Sergeant Mesa checked in?"

"No, sir, he hasn't, and I am worried about him. I've asked all the local police to be on the watch for him and let him know to check in. He is under a lot of strain, but sir, he is a ranger. He will bounce back. He is the last of that breed of men who made this country. I will call you as soon as we hear anything."

In Lordsburg, New Mexico, at a small cantina, a small man sits eating a meal. He is dressed in Levis, a gray western shirt, brown boots, and a white Stetson. His face is drawn, and his eyes seem to burn through the soul. There is a star on his chest and a gun that seems to be as much a part of him as the hat. He has spoken only once, and that was to order a meal.

A waitress approaches the man, "Señor, would you like more iced tea or something stronger?"

"No, thank you. I will be moving on. It seems like you have some trouble brewing over there."

"Señor, you are a ranger, and from your looks, I say you know how to handle yourself. Please stay a while until they leave. I have called the police, but they are slow getting here. They frighten me."

"Ma'am, I will stay for a while. They won't bother you."

"Hey, lady, we want service too," one of the men says. "Tell your little boyfriend to wait. Hey, I am talking to you." The big man rises to his feet and makes a move toward the waitress.

Mesa takes a deep breath and stands up. He walks over to the table, and before anyone can move, he slaps the talker twice as fast as he can and steps back. The fire in his eyes is blazing out of control, and his small, wiry frame is poised.

He speaks in a deep, throaty voice, "You have exactly two minutes to apologize to her, and one minute has passed already."

The three men rise.

The talker says, "Little man, I am going to tear you apart."

He moves, and suddenly, there is blood on his face. His nose is broken, and two teeth are missing. No one saw what happened. Mesa walks over to the wall and takes down a piece of rope about ten feet long. He coils the rope, and in less than five minutes, he has laid open the faces of the other two men. He ties them up.

"The three of you need to find a new occupation," he says. "You aren't as tough as you think. Tell Carlos you weren't tough enough. Also, tell him I am coming after him and I will kill him."

With those words, he turns and walks away.

The police arrive to find three men tied up who have been severely beaten.

A policeman says, "Juanita, what happened here? We came as quickly as we could."

"Jim, those guys were making trouble, and there was this other fellow in here. He sat over there eating, a small man who looked to be African American. When these guys started harassing me, I asked him to wait until you arrived, and he stayed. They started making nasty remarks to me, and this fellow told them to apologize and they refused. The next thing I saw was his hand move, and then there was blood all over the big fellow. He walked over to the wall and took down that coil of rope and went to work. He could easily have killed those guys, but he didn't. He told them they weren't tough enough to do the job and to tell Carlos he was coming after him. I believe he was a cop. He wore a star and was dressed in jeans, a western shirt, boots, and a white Stetson. I am sure he carried a gun, but I didn't see it. He just said good-bye and left. He drove a Jeep Wrangler, and it was new. Jim, that fella is someone to be left alone. He is carrying around a lot of anger. It seemed as if he just didn't give a damn about anything."

"If he is who I think he is, he's an Arizona ranger, and his people are looking for him. He is the one who was in the news a couple of months ago. He was involved in that shoot-out in Albuquerque. Recently, his girlfriend was kidnapped and murdered. He is looking for the men involved in it," the policeman says.

The policeman turns toward the men saying; "Gentlemen, you are under arrest for disturbing the peace, harassment, and anything else I can think of. You are lucky to be alive. That fellow you pissed off could have killed you. That was Ranger Dan Mesa. I am advising you to leave this part of the country or your life won't be worth a plugged nickel."

In a motel room in Tucumcari, New Mexico, Carlos and Antonio are resting and wondering about their fate.

"Antonio, I never knew it would be like this. We have tried every way possible to kill him or just stop him, and nothing has worked. It is time for us to split up and go different ways. I am heading for the border, and you should go and visit your relatives on the reservation in Mesa, Arizona. He can't touch you there."

"Boss, I don't think it is wise to split up. Together, we can watch each other's backs. Two sets of eyes are better than one at all times."

"Antonio, you may be right. I can't think straight now. I need a drink, so let's to go downstairs to the bar."

In Yuma, Alana Osborne is off duty and is home with her mother.

"Mom, this whole thing has taken on the weirdest face. Now we are dealing with ghosts. I can't make any sense of any of this. I am a trained investigator, and I feel like a little kid."

"My darling daughter, this case is not about you, and you shouldn't let it get to you. You have done a good job, and you have nothing to be ashamed of. The life of a ranger is a dangerous one, and things don't always go as you plan. You know that. So, let it go, and let's have dinner. Now tell me what the status of Daniel is. Have the two of you gotten any closer?"

"Mom, I am going to tell you about something that happened to me today. I received a letter from someone." Alana goes on to tell her mom about the letter. "Now tell me what you think."

'Honey, there are so many things in this world that can't be explained, and I can't explain it either. You said others have seen her, including Dan, the major, and his boys from San Antonio. Based on those things, I can only conclude that all of you saw Sonia. For some reason, God has granted her this time to tie up loose ends. Do as she requested: look after him. He likes you a lot, and maybe he loves you, but you have to be patient with him. He has a lot of baggage that he carries around," she says. "Where is he now?"

"That's the problem. No one knows where he is. He is running around half-cocked and ready to destroy anyone who challenges him. There is a lot of anger and energy in that little body of his. If he ever gets over this, I believe he will make an excellent friend or, even better, a great lover."

In Tucumcari, Carlos has had a few drinks too many and has to be carried to his room by Antonio.

When morning comes, they check out and start on the road to Albuquerque. As they are listening to the news, the local commentator says, "Now for the lighter side of the news. It seems that three tough guys were giving a waitress a hard time in Lordsburg, when this fellow who looked to be a ranger intervened and stopped them. He stopped them the hard way. He broke one's nose, and when he finished with the other two, he tied them up with a rope and left them for the police. According to the waitress, the man never said anything, but that rope he beat them with spoke volumes. He was a small fellow about five feet five inches tall and not over one hundred fifty pounds. The waitress, whose name is Juanita, would like to say thanks to her knight in shining armor. So fella, if you are listening, Juanita sends you her thanks."

Carlos turns to Antonio and says, "Doesn't that sound like somebody we know? How did he find out we were going back to Arizona?"

"Boss, I doubt he knows we are heading back home. It is just coincidence. Mesa is the best, but even he isn't that lucky. Thanksgiving is approaching, and we haven't made any plans for it. I plan to go to the reservation and spend time with my father's family. It has been some time since I saw them last. Dad is a great guy, although, I am not on his list of favorite people. But I am still welcome there."

"Antonio, I guess I will visit this lady I know. She has been begging me to spend some time with her. I put it off for a while, but maybe it is time. I may not get a chance to see her again. I have a feeling Dan Mesa is going to be after us when this holiday is over. He will never give up until he catches us. Maybe, I should get in touch with Sandoval again and see if he can cancel Mr. Dan Mesa's ticket."

On I-10 heading west is a black Jeep Wrangler with the solemn figure of a man whose face seldom smiles. The radio is tuned to a country station playing a Patsy Cline song, "Crazy." The man driving is concentrating on the road and on the situation he is facing. His minds wonders back over the last six months. In his mind's eye, he sees Sonia for the first time. He remembers the night she handed him her phone number on a piece of crumbled up paper. He can still remember how she looked in a pair of jeans and how she danced with him and how her body felt when she pressed against him. Deep down in the recesses of his heart, the pain comes back, and tears begin to flow down his face.

The song ends, and a Bob Wills song begins to play. Daniel Mesa continues driving westward. A road sign says, "Welcome to

Arizona." He drives on. He sees a church and pulls off the road and into the churchyard. He is Methodist, but in his state of mind, any church will do. He walks in and sits in the front row with tears in his eyes. He prays.

"Lord, you and I talk often, as we have since I can remember. You know me better than anyone, and I thank you for all of your blessings and for saving me so many times from death. The job I do is a dangerous one, and I have had to kill other human beings to save either my life or someone else's life. I know there is a commandment that says 'Thou shall not kill,' and I have tried not to take another's life, but in war I had to kill, and as a ranger, I have had to kill. I ask your forgiveness for my sins. Father, Sonia was an innocent one, and I let her down. I did not protect her as I should have. I should have been there for her, and I wasn't. It seems that I let Garnett and Devlin down as well. I should have made changes in my life for them, and I didn't. I am so sorry for my failures. Lord, it is hard to let go of Sonia. I loved her so much, and now she is gone, and I have to find the men who are responsible for her death. I ask you not to let me kill these men, but let the court decide their fate. Help me to find a way to find peace and forgiveness for my sins. Lord, take care of her. She belongs to you now. Amen."

"My son, you seem troubled. I heard you praying and saw you crying. I am Father Paul, and this is Saint Phillips Cathedral," a priest says.

"Sir, I apologize for my presence here. I am Protestant, but I needed a place to pray, and this church looked inviting. I seem to be at the end of my rope. I am Sergeant Dan Mesa of—"

"My son, I know who you are. She was here; she told me you'd be stopping by."

"Who was here?"

"Sonia was here, or her spirit was here. Son, she loved you dearly, and she knows it wasn't your fault, what happened. She said to tell you that you have to forgive yourself. She also said you have to move on with your life but don't forget her. She will see you again when it is your time."

Mesa falls to his knees, sobbing as Father Paul kneels and prays for him and with him.

"Daniel, you are a good man, just as she said you are," he says. "It seems as if I know all about you. I know about Garnett and Devlin. I also know about Vietnam and all the things you have been through. You are carrying around a lot of guilt and pain. You should leave it here, and let our Lord and savior carry the burden for you. I know you believe in him, and I know you try to be good and perfect, but remember that none of us is perfect. You just be what you are and continue your relationship with our Lord and savior. Now as for your mission, only you can make the decision to kill or not to kill Carlos and Antonio. Your quest is slowly winding up. Trust in God and go in peace."

Dan slowly stands up and wipes away the tears. He looks into the priest's eyes and sees a reflection of something, but he doesn't know what he has seen.

"Thank you, father. If you see her again, tell her I love her dearly and always will, no matter what."

"My boy, she knows. She is listening because she is right here. No, don't try to find her. You won't be able to see her, but she is here. Now you go on your way and vaya con díos."

Dan Mesa climbs into the Jeep and heads west. He looks back, but the church is gone. He stops the Jeep and gets out. He smiles a crooked smile, gets back in, and drives on.

The sun is setting in the west, and there is a chill in the air. Mesa stops at a rest stop and puts on his jacket. Then he continues driving westward. It is two a.m. when he pulls into the lot of ranger headquarters in Nogales, Arizona. He walks into the office as Captain Johnson is about to call Tucson. Johnson puts down the phone and turns to Mesa.

"Sergeant, it is good to see you. You had us worried about you. Are you okay?"

"I am fine, sir. I have my report written about what happened in Texas. I also believe you are aware of some of the things that happened while I was there. Captain, am I losing my mind? Sonia is dead, yet I have seen her with my own eyes. How do I explain all of this to anyone?"

"Dan, I don't know how you explain it. Maybe it isn't for explanation. It happened; why not accept it? The longer I live, the more I realize there is so much we don't understand. Maybe we aren't meant to know everything or to understand everything. You look beat, so why don't you just crash in the spare room? Dan, the day after tomorrow is Thanksgiving; what do you plan to do? I think you should either spend time with Alana or that friend of yours in Sierra Vista."

"Yes, sir, I have thought about it. I guess I have been so caught up with this case until I just pushed it to the back of my mind. I am not so good at family dinners and get-togethers. But I have been spending a lot of time by myself, and maybe you are right."

Mesa walk to the spare room and in a few minutes he is fast asleep, and his mind is clouded with visions from his past. His sleep is intermittent. He sees Sonia and tries to get to her, but the faster he runs, the farther away she moves. He screams and wakes to find the captain staring at him.

"Dan, are you okay? Man, you need some time off. Starting right now, you get in that Jeep and head toward Yuma. That is an order, sergeant. Go someplace and relax. You are wound much too tightly. You need to spend time with people, sergeant, people who only want to be friendly. Do you understand what I am saying?"

"Yes, sir, I understand what you mean, and I will obey."

Mesa smiles one of his crooked smiles. He gets up, packs his bag and walks away.

In Yuma, Alana is finishing up the day when the phone rings.

"Lieutenant Osborne speaking."

"Lieutenant, this is Corporal Santiago, and there is a phone call for you on line two from Captain Johnson in Nogales."

"Thank you, corporal, I'll take it." Osborne changes lines. "Hello, captain, how are things in Nogales?"

"All is well here, Alana. The reason I am calling is because Sergeant Mesa is back, and I promised you I would let you know when he returned. Alana, he needs to spend time with people who care about him. I am hoping that you have considered inviting him to join you and your mom for Thanksgiving."

"Captain, you must have read my mind, because that is just what I planned to do. How is he really?"

"Alana, he is okay on the surface, but deep down, the turmoil is there. He needs to spend time with you away from here, where it all happened. Maybe he can get his mind off of it."

"Sir, I will do everything I can for him. As you have guessed, he means a lot to me. Thanks for being his friend and caring about him. Bye, sir."

Lieutenant Osborne takes her weapon from her desk and departs for home. The ride home is pleasant and allows her time to reassess her feelings for Daniel Mesa. She thinks, *I was happy before I met him, but there wasn't a steady man in my life. Since I met him, I am still happy, but I have this feeling that tells me I would be extremely happy if he was a permanent fixture in my life. The problem is how you get a man like Dan Mesa to forget the problems he has faced the last few months. It is hard to forget.*

She in so engrossed in her thoughts that she doesn't see the light turn green, and the car behind her blows his horn. She turns around, smiles, waves, and drives on. *I love him so dearly, but the question is does he love me enough to try to forget what happened to Sonia and get on with his life? Maybe the answer is to take it easy and just make sure I am there for him and make myself a major part of his life without him realizing it.*

Alana shifts into third gear, gathers speed, and drives home. As she pulls into the drive, she remembers she hasn't ridden the horses in over two weeks. She also notices that her mom is not home, so she decides to change into jeans and go for a ride. The afternoon has a chill so she puts on a duster with a sheepskin lining and heads for the barn. He opens a stall and walks in. Standing there is a tall horse of about seventeen hands high.

"Well, Ben, it has been a while since you've been ridden," she says to her horse. "What do you think of a quiet ride along that mesa over there?" The horse's ears perk up as if he understands her.

He begins prancing. Hurriedly, she saddles the big bay and canters him around the pen. Then they head down the trail at a trot. He is a spirited horse and puts her through the paces. Then he settles down to a nice trail trot.

The cattle are healthy, and there is plenty of grass, but it is time to reduce the size of the herd. They have close to a thousand head of Santa Gertrudis on fifteen hundred acres of land. They probably should reduce the herd to eight hundred. She thinks about it and decides to ask her mom about it. *Mom is the cattle expert. She is better than Dad was. How does a lady with so much class know so much about cattle?*

Alana smiles and rides on. She spies a family of coyotes, and overhead, a lone eagle rides on the currents of air as if he owns the sky. Maybe he does. In the distance, she hears the sound that reminds her of Dan Mesa. It is the sound of wolf in the distance. In some ways, the wolf and Mesa belong to this land; they complement each other—neither one wanting to be tamed but both knowing their way of life is on its way out. It brings a tinge of sadness to her heart.

The ride extends into hours, and before she realizes it, she has ridden several miles. She stops at a stream and and climbs down from the saddle allowing the bay to drink. She takes the Winchester out of the scabbard and checks the load and its action and returns it. She climbs back into the saddle and heads home. As she rides into the yard, Matilda arrives.

"Hi, Mom. Let me put Ben away. Then I need to talk to you about something."

Okay, I'll get dinner started. I am hungry, and I have a new recipe I want to try out on you."

Alana takes the horse to the stall, washes him down, and dries him off.

"Ben, you are getting fat, and you need exercise. I have to take a few days off and do some work around here. I know what! It will be good for Dan to ride these horses and help me clean out the stalls. Now that you are all clean and fed, I must do the same for me. Bye, big fella."

As she walks into the kitchen, she smells Italian food.

"Mommy, something smells good in here," she says.

She gives her mom a big hug and a kiss.

"Now, young lady what do you want to talk to me about?"

"Mom, I was looking at our herd, and we are running about a thousand head on one thousand five hundred acres. I was thinking we should probably reduce it to eight hundred, just in case next summer brings a drought. What do you think?"

"Well, you know, I rode out the other day, and I reached the same conclusion. I think we should load up two hundred and take them to the auction. I believe we could get a tidy sum of money for them. They are blooded stock; your dad made sure of that. Alana, do you think Dan would enjoy helping us round up the stock? It would take his mind off his troubles."

"Yes, I was thinking along those same lines. Captain Johnson called me today and said Dan was headed this way."

The phone rings, and Alana picks it up and say, "Hello."

"Alana, Dan Mesa here. I am wondering if you and your mom would mind if I came for a visit."

"Dan Mesa, you know you are welcome anytime. Where are you now?"

She hears him laugh.

"Well, if you look out your door, you will see me."

Alana hangs up the phone and rushes to Matilda saying "Mom, it's Dan. He is parked in the yard."

They rush to the door. Standing there larger than life is Dan Mesa. Matilda gives him a hug and steps back to look at him.

"Dan, you have lost weight. You look like a lean wolf that is ready to turn on anyone or anything that moves. I am glad you are here. You need to be with us."

"Thank you, ma'am," Mesa says. "I am happy to be here. I can't think of any place I'd rather be. I hope you don't mind if I bunk with you for a few days. Captain Johnson seems to think I need some time off. He says I am too caught up in this investigation. I know he is right, but I can't let it go. Anyway, I decided to come for a visit. To tell you the truth, I am tired. I haven't slept in a week, and I am living on coffee and pure cussed anger."

Alana walks forward and hugs him as Matilda looks at them and just smiles. Alana starts to speak, but only tears come. Dan Mesa stands there not knowing what to do.

He stammers and says, "Alana, I didn't mean to make you cry. If my being here is going to cause you pain, then I should leave."

"Daniel Mesa, you make me so *darn* angry at times. Can't you tell the difference between pain and joy? I am just happy you are here. You big ape, don't you know I am madly in love with you? Oops. Mom, I am sorry for my language."

"Honey, you don't have to apologize, because I know your heart better than you do. It gives me great joy to see the two of you together. Dan, get your bags and come in. I see you have a new Jeep. I didn't know you were the Jeep type."

"No, ma'am, I'm not. That was given to me, and I will tell you about it, but not right now. It has heartbreak with it." Mesa retrieves his bags and walks into the house. "Ma'am, could I trouble you for a bath? I smell like a goat. I didn't get a chance to shower; I just packed my bags and headed out."

Alana show Dan to his room and to the bath and I will continue making dinner.

Alana takes him to his room and lays out some towels.

"Now take a bath while we get supper ready."

She closes the door, flies into him arms, and kisses him passionately while rubbing against him in a way a lady shouldn't.

"Alana, you shouldn't do that to me. I won't be responsible for my actions, and your mom would kill me."

"Dan Mesa, I am a grown woman, but you are right. You owe me, though; don't forget it. I will leave you to take your bath. Hurry up, because supper is almost ready. I was serious about the way I feel about you. I almost lost you when my memory was gone. I don't ever want to lose you again. I know you still have some forgetting to do, but I am here for you, and I will wait for you to heal both physically and emotionally. You paid a heavy price, and I wish I could erase some of it, but I can't and neither can you. So take your bath and join us. You are a lucky man, because you have two women who love you dearly."

Sergeant Daniel Mesa of the Arizona rangers suddenly feels the weight of the world settling on his shoulders. He looks at Alana and starts to speak. Suddenly, the floor zooms up at him. He hears voices and tries to get up.

A familiar voice says, "Lie still for a moment. You fainted from exhaustion."

He sits up and looks into Alana's face. There are tears in her eyes and Matilda's.

"I guess I was worse off than I knew. I must apologize for my behavior. I am exhausted, but I think hunger is the main thing. I hate to say it, but it has been almost five days since I've eaten. Something smells great. I believe I could eat a horse. So if you will help me to my feet, I will shower and meet you in the kitchen."

Both women help him to his feet and help him regain his composure. Matilda smacks him on the arm, saying, "If you scare me like that again, I will break you darn neck. You aren't ten feet tall and bulletproof. You are just a man who is slowly destroying himself. I love you, fella, and so does Alana. Now get your butt in the kitchen, and we will eat."

Alana laughs and leads him to the dining room as happy as a schoolgirl. Mesa follows, holding tightly to her hand as if he might lose her. He becomes aware of it and relaxes his grip, smiling and apologizing.

The food is good and the expression on his face tells them that he is relaxing and is no longer the ranger but just a man with friends.

Matilda opens a bottle of wine and pours a glass for Mesa, saying, "I know your drinking habits, but this is a special occasion, and you are not on duty so drink and enjoy it. The meal is Italian with chicken breast grilled with tomatoes and basil with baked eggplant and stuffed mushrooms. There are green beans and Italian salad and garlic bread. As they eat, the conversation turns to ranching.

"Dan, while you are here," Alana asks, "will you help me with the horses? They need riding and a good workout, and there are too many for me to do it alone."

Mesa smiles and says, "Sure I will be happy to help out. I haven't done much riding lately, and I need the exercise as well. How are the cattle doing this year?"

"I was talking with Mom earlier, and we are thinking about thinning the herd out some. We are running about a thousand head on one thousand five hundred acres, and that crowds the range a little. I am thinking maybe we should sell about two hundred head. That will bring in a tidy sum of money as they are Santa Gertrudis and they are expensive. I am sure the King Ranch will buy them. I'd like to take them to the auction on Friday, if you don't mind going with me."

"I'd love to help out," Mesa says, smiling. "I haven't been on a roundup in many years. It will be good to get back in the saddle again. I only hope I can stand the pace of the work. I am not as young as I once was, but I believe I still have it. I'll give it my best. Now, do you have any dessert? I have a sweet tooth this evening."

Matilda serves cake and ice cream. For once, Dan Mesa relaxes and lets his hair down. He is with people who care about him and want nothing from him. He smiles and enjoys the moment. It is a rarity in his life.

Meanwhile a plan is being put into action in Phoenix. A phone call is placed to a motel in Toronto, Canada, to Armanti Sandoval.

"Armanti, I need your help again. It is the same situation as before," Carlos says. "Can you help me?"

"Yes, I am sure I can, and because I failed you the last time, this time it will cost you nothing. I hate to fail at anything I attempt. Where is he now?"

"He is probably in Nogales at his ranch. Sandoval, that man has eyes on the back of his head. Remember, he will not be merciful. So if you go after him, you had better be prepared to kill him or die trying. When do you plan to go after him?"

"Carlos, the less you know, the better it will be for you. I will go after him when he least expects it. Although, from what I know of him, I doubt I will be able to surprise him. After this job, I am going to disappear. I will contact you when the job is done."

An unknown figure was listening and recording the conversation places a call to FBI headquarters in Washington, DC.

A private phone rings in the office of the director.

"Sir, this is Agent Duvall, and I just intercepted a call from Carlos Meana to Armanti Sandoval in Toronto, Canada. They are planning to kill that ranger friend of Scotty's. Should I pass that information on to Agent Ortiz?"

"Yes, that ranger is temporarily one of us, and you know I like the way he handles himself. He would have made a damned good agent. Too bad he was over the age when he applied to us. Yes, go ahead and tell Scotty about everything."

Scotty is working at his desk when his private phone rings.

"This is Scotty. What can I do for you?"

"Scotty, this is Duvall. I have some information for you. I intercepted a phone call from Carlos to Armanti Sandoval in Toronto, Canada. They are planning to assassinate your ranger friend, Dan Mesa. They didn't say when, but they are planning to do it at a time when he least expects."

"Thanks, Bob," Scotty says. "I owe you one. I will contact Dan right away. Do me a favor and put an agent on Ranger Mesa. Find someone who is a native of Arizona and can blend in and follow Mesa without standing out like a sore thumb. Tell them not to follow too close and to be careful. Dan Mesa is smart, and he has eyes on the back of his head. I want to keep him alive."

"Okay, Scotty you got it. I will personally see to it that the right person is put on the job."

Duvall calls ranger headquarters in Nogales.

"Captain Johnson, I am Agent Robert Duvall of the FBI, and I have been authorized to tell you that Carlos Meana called Armanti Sandoval in Toronto, Canada. They plan to assassinate Ranger Mesa within the next few weeks. It would be my guess that the hit is planned around Christmas or New Year's. I have been told by Agent Ortiz to place an FBI tail on Sergeant Mesa without his knowledge. The agent in question will be Agent Dolores Maldinado. She will make herself known to you and you only."

"Agent Duvall, I thank you," Johnson says. "Please tell Scotty thanks for me also. Mesa is in Yuma on rest and recuperation. I will tell him about Carlos and Sandoval but not about Agent Maldinado.

Captain Johnson put the phone down and ponders the thought of calling Colonel Grant. He decides to place the call.

"Hello, Sam. I was about to call you. My sources tell me there is another contract on Sergeant Mesa, probably put out by Carlos. We probably need to put a tail on Mesa without his knowledge."

"Sir, that is why I am calling. I was notified that there would be an assassination attempt as well. I want to assign a two-person tail to Mesa. The FBI has an undercover agent assign to watch over him too. Mesa is not aware of any of this yet. I will tell him about the contract, but everything else should be kept quiet, because if he knew we were watching he would go nuts."

"Okay, Sam. Do what you think is best and keep me informed."

"What are you doing for Thanksgiving?" Johnson asks. "I will probably visit Major Boca of the Texas rangers. He wants me to go hunting with him. What are your plans?"

"My friend, I am going to Vegas to the casinos for the entertainment; maybe I will gamble a little bit. Have a great hunting trip, because I have a feeling all hell is about to break loose. Take care."

Captain Johnson then places a call to Lieutenant Osborne at home.

The phone rings and Matilda answers, "Hello."

"Hello, I'm Captain Johnson of the rangers in Nogales. May I speak to Lieutenant Osborne? I know Sergeant Mesa is there, but don't tell him I am on the line. Alana will explain everything later."

"I understand, captain. I will get her for you."

Matilda walks into the kitchen.

"Alana, there is a call for you from the rangers."

Mesa is eating. He stops and gets up slowly. Alana goes into the hallway to answer the phone.

"Lieutenant Osborne here."

"Lieutenant Osborne, listen carefully. This is Captain Johnson. Is Dan there? If he is, don't let on that I am on the line. There is another contract on his life put out by Carlos Meana. They will probably try close to Christmas. I am placing a tail on him for his protection. Don't tell him about the tail, but do tell him about the contract. If he knew I had a tail on him he'd go nuts and I want him safe and I don't want him trigger happy. The assassin is Sandoval. Let him have a few days of peace before he has to face reality again. Tell him to be careful. I will be with Major Boca in San Antonio, hunting deer."

She hangs up the phone and walks back into the kitchen.

Mesa is watching her as she enters the kitchen.

"Okay, Alana, what's going on? I can read the expressions on your faces."

Alana smiles and says, "Captain Johnson called to tell me that there is another contract on you. Carlos put it out. The assassin is Sandoval."

"I knew it was only a matter of time before they tried again. This time I will stop Sandoval permanently, and then I will finish up with Carlos and Antonio. This situation has gone on long enough. It is time to put an end to it. After the holidays are over, Carlos's time will be over too."

Matilda and Alana stares at Mesa without commenting. They return to the table for dessert and coffee. After that is over, Mesa dries the dishes as Matilda and Alana wash them.

Afterward, Mesa straps on his pistol and puts on a jacket.

"Dan, where are you going?" Matilda asks.

"I was thinking about just walking out to do a look around to make sure that things are as they should be."

"Dan, I know you follow a certain procedure in all you do, but seriously, you need to relax and just enjoy life sometimes. We will turn the dogs loose and let them roam around. They will alert us if anyone is about."

"Just give me five minutes to walk out and listen to the night. I will be okay."

Mesa smiles and slides out the door like a ghost. He blends into the night as if he was a part of it. Alana walks to the window and looks for him, but he is not there. She stares into the dark and notices a slight movement and knows he's there.

"Mom, he is like a ghost. I sometimes wonder what it is that makes a man become a person like Daniel Mesa. What happened in his life that made him as he is? If I was a psychologist, he would make an interesting subject for study."

Matilda smiles and says, "Your dad was the same in a way, but he was more trusting than Dan, and I think that was the difference. Dan Mesa doesn't trust anyone, and that is a flaw in his character, but it is a flaw that has been to his advantage. By being distrustful of others, he never allows himself to get too close, and that always gives him an advantage. One day, when you are with him, try to get him to talk about himself and find out what he is after or looking for in his life."

The door opens, and Mesa walks in.

"It is quiet outside and a beautiful night. The horses are quiet, and the dogs are dozing. It reminds me of a story I read when I was a kid."

"Children, I am going to bed to finish a book I started," Matilda says. "Good night."

"Dan, would you like a drink or coffee maybe?" Alana asks.

"Yes, I'd like a drink. Do you have Amaretto or something of that nature?"

"No, but I do have some brandy I believe you will like. It is Presidente brandy made in Mexico, and I will make you a brandy sour. I know you like Amaretto sours, but this will be good too."

She makes the drinks and they stand there just looking at each other and smiling.

Chapter Eleven

In an apartment complex in Phoenix, four women who look like Marilyn Monroe, Jane Mansfield, Sophia Loren, and Susan Pleshette are laughing about their recent exploit.

"I have a feeling the rangers are stalking us. We had best be very careful about everything we do. That ranger . . . Daniel Mesa, that's it. I don't want him after us. He is bad news, and I don't want to get into a shoot-out with him. I personally don't want a shoot-out—period."

"Jane, none of us wants trouble with the rangers. That is why we should lay low for a few weeks. We have over five hundred thousand dollars in old money that is hard to trace. What we should do is clean this money by depositing it into various banks. We will deposit it weekly or every two weeks. We all have jobs—I teach school; Susan is a dental hygienist; you are a cop; and Sophia is a lawyer. There isn't anything that ties us together. We are black, white, Asian, and Hispanic. Although, Jane, you may be black, but honey, you look to be white, and that works to our advantage."

"I like the idea of spreading the money around in small amounts," Sophia says. "We can always claim we won it at the casino. Maybe we should buy money orders in various cities and make them out to each other. We will go to Albuquerque, San Antonio, even Nogales and Mexico. There, we will exchange some of the money, bring it back, and deposit it in various banks. We will continue to live as we always have. We will not change anything we've done in the past, and that way, we will not bring attention to ourselves."

Marilyn smiles and says, "The crazy thing about all of this is that we all have authentic names, and we look the part. How did this ever happen? It's like the hand of fate took hold, and we became a part of destiny. I want to thank you guys for making the last few months of my life exciting. All of you have beaten cancer, and I guess it is just my time. You are my friends, and I love you. Since I am Marilyn when my time comes, I don't want you to cry over me. My family knows what to do. Now, let's do as we suggested and lay low for a while. The holidays are coming and visiting the cities we suggested would be appropriate and not out of the ordinary."

Jane is smiling, but inside she is crying. They are individuals, but collectively, they operate as one. It is as if they read each other's minds. She thinks, *Marilyn is closer to me than my own sister. What will I do without her? What would I do if something happen to either one of us?*

She looks into their faces and knows they are all thinking the same thoughts. They burst out laughing. They are the girls. They get dressed, making sure to change their appearances just enough so as not to draw attention. Then off to the symphony they go.

In Tucson at ranger headquarters, Colonel Grant is in conference with the district attorney, Emmett Rodgers; the lieutenant governor; and the commander of the state police, Colonel Hamilton Ellis.

"Gentlemen, my men have looked high and low for those female bank robbers, and so far—nothing. It is as if they have just disappeared. Have any of your people turned up anything?"

Colonel Ellis's men have also been busy, and they haven't turned anything. Ellis has lost two patrolmen in the last two months. One was his godson, and he hasn't gotten over it yet. His face is drawn and thin as he speaks.

"Joe, we've turned over every rock looking for them. We interviewed the personnel of the banks they robbed, and everyone says the same things, and that is that these women look just like the actresses they claim to be. We had an expert look at the photos, and they aren't wearing makeup. They really do resemble those people."

"Yes, I know. We ran the plates on those cars, and the plates don't exist. There are about a thousand Corvettes of that design in Phoenix and Tucson alone."

Colonel Ellis looks at the lieutenant governor and says, "Sir, what do you suggest?"

"I suggest we lay low and wait to see if they strike again," the lieutenant governor says. "If they are greedy, they'll strike again. But I have a hunch these ladies aren't greedy. There is something about them that leads me to believe they aren't doing it for the money. They are polite, and they never harm anyone. They are good, and everything is timed to the second. They operate like a military unit. Now there is a possibility they are ex-military. I will send a letter to the FBI and ask them to check on the possibility of a link."

"Thanks, sir. Tell her honor, the governor, we are working the case, but so far nothing."

"Joe, regardless of what the press and Senator Ibarra say, the people support the rangers. If the Governor has her way, there will always be rangers in Arizona. They are doing a good job. Sergeant Mesa has turned the rangers into celebrities and folk heroes, like the Texas rangers. One may not always agree with Dan Mesa, but he is resourceful, and he gets the job done. The publicity he has generated has been the best thing for the rangers. The public, with the exception of some members of the press and the state legislature, support them."

Joe Grant, a former brigadier general in the army, is a veteran of many fights, and he feels the weight of responsibility associated with the rangers. He loves the job and is aware he spends too much time at it. He needs to have a life too. He knows the price of responsibility. His wife divorced him ten years prior, and he hasn't remarried. She blamed his job for the divorce, and though they are on friendly terms, the chance of reconcile doesn't exist. He is sixty years old, but he is fit. There is a touch of hypertension, but he keeps it under control through exercise, diet, and medication. He worries about the future of the rangers. He picks up the phone and dials his ex-wife's number.

"Hello?" she says.

"Joan, it's Joe."

"Oh, hello, Joe. It has been a while since you called."

"Hello Joan, I know it has been a while, but calling you always makes me remember a different time, and that makes me sad. Sometimes, I have to get away and allow myself to settle down. I guess . . . well, I know that I haven't gotten over you, and it has been ten years."

"I know, Joe, and there are times when I wish I could redo my life for the last ten years. I am not exactly happy these days either."

"Honey, I thought this was what you wanted. I never wanted to be divorced—"

"Joe, hold on now. I know it was me who started it. I was very sure for about the first five or six years; however, these last two years have been hell without you. I must admit I live for your calls."

"Joan, I have an idea. Why not move back to Tucson, and let's try dating and being together to see if we can make it work again. I can rent you an apartment or house, and I am sure the bureau will allow you to relocate here. I know the kids will be happy, and I know I will. What do you say?"

There is silence on the other end. Then slowly she answers, "Joseph, are you sure you want me back into your life? I know I want you back, but are you sure you want me back?"

"Joan the answer is yes, so when can you be ready to move back?"

She laughs and cries at the same time.

"I will be down to visit this weekend, and we can figure out all the details. Just in case you don't know, I have been in love with you all this time."

Joe Grant, retired brigadier general and Colonel in the Arizona rangers, smiles and says something he hasn't said to anyone for a long time: "I love you just as much and just as long. I will see you when you get here."

In a spacious house located in the foothills of Mount Lemon in Tucson, Carlos and Antonio are having breakfast. They have hired help to guard the place. Both are armed with pistols and M16s.

"Antonio, we have to get across the border into Mexico. That is the only way we will be secure. Sandoval is good, but you and I both know he will not kill Mesa. He may get lucky and injure Mesa, but he isn't good enough to take him. Dan will kill Sandoval and keep coming after us. We will have to disguise ourselves and contact our friends and see if they can smuggle us across the border."

"Boss, it will not be easy, and it will be expensive. We are approaching the holidays. Tomorrow is Thanksgiving, and it will the right time to sneak out and see what can be accomplished. The police will be out, but they will be looking for speeders. If we disguise ourselves properly, we should be able to get away with it."

"I wonder where Sandoval is right now. That fellow is creepy, and he is extremely dangerous. I would not want him after me. Just maybe, he will be lucky and kill Mesa and Mesa will kill him, and we can escape to Mexico or maybe Columbia. Even if Mesa is killed, the rangers will never stop looking for us no matter where we go. We will never be safe anywhere for a long period of time. We will have to find a place where they cannot extradite us back to the United States. Maybe Cuba is the place to go." The morning passes and it is time for Carlos and Antonio drive to Carlos' brother house to celebrate Thanksgiving with their family. His mother and sister in-law have been waiting for their arrival, and the Thanksgiving feast is on. Carlos and Antonio are unaware that this is the last Thanksgiving they will ever enjoy together. Carlos's brother and wife have arrived, and so have members of Antonio's family from the reservation. They watch the parades and the games while the women prepare the food.

Carlos is watchful, because he suspects they are being watched. He makes an excuse to go out and look around. He takes his rifle and is gone for about fifteen minutes before he returns. Everyone is aware that he is a wanted man, and therefore, they don't ask questions.

The day progresses, and Carlos finds himself falling in love with Darla Estefan, a beauty from Monterey and the sister of his brother's wife. He knows a life with her is impossible. But yet the feelings are there. Suddenly, he feels and understands how Sergeant Dan Mesa must feel. This is something new for him, because previously he would not have cared. He knows he must kill Mesa if he is to enjoy any type of life.

Antonio has been watching his boss and smiles, realizing that the playboy of the underworld has just gotten himself hooked by a woman. He never thought he'd see the day that Carlos Meana would be brought to his knees by a skirt.

Meanwhile at Matilda Osborne's ranch in Yuma, Dan Mesa is enjoying a respite from enforcing the law. He is dressed in a sweat suit three miles into a jog around the ranch. He realizes how peaceful it is on the ranch. It is five a.m., and Alana and Matilda are still asleep. He finishes his three miles of roadwork and is cooling down.

"It is good that you are staying in shape because you will need it before this is over," someone says.

Mesa turns around quickly, but no one is around. There is a whiff of perfume in the air. It is a fragrance with which he is familiar. He smiles a sad smile and jogs on. Again the voice says, "I don't like it when you are sad. You should smile more, because your face lights up when you smile. Remember, I am still watching over you."

As suddenly as it appeared, the fragrance disappears. He knows whomever she is has departed.

When he arrives back at the ranch, everyone is still asleep. He showers and makes coffee. He pours two cups and takes one to Alana's room. He knocks on the door and is greeted by a very sleepy-eyed Alana.

"Dan, what are you doing up so early. It is six thirty in the morning. You should be asleep."

"No, I shouldn't. I am always up by five a.m. I have done my three miles, and I have had a shower. Here is your coffee and a cup for your mom. Will you please take it to her? I'd feel uncomfortable doing it."

"Okay chicken. You are one in a million, Dan Mea. It is nice to know you respect people, especially my mom. I know she likes you, and I know you like both of us. It is so cute to watch you squirm when we talk about it."

Mesa blushes and smiles.

"Alana, take your mom her coffee."

She smiles and takes Matilda her coffee. Alana enters her mother's room smiling. Matilda has been awake all along.

"Alana, what am I going to do with you? You little rat."

"Good morning, Mom. How are you this Thanksgiving Day?" she asks with a big grin.

"Alana, I am going to break your neck. I will admit he is a special person, and that is all you will get from me."

Both women are laughing like crazy. Alana crawls into her mom's bed. They are acting like teenagers.

Dan walks to the door and smiles. He thinks to himself how nice the sound of laughter is. It is good to watch happiness take place. He has had little of it in his adult life. There have been episodes of happiness, but nothing continual.

He surprises them by saying, "It is so nice to see the two of you together. I wish the peace I find here would follow me always. There has to be a place for a man like me in this world. Here, on this ranch, I find more happiness and peace than I have seen since I was a kid."

Matilda smiles and comments, "Sometimes, you have to make your own happiness. You simply say to yourself, 'Today I will be happy' and let it be so. I have found that it works for me. In your line of work, it can be difficult to be happy. A lot of the sadness you have experienced comes from things you had no control over, so why worry about it. Make your own happiness."

"I know what you are saying is true, and I have often tried just that, but so far I haven't been successful. Maybe my time hasn't arrived yet."

Thanksgiving comes and goes without any significant events. Dan returns to Nogales and goes back to work.

December arrives and the cities of Nogales, Tucson, and Yuma are putting up Christmas decorations.

In Sierra Vista, Janie Olivetti is decorating her restaurant for the holidays. Christmas with a cowboy flare is an event to behold. She has wagon wheel chandeliers, barbed wire Christmas wreaths, and everything decorated in Christmas colors. The Chardon Blieu has taken on all the trappings of Christmas, and it is a beautiful sight to see. Inside, there is dining and dancing.

A black Ford F150 pulls into the parking lot. It has dual exhaust, four by four, and an extended cab. As she looks at it she discovers it is not black but midnight purple. A small man steps down from the truck dressed in a brown western suit with brown boots and a beige hat. There is the hint of a smile. But upon a closer look it does not look like a smile at all; it is a frown. His eyes are brown and unsmiling. He opens the door and steps in.

"Good evening, sir. May I help you?"

"Yes, one for dinner. Nonsmoking please."

"Please, follow me. Is this table okay?"

"Yes, this is good," he says. He takes his seat and receives a menu. The lady leaves and a waitress appears.

"Sir, would you like a drink from the bar?"

"Yes, an Amaretto sour will do."

When she returns with the drink, she asks, "Have you decided what you want to eat? Our special tonight is lamb chops with mint sauce, a Greek salad with green beans, new potatoes, and cocktail onions."

"Thank you, but how about the grilled trout with the vegetable medley and the Greek salad?"

"Very good, sir. I will get your salad."

As she departs, she turns around for a second look at the man. She tries to remember where she has seen him before.

She turns to Charley Grey and says, "Charley who is that fellow at table twenty-two? I have seen him before, I am sure."

"Honey, go and get Miss Olivetti. She will be happy to know he is here."

"Charley, who is he? He isn't Mexican and definitely isn't white. He looks to be a Negro."

"Honey, don't ever let him hear you call him a negro. The correct term is African American and *he* is Sergeant Daniel Mesa of the Arizona rangers."

"He is that gunslinging ranger I have heard so much about! He has killed a lot of people, and they say he is looking for Carlos Meana and Antonio Blackbear. They say he plans to kill them for killing his girlfriend."

"Just go and get Miss Olivetti."

Charley walks over to the table, smiling and says, "Hello, Dan, how are you?"

Mesa stands up and smiles a quick smile.

"Hello, Charley, how are you?"

"I am well, and it is good to see you again. Have you recovered from your injuries? Oh, Janie will be here in a minute."

"Janie is here," a voice says from behind Mesa. Dan turns around and what he sees makes him weak in the knees. She is dressed in a soft beige pantsuit with a green trim. The suit is somewhat revealing but in a tasteful manner.

"Hello, Janie. How are you? You are absolutely beautiful as always."

He seats her and then takes his seat. He stares into her eyes, sees his reflection, and the hurt returns. He looks away quickly to prevent her from seeing what is in his heart. It is too late. She has already seen his eyes and smiles a sweet smile.

"Dan, have you fully recovered from your injuries? You had me very frightened."

"Janie, I'm totally recovered and back at work. A lot of strange things have happened since I saw you last, but I am well and am handling things as they come. I just wanted to come down for dinner and spend a couple of days with you—that is, if you don't mind?"

"Daniel Mesa, of course I don't mind. You are welcome at my house any day. What are your plans for Christmas? How about spending it with my sister and me?" Janie asks. "That's right, I never told you about her. Well, she really isn't my sister. I was adopted when I was a year old by her parents. We are the same age. I am three months older than she is. She is a criminologist with the Denver police department working with CSI. Although, we are not blood related, we are as close as blood sisters. She is a lot of fun, and you will like her. Her husband was born blind, but he never allowed that to stop him. He is a professor of international politics at the University of Denver. The two of you should have a lot to talk about. What do you think?"

"I accept your invitation, and I thank you for inviting me. I think being around you is a plus in itself. I really do enjoy spending time with you. Some of the best hours of my life have been spent with you. I find that I miss you a lot."

"Dan, allow me to treat you to dinner. We have a grilled trout that is flavored with herbs and spices from Greece with Mediterranean vegetables, a sweet potato cooked in paper, and a Greek salad. If you don't like that, we have other dishes to choose from. I believe you will enjoy the trout."

"Okay, that sounds great. I am hungry. I find that I miss a lot of meals these days. I need to just sit and talk with you. I am at the end of my rope. My anger at what happened is all-consuming. The only time I don't think of it is when I am asleep. Killing is becoming too easy for me. I don't want to kill anyone, but lately, every situation turns to killing. It is as if every would-be tough guy wants to make a play for me."

Dinner is served, and Mesa realizes he is very hungry indeed. He eats with gusto.

Meanwhile back in Tucson, the authorities still haven't found a clue as to who the female bank robbers are. They do have information that Armanti Sandoval is in Arizona and possibly in the Tucson area.

Dan and Janie leave the restaurant and go to her house. They are enjoying the evening listening to music by Glenn Miller when the phone rings.

"Hello?" she answers.

"Janie this is Captain Johnson. Is Dan with you?"

"Oh, hello, Captain Johnson. Yes, Dan is here. Just a moment and I will get him for you."

"Dan, your captain is on the line."

Mesa accepts the phone saying," Sir, Sergeant Mesa here."

"Dan, the state police received word that Sandoval is in Tucson, and he is looking for you. He is the one with the contract to kill you. What do you want to do?"

"Sir, I won't hide or run from him or anyone. I will face him at my choosing and at the time and place that is convenient for me. I am leaving now for Nogales and I will see you in about three hours. Mesa hangs up the phone and turns to Janie and says, "Janie, I have to leave for Nogales. There is a contract on me, and the man trying to collect is a killer. He would kill you to get to me, and I can't have that, so I am leaving right now. I will return to Nogales through Tucson, the long way around. I don't want anyone to know I was here."

She looks at him and tears fill her eyes.

"Dan, be careful. I have a bad feeling about this one. You will be shot, so wear your vest. I have a premonition, so humor me and do as I request, okay?"

"Honey, I wear it most of the time, but for now, I will wear it all the time. I must leave now."

Mesa packs his duffle and walks to the door. He turns, kisses Janie and says good-bye and drives away.

The drive back to Nogales is uneventful. When Mesa arrives in Nogales at his ranch, he steps from the truck and notices that his dog is nowhere to be seen. He gets back into the truck, drives down the road, and stops. He walks quietly back and stands in the shadows. He notices movement next to the horse barn, and he moves in. He throws a rock and hits the figure. The man turns, and Mesa clobbers him hard. The man drops hard to the ground. Mesa moves like a ghost in the night and attacks without warning. A second man turns to run, but he runs straight into Mesa, who hits the man in his kidneys with a punch and kicks the man's knees. He falls, and Mesa is on him like a vulture. He handcuffs the fellow's left hand to his right ankle.

He searches the ranch for others but finds the tracks of only two vehicles and nothing else. Yet there is something else. There is an aroma that lingers at the corners of his mind. It is something he has smelled before but where?

He calls the rangers and they arrive with the local police. The two assassins are taken away and the forensics team arrives and does an inch-by-inch search of Mesa's ranch. Alvina Venable is in charge of forensics, and she doesn't miss much. A cigar stub is collected. A cast is made of footprints and another of tire markings. The tire has strange markings and should be easy to trace. Alvina walks toward Captain Johnson.

"Captain Johnson, these guys were playing for keeps. They dropped a bag, and inside I found this." She opens the bag and produces plastic explosives, the military type. "Those guys are pros, and they planned to kill the sergeant and not leave a trace."

Mesa says, "Sir, give me five minutes with them, and I promise you they will tell you everything you want to know."

"Sergeant, you know I can't and won't do it. This has to be done by the book, because I don't want some smart lawyer to get them off on a technicality. I want them to pay for their transgressions."

"You are right, captain, but I just get tired of these characters getting away with their dastardly deeds."

"Come along, sergeant, and let Alvina do her thing. If there is any evidence to be found, she will find it."

"Sergeant, how did you know something was wrong when you drove up?"

Mesa smiles and says, "The dog was missing. If he had been alive, he would have greeted me with barking. So I took it as a warning and drove away."

"Dan, this is the strangest case I have ever worked on. We have ghosts appearing and disappearing. To top it all, we have a second case involving female bank robbers, and they all are replicas of famous movie stars. It has to be a full moon, because there are lunatics everywhere I turn."

The crime scene is secured, and the CSI team is combing the area with the hope of find more evidence.

In a house in the hills northwest of Tucson, Armanti Sandoval is figuring out his next move.

"There has to be a way of tricking Mesa into meeting me some place. I don't want a fist fight with him. I am not so sure I will win. He has proven to be quite handy with his fists and with most weapons. This will require simple sniper tactics."

Sandoval is aware of Mesa's feelings for Alana Osborne and her mother and decides to use that to his advantage. The idea is to trick them into bringing Mesa out into the open. Maybe he can follow them to dinner and there attack. Christmas is only a few days away. The idea is to finish up everything before the New Year. It makes for messy bookkeeping to carry it over to the next year.

In another part of Tucson, Colonel Grant is meeting his ex-wife at the airport. As she steps through the entrance, Joan sees Joe standing there looking like a huge cuddly bear. He has a smile on his face, but she can see the apprehension in his eyes. She walks toward him and gives him a hug. She looks into his eyes and says, "Joe I was afraid that you'd change your mind and not be here after the way I acted years ago."

He smiles and says, "I was afraid you'd change your mind and not come. I prayed last night and asked God to guide you and me back together. I haven't done much praying over the years, but I think it will become a big part my life from now on. I promised him I'd start serving him better than I have been."

"Joseph, you think we can make it this time? Can we find a place for us to meet and be husband and wife?"

"Honey, I looked at my life and decided that compromising will be a big part of my life with you. There were times before when I should have been more in tune with you, and I wasn't. That changes as of now, and that is a promise. Remember some months ago when I told you about one of my rangers, a Sergeant Mesa? I've seen what he has gone through with the loss of his lady friend, and I don't ever want to experience what he is facing."

"Joe, is he the one who has been in the news so much of late? The bureau has a file on him. He is something of a folk hero, but no one knows much about him. He doesn't give interviews. He has a friend in DC, an Agent Ortiz, who is worried about him. I've known

Scott Ortiz for a few years, and he is a darn good agent. He asked me to keep tabs on him. I will leave that to you, my darling."

They gather her bags and depart the airport. Joe Grant is happier than he has been in many years. He silently gives thanks to God for bringing them back together.

They arrive at Joe's house, and the children are there to greet her, as they are all aware that their parents are back together. Peter, the oldest, hugs his mom and gives his dad a big bear hug. Gilda and Patrice, the twins, just smile and tears roll down their cheeks. They notice that, for the first time in their lives, their father is crying, but crying happy tears.

It is said even God smiles when families pray together. Joseph Grant falls on his knees and thanks God for his goodness and his many blessings. Grant remembers Sergeant Dan Mesa and wishes he could pass some of his happiness on to him.

In Yuma, Matilda receives a phone call telling her to meet her daughter in Tucson at the hospital. Alana and Sergeant Mesa receive the same call. All three speed toward Tucson.

Dan Mesa is suspicious of the call and puts on his vest; he remembers Janie's warning. He adds his 9-mm pistol to his arsenal. He arrives at the hospital to find both Matilda and Alana there waiting. Just as he steps out of his truck, someone opens fire and hits Matilda and Alana. Dan Mesa locates the shooter and opens fire. He sees the shooter go down. He stands up, knowing he is going to be hit. He feels the impact of the bullet, but thanks to the vest, he is unharmed.

The sound of sirens is everywhere, but Mesa is steadily shooting and moving. He finds the shooter, Armanti Sandoval. He is almost shot to pieces. He is still alive when Mesa arrives.

"You are Dan Mesa," he says, struggling to speak. "They told me you were tough. I should have listened. Carlos should pay for the trouble . . ." He dies before finishing what he started to say.

Mesa rushes back to Matilda and Alana. They are being taken inside the hospital to the emergency room. He rushes to the emergency room only to be stopped by a nurse.

"Ranger, you can't go in there now."

"Look, lady, two of my friends are in there, and I am going in with or without your approval. Now get the hell out of the way!"

The nurse sees something in his eyes that frightens her, and she immediately backs away. Mesa rushes in and sees blood everywhere.

"How are they?" he asks.

No one says anything. He moves forward like a crouching tiger ready to pounce on someone. His voice suddenly changes, and each word sounds like thunder.

"I asked you how they are doing! I won't ask again!"

The attending physician suddenly becomes aware that the man is about ready to attack him.

"Ranger, they are in serious condition. Now, please let us try to save them. I promise as soon as we stabilize them and find out their injuries and how serious, we will let you know. You have my word on that."

"I will hold you to that."

Mesa turns and walks out. He uses his phone to call Major McMasters.

"Hello, this is Sergeant Dan Mesa of the Santa Cruz detachment. May I speak to the major?"

"Sergeant Mesa, this is Ranger Aliente. I will see if the major is in."

"Sergeant, what can I do for you?" McMasters asks.

"Sir, Lieutenant Osborne and her mother have been shot, and they are in the hospital here in Tucson. They are in serious condition, and I don't know if they will pull through. I don't know what happened. I received a call that said I should rush to the hospital, and when I arrived and saw them, suddenly shooting started. They were hit. I saw the shooter and took him out. It was Armanti Sandoval."

"Okay, Dan, I will be arriving by helicopter shortly. Have you notified Captain Johnson yet?"

"No, sir, I haven't. You are the first one I have called. I will call him now."

"Dan, I will call him. You just hold tight where you are and keep an eye on them."

The phone rings at Ranger Headquarters in Nogales and Bonefacio Hernandez answers saying, "Ranger Station."

"Yes, I'm Major McMasters from Yuma. May I speak to Captain Johnson please."

"Yes, sir, I will get him for you."

"Captain, Major McMasters in on the phone, and he is a little upset."

"Okay, Bonnie, I will take it. Captain Johnson picks up the phone and says, "Yes, major, what can I do for you?"

"Sam, Alana and her mother have been shot. They are in the hospital in Tucson, and Sergeant Mesa is there. Sam, he doesn't believe they will make it through the night. Sandoval did the shooting, and Mesa killed him. I don't know if he was injured or not. He never said. I am flying down by helicopter, and I will see you there."

Sam Johnson feels gut-wrenching anger. Bonnie sees him, and what he sees scares the daylights out of him. Captain Johnson's face is like beige stone, and his eyes are as dark as the pits of Hell. The captain takes down his .44 Magnum and straps it on.

"Bonnie, Lieutenant Osborne and her mother have been shot, and they are in the hospital in Tucson. Sergeant Mesa is there also. I don't know if he has been shot or injured. Please call the colonel and tell him. I am on my way to Tucson. Call my wife and tell her."

"Yes, sir. What should I tell the guys?"

"Just tell them what I told you and that, as soon as I get more information, I will call."

With those last words, Sam Johnson leaves for Tucson.

Meanwhile back in Tucson, the police are everywhere asking questions. Sergeant Dan Mesa has written a statement explaining what happened, and he isn't any too pleased. He is trying to control his anger and finding it extremely hard to do.

Sergeant Sheila Burke arrives and takes over. She walks over to Mesa.

"Dan, how is the lieutenant and her mother?"

"Hello, Sheila. They are still in the emergency room. The doctor on call said he would tell me something as soon as he could."

Sergeant Burke notices that Mesa is covered in blood and suggests he go wash some of it off.

Mesa becomes aware of his situation and complies. He returns with the blood removed from his face and hand, but he could not do much with his shirt. There is a bullet burn on his neck and another on his arm, but he isn't really aware of them.

Sheila returns with a nurse and says, "Dan, you have been wounded. Let the nurse take a look you."

Mesa turns around, and what Sergeant Burke sees scares her; there isn't anything human about the man she is facing. His face and entire demeanor are those of a dangerous animal.

"Dan, you have been wounded. Let the nurse have a look," she says again.

Mesa relaxes and never says a word. It has been two hours since the shooting, and he hasn't sat down yet. As the nurse is working on him, Major McMasters walks in.

Mesa attempts to stand, but the major says, "No, Dan, you stay seated. Are you badly injured?"

The nurse answers, "No, his injures are not life-threatening, but they are of concern, because the bullet burn on his neck barely missed an artery. The one on his arm came close to an artery too. I have disinfected the wound, and these bandages will protect them and allow them to heal. Ranger, you are a lucky man."

Major McMasters has the look of a worried man.

"Nurse, could you please check on the condition of Lieutenant Osborne and her mother?"

The nurse leaves and goes to the emergency room.

"Doctor, how are those two patients who were shot? The younger one is an Arizona ranger, and the older lady is her mother."

Doctor Burke is the on-scene doctor. He looks at the nurse and shakes his head.

"The ranger's mother didn't make it, and it is doubtful if the ranger will make it, although she is fighting for her life."

"What should I tell the rangers?"

"Nurse, that is my job. I will have to bear the sad news."

Dr. Burke arrives in the waiting room to find it filled with rangers, the police, the FBI, and news reporters. He calls the major and Captain Johnson to one side.

"Gentlemen, Lieutenant Osborne is in critical condition, and her mother died on the operating table. If we can stop the bleeding, there is a possibility we can save Lieutenant Osborne. She was shot once in the back and once in the chest. Her mother took two shots in the back and both would have been fatal. She said, 'Tell Dan good-bye and that it is just my time.' Captain, I assume that Dan is Sergeant Mesa? I think you should come with me when I tell him. I saw how he was when they brought them in, and I would not want to get on his bad side."

Major McMasters's face is like a mask. He hasn't said much. They walk over to Sergeant Mesa, who is still seated. He stands as they approach.

"Hello, major. Hello, captain. I am sorry this happened. They were shot because of me. How are Matilda and Alana?"

"Dan, this is Doctor Burke, whom you already know. Listen to what he has to say."

"Ranger Mesa, Matilda died on the operating table. I couldn't save her. She told me to tell you it wasn't your fault. It was just her time. Alana is in critical condition, and I won't lie to you. I honestly don't know if I can save her, but we are trying like crazy. A few prayers wouldn't hurt."

Mesa's whole world is spinning out of control, and all he can do is watch it fall apart. All eyes seem to be on him. Then suddenly the doors burst open, and a nurse rushes in.

"Doctor! Doctor! That lady is still alive. She is talking."

"Nurse, what are you talking about?"

"Doctor, Mrs. Osborne is still alive and talking."

It takes a few second for what has been said to register with those listening. Suddenly, it dawns on them what has taken place.

Sergeant Dan Mesa of the Arizona rangers does something few people have ever seen him do. He smiles. He really smiles, with teeth showing and everything.

Dr. Burke is so shocked he can barely talk.

"Nurse, let's get back in there and save a women's life."

He rushes into the emergency room.

Major McMasters and Captain Johnson sit down and show signs of relief. Now the waiting begins as the police and the FBI continue to ask questions of everyone.

"Sergeant, I know this is a bad time to be asking questions, but could you give us a quick and dirty idea of what happened?"

Mesa explains again what happened in a straight-to-the-point way.

Sergeant Burke looks at Mesa and smiles, saying, "Ranger, there must be an angel looking after you. You have escaped death so many times. Those news reporters who constantly belittle the rangers and the police should have been here to see how a servant of the people saves the lives of our citizens. They seem to only see the brutal side of us."

Everyone is nodding his or her head in agreement. One person standing to the side taking notes asks, "Sergeant Burke, can I quote what you said in my article? I am Jim Landry of the *Phoenix Herald*. I agree with what you said, and I promise to write an article that is fair and honest. I won't lie for you or against you."

"Yes, Mr. Landry, you can quote me. But if you do misrepresent the truth of what I said, I will sue you and your paper, and I promise all of us standing here: I will win."

"Sergeant, you have my word of honor on what I have said."

The smile on Mesa's face fades, and he returns to being Daniel Mesa. They wait some more. The FBI takes Mesa's statement and the statements of some of the bystanders. Sandoval's body has been removed, and the hazardous materials crew is cleaning up the blood and debris. There is still much work to be done.

The local TV stations are broadcasting the shooting at the Tucson Medical Center. The TV echoes, "This is Laura Denton of *Channel 14 News*. There has been a shooting at the Tucson Medical

Center involving the Arizona rangers. Chuck Garrison is on the scene. Chuck, can you tell us what happened?"

"Laura, apparently two women—mother and daughter—were shot as they arrived at the medical center. The younger lady is a lieutenant in the rangers, and the older lady is her mother. Someone opened fire on them, hitting the mother in the back and the daughter in the chest and back as she tried to shield her mother. Ranger Dan Mesa was at the hospital, and he opened fire, killing the shooter. The shooter has been identified as Armanti Sandoval, the notorious assassin wanted in several countries, including the United States, for murder. He is—or I should say *was*—a paid assassin. The names of the two ladies are being withheld, pending further investigation. The ranger who shot Sandoval is Sergeant Dan Mesa, who has been in the news several times over the past year as you and our viewers are aware. We do not know if Ranger Mesa was injured or not, but he was covered in blood, possibly from rendering assistance to the two ladies. That is all we know at this point."

"Thanks, Chuck," Laura says, "and please keep us inform of anything happening there. This has been a breaking news story from the scene at the Tucson Medical Center. I am Laura Denton of *Channel 14 News*."

The regular program resumes. Mesa looks at the TV and leaves for coffee. Sergeant Burke follows him. Mesa goes to the coffee machine and gets a cup of coffee

"Dan, are you okay?" she asks.

Mesa turns around and says, "No, I am not okay. They were shot because of me. Somehow, he knew they were my friends. He shot them to get at me. But the people responsible are Carlos Meana and Antonio Blackbear. I will catch up with them very soon, and I will end this whole affair. Matilda and Alana had a great life until I walked in. Now, I don't know what to do."

"Sergeant, it wasn't your fault," Sergeant Burke says. "We can only do so much to protect the ones we love, and that is all we can do. Someone greater than you and I has control, so let him do his job. Dan, I am a good listener if you need someone to talk to. Call anytime."

Sergeant Burke walks away, leaving Mesa alone to drink his coffee and think. He makes his way back to the emergency room. Everyone is still waiting. It has been six hours since the shooting, and the doctors are still in the operating room.

Everyone is in deep thought when the doors burst open and Dr. Burke enters with a smile on his face.

"Ladies and gentlemen, we have stopped the internal bleed in Lieutenant Osborne, and I believe we can save her life. Matilda is getting better every hour. I can't explain any of this! It is beyond anything I have ever come across. By all accounts, they should be dead, but thanks to God, they are still alive. It has to be a miracle."

Everyone is smiling but Daniel Mesa. He walks down the hall to the hospital chapel. He walks inside and kneels to give thanks, but he knows that, come tomorrow, he will enter the day with hatred in his heart. He plans to kill at least two men and maybe more. He walks away from the chapel and leaves the hospital without saying a word. He climbs into his vehicle and heads toward Nogales.

In Phoenix, the local TV station is broadcasting the news about the shooting in Tucson. Carlos and Antonio are listening to the news.

Carlos bangs the table, saying, "Can't anyone kill that man? Now he will be coming after us. There isn't any place for us to hide, so let's go after him."

Unknown to them, they are being watched by an undercover FBI agent using night vision binoculars. The officer observes what appears to be the beginning of preparation for a road trip. The suspects are packing bags and using a checklist, something quite original for such people. He observes them packing several weapons, including some type of explosive.

At a bank in Phoenix, two women are making deposits into their accounts. Jane deposits a thousand dollars, and Marilyn deposits eight hundred fifty dollars. The teller remembers them and smiles as always, and they make small talk as usual about their jobs.

Christmas is just around the corner, only about ten days away. Jane looks at Marilyn and notices that her face is contorted with pain.

"Honey, are you okay?"

"Jane, get me home as quickly as possible."

Jane presses the accelerator and the Chevy Corvette moves on down the interstate at a fast pace. An Arizona highway patrolman notices the yellow Corvette and goes after it. Jane sees the car and slows down and pulls over to the side.

"Marilyn, are you okay?"

"No, I hurt badly."

The patrolman walks to the car, and as he looks into the car, he sees the lady in pain.

"Good afternoon, ladies. I noticed you speeding down the highway, and your friend appears to be in pain. What can I do to help?"

Jane cries.

"Officer," she says, "my friend is extremely ill. She has cancer, and we live in Tucson. I need to get her to the hospital quickly. Will you please escort us to the Tucson Medical Center?"

"Ma'am, pull in behind me and stay on my bumper, and I will get you there pronto. He walks back to his car and says, "Patrol fifteen to headquarters, this is Trooper Crawford, and I have an emergency situation. I will be escorting two citizens to the Tucson Medical Center. I will stay in touch as I go."

"Headquarters to Patrol fifteen, should we notify the hospital and have them waiting?"

"Yes, we will be arriving at the emergency entrance."

When they arrive, a team of doctors and nurses are waiting. Dr. Burke is the doctor on duty when they arrive. He is also Marilyn's personal doctor and is familiar with her illness. Marilyn is wheeled into the emergency room, and Jane waits. They have disguised their appearances so that people would not be completely surprised when they are seen.

Jane waits in the emergency room and calls the girls and Marilyn's parents. The girls decide it would be safer not to show up. Dr. Burke walks into the waiting room with a grim face.

"Jane, her condition is getting worse. It is progressing faster than I thought. At this rate, the best I can give her is six months, and that is really stretching it. I have known you two for a couple of years, and I know how close you are. If you can, make the next few months the best for her. It is my guess that she will start showing signs of fatigue around the fourth month. She won't suffer. It will happen all of a sudden, and then it will be over."

Jane's heart is breaking, but she maintains her composure.

"Doctor Burke, what can I do for her? How do I make her comfortable?"

"Just make sure she enjoys life as much as possible. Marilyn will not just sit back and die. She will try to enjoy life as much as possible, so let her enjoy it. Now, go on in and be with your friend."

Jane regains her composure and walks in to where Marilyn is.

"Hey there, girlfriend," she says, "and how are you?"

"I'm okay. It was just another warning from God, telling me I don't have long to hang out with you guys. So, for the next few months I want to enjoy my life. Now don't give me that surprised look. I know I have only about six months left. I plan to make the most of the next three or four months. If my guess is right, I figure that around the fourth or fifth month, I will be too weak to do much."

"Marilyn, what will I do without you? We are sisters through and through. I know God knows what is best, but I wish he'd reconsider and let you stay with us. You are my best friend, and if I could take your place, I would."

"Jane, if it was possible, I wouldn't allow you to take my place. This is my fate, and I must do as God has planned. Now get me out of this meat factory, and let's find food. I am hungry."

When they arrive at the apartment, Susan and Sophia meet them, and all laugh and cry together.

Sophia turns to Jane and asks, "What do we do next? Do we need to take down any more banks?"

"No, I think we have enough money if we manage it right. Also, I have this feeling that tells me it is dangerous to try it again. We were lucky; we didn't have to shoot anyone. Our luck could run out any day."

Marilyn looks at them and says, "I believe Ranger Mesa will be after us once he clears his current case up. I don't want Mesa as an enemy. He is trouble, and trouble is something we don't need right now. Let's just go back to work and act as if nothing has ever happened. We will disguise ourselves just enough to prevent anyone from associating us with the movie star bandits."

Sophia stands with a strange smile on her face and says, "I wonder what Ranger Mesa would do if I just sort of brushed into him one day. He is handsome in a western sort of way. He isn't Robert Redford or Sidney Poitier, but there is something about that man that gets to me."

The girls all respond at the same time, saying, "Are you crazy or have you bumped your head one time too many? If he discovers who you are, he will arrest you and send you to prison!"

"All right, I was only thinking out loud. I am not going to look him up. I was just thinking about him."

Marilyn smiles.

"Sophia," she says, "now is not the time. After I am gone, then it will be okay. I know what you are thinking, but trust me. I know what I am talking about. If you do as I say, we will not be caught, but if you fail to do so, we will all go to jail. I don't want to die in prison."

Jane cries softly, and they all hug Marilyn. It is a scene that would make even a ranger like Mesa cry.

The news comes on the TV, and the local commentator is talking about the shooting in Tucson.

"Good evening, I am Laura Denton."

"And I am Chuck Garrison and this is the evening news. Our lead-off story is about the shooting that took place in Tucson yesterday. An assailant viciously shot down Lieutenant Alana Osborne of the Arizona rangers and her mother Matilda Osborne. Mrs. Osborne almost died on the operating table, but due to the work of the attending doctors, she has survived. Her daughter the lieutenant survived but is in critical condition. The assailant was shot and killed by another ranger, Sergeant Daniel Mesa. The assailant was Armanti Sandoval, a notorious assassin wanted by the FBI and INTERPOL. We will continue to keep you posted on this situation."

Susan walks over and turns off the TV and sits down quietly.

"How is it that one man can be a part of so much violence?" she asks. "That Ranger Mesa seems to be wherever there is violence and shooting. It is as if he is cursed. I would not want to be married to him. I would always be afraid of that knock on the door and someone telling me he had been killed. My dad was an air force pilot during Vietnam, and I will always remember that knock on the door when they told my mother he had been shot down and killed over North Vietnam. They loved each other so much. It took her ten years to let go of him. That was in 1968, and I was a sophomore in high school. In 1978, she finally started dating this nice guy, and they got married in 1980. They are happy, and amazingly, he was a pilot also. But I am not my mom.

Marilyn smiles and says, "If he loved me, I would just love him back and pray for his safety and trust that God would protect him. I would just want to be happy."

The group smiles and nods in agreement.

Chapter Twelve

Thirty-six hours have passed since the shooting by the time Mesa arrives in Nogales and checks in at ranger headquarters. He knocks on the captain's door and walks in.

"Captain, I am going after Carlos and Antonio, and I won't be back until I have them in custody. Please do me a favor and check on Alana and Matilda and keep me posted. This whole affair has gone on too long. It is time to bring it to an end, one way or another.'

"Dan, the colonel just called me, and I have been promoted to major," Johnson says. "I need another lieutenant in the unit. You have earned the rank of lieutenant, so how about taking the promotion?"

"Sir, I'm grateful to you, and I'd like the rank, but I have to finish this up before I can accept it. Do me a favor and let me finish what I have begun, and then we'll sit down and talk about it."

Captain Johnson looks at Mesa and almost chews him out, but he decides against it.

"Sergeant, go and do what you have to do. After this case is over, we will talk, and for once in your life, you will listen while I talk. Do we understand each other?"

"Yes, I understand, and thanks, sir. I know I sometimes push too hard, but this case has hit home in too many ways."

Mesa turns and leaves the office. He is thinking about his friend Ranger Savalas when suddenly he smells a familiar fragrance. He begins searching and hoping. Then the smell is gone. He feels that familiar tug at his heart.

He climbs into his truck and heads toward home. He thinks about all the people he has been acquainted with who have died. He thinks of Jose, Sonia, and Savalas, and he remembers what has happened to Alana and Matilda. He thinks of the men he has killed and finds that he regrets killing them; but if he had it to do over, he would do the same thing.

He arrives home and calls for the dog, but he remembers that the dog is dead.

"I need to get another dog. I guess I'll get me a hound dog. They make great pets and great watchdogs."

Mesa goes to the stables and feed the horses and reminds himself he needs to start riding them more. He gives each one grain and some hay and checks the water. The barn is new and has a concrete floor with built-in drains and feed bins. He takes down the brush and comb and brushes the coats of the horses, taking his time and talking to them as if they were human. When the chore is finished, he goes into the house.

He starts to prepare food, and then suddenly the smell of Chanel No. 5 is strong. He turns, and she is standing there. He smiles.

"I was hoping I would see you again," he says. "I miss you so much."

"Dan, I will always be with you, and nothing will stop that. One day, I won't be around as much I am now, but when you need me, I will be there. I am your guardian angel, and believe me, you need one. You must take better care of yourself. Don't worry so much. Enjoy life."

Mesa looks at his watch, and it is four a.m. It was only eleven p.m. when she appeared. He wonders if he dreamed the whole thing. Then suddenly the fragrance is strong again, and he knows that he wasn't dreaming. He gets up, takes a bath, and dresses in gray slacks with a green shirt and a gray western tie. He straps on that familiar peace of gear, the .357 magnum, and climbs into his truck with the destination of Tucson. Mesa puts in a call to the Arizona state police and finds that Carlos is in the foot hills of Mount Lemon. He calls the telephone company and gets a number for the location.

Carlos is eating breakfast when the phone rings. "Hello, Hello. Who is this?"

"Carlos, this is your worst enemy, Daniel Mesa, and I am coming for you. You should change from those ridiculous pajamas into running clothing, because you have only a few hours left in this world. Pray that I don't catch you. Now run, damn you."

Antonio has been watching Carlos and asks, "Boss, who was that?"

"Antonio, that was Dan Mesa, and he is coming after us. He knew that I was wearing these pajamas! How in the hell does he know that? Let's pack and get out of here. Get every gun we have and all of the ammunition. We are heading for Mexico. Let's see if he can find us in Mexico."

"Carlos, how will we cross the border? You know they have pictures of us at every exit point."

"My friend, we will cross where there aren't any patrols. Do you remember that old abandoned silver mine out there by the golf course in Nogales? Well, that is where we will cross the border, but first I must make a phone call."

He places a call to a number in Chicago. A voice answers, "Hello?"

"Rudy, this is Carlos, and I need your help."

"Carlos, you are trouble. The kind of trouble we don't need right now. We are watched too."

"Rudy, I need someone who is discreet and who can take care of a package for me. I am transferring two hundred fifty thousand dollars to your account now and another when the job is done. The package must be mailed, whether I am around or not."

"Carlos, after this, I don't ever want to hear from again. Our association is over. You have angered many people. Your actions have caused us much discomfort."

The line dies, and Carlos and Antonio drive away with the conviction that their troubles will soon be over.

As they drive away, a dark truck follows at a comfortable distance. The driver places a call to ranger headquarters.

"This is Ranger Mesa," the driver says.

"Go ahead, Sergeant Mesa."

"I am following Carlos Meana and Antonio Blackbear on I-19, and they are headed toward the border. I suspect they will detour and head toward Patagonia and try to cross the border in that area around the old silver mine. I will need assistance. Please notify the local police and the state boys to be on the watch for them. They are traveling in Carlos's Dodge truck, and they are heavily armed."

"Dan, this is Major Johnson, you be careful. Don't take any foolish chances. We don't need any more dead rangers."

"I understand, sir, and I promise to be careful."

Major Johnson alerts the local police and the state police. He turns to the desk sergeant and says, "Log me out, and I will be on the radio. This is not going to be nice."

The major takes an M16 and one hundred rounds of 9-mm ammo. He knows it will be a tough take-down.

On I-19 headed south to Nogales, Carlos and Antonio are speeding along at the posted speed limit, not wanting to attract attention. Suddenly they notice a dark Ford truck on their tail and closing in.

"Carlos, we have trouble behind us, and it looks like that darn ranger," Antonio says. "What should I do?"

"Take him out if you can. I will try to outrun him."

Antonio begins firing at Mesa's truck, but he is unable to score a hit. Carlos takes the Nogales exit and speeds toward Patagonia. He misses the golf course turn-in and continues toward Patagonia. Carlos suddenly takes a side road, and Mesa follows. Carlos ditches the truck, and they begin running. Mesa stops his truck and is aware that other police cars have arrived. They begin following Carlos and Antonio.

"Carlos, what is your plan?"

"I plan to kill Dan Mesa once and for all. Now watch and learn."

Carlos takes several grenades and goes back down the trail. Antonio follows.

Mesa is coming up the trail in a very careful manner. He stops and turns to those behind him.

"Carlos is no fool. He will try to ambush us, and if I were he, I would use some kind of explosive, probably grenades so let's wait here for a few minutes. I have a feeling we are about to have his presence."

Carlos is moving down the trail carefully when he hears, "Carlos, this is Dan Mesa of the rangers. Stop where you are and give yourself up. If you do not, you will die, and that is a promise."

Carlos lobs a grenade at the police. There is an explosion, and a young rookie policeman is injured. His left arm is mangled, and another officer is also injured. They open fire, and Carlos retreats, throwing grenades as he runs.

Major Johnson arrives on the scene and is a witness to the action. He watches as Mesa charges forward, firing every step of the way. Major Johnson yells at Mesa, "Sergeant Mesa, get back here," but due to the noise from the explosion, Mesa doesn't hear him and continues to charge forward. The police and the rangers charge forward.

Carlos stops as Mesa approaches.

"Okay, Sergeant Mesa, people are always talking about how tough you are. Well, I am tough too, so let's settle it right here. Or are you just a lot of hot air? Well, what will it be?"

"Carlos, you have an opportunity to live, and if I were you, I'd take it. If you face me today, you will die, and so will Antonio. Antonio killed her, but you are responsible, and both of you will die today unless you give up and disarm yourselves."

"No, Mesa, it ends here today. Not tomorrow, now!"

Mesa stands up and moves forward, carrying a pump shotgun loaded with double loads of buckshot. Everyone is watching this turn of events. Mesa walks at an even pace, almost as if he is floating on air.

One ranger says, "I smell perfume. Where is it coming from?"

"Ranger, I suggest you pay attention to what is happening here and not become fixated with perfume," comments an older ranger.

Suddenly, Mesa stops, and Carlos appears. He drops his gun and grenades.

"Okay, Ranger Mesa let see how tough you really are."

"Carlos, are you sure you want it this way?"

"Yes, I am sure. Either I kill you, or you kill me. So, tough guy, let's get it on."

Mesa is leery of a trap, so he slowly drops the shotgun and discards the pistol. Carlos charges Mesa, not giving him time to prepare. Dan sees what is happening and braces for the attack. Carlos leaves his feet in a flying tackle, something he used during his football days at the University of Texas. He hits Mesa with his shoulder, and Dan is knocked backward and is dazed. Carlos throws a kick and hits Mesa in the ribs, but Mesa continues to get up and smiles at Carlos.

"If that is your best, then you are in trouble."

Carlos throws a left punch and hits Mesa on the jaw. He follows that with a right cross that knocks the ranger down again.

"Come on, ranger. I thought you were tough!"

Mesa stands up, rips his shirt off, and goes after Carlos. Carlos throws a roundhouse kick, and Mesa dodges it and counters with a kick to the groin. Carlos falls to his knees, and Mesa waits until he stands. Then he methodically takes the man apart piece by piece. He smashes his kneecaps with a swift kick and then breaks his nose with an open-handed smash to the face.

Antonio rushes forward with a knife, and Mesa braces for the attack. As Antonio lunges, Mesa sidesteps and kicks the man in the face. Antonio drops the knife, and Mesa goes to work on Antonio. Carlos gets up slowly and goes after Mesa. Mesa fights like a cornered tiger. He lifts Antonio off the ground by the neck and body slams him, breaking Antonio's arm. He kicks Carlos in the stomach and again in the face.

Mesa is bleeding from a cut in the side, and he has a broken rib. He walks over, lifts Carlos off the ground, and throws him about five feet. Carlos is no coward; he gets up. He throws a wicked left hook that knocks Mesa to his knees. Carlos is sure he has beaten Mesa. He charges forward but is surprised when Mesa stands up and smiles at him.

"You had her killed, and now I am going to kill you and your friend."

Dan summons all his reserved strength and fights like a caged animal. He slaps Carlos's face, drawing blood and clearly making him angry. Carlos attempts a roundhouse kick, but Mesa blocks the kick and smashes an elbow to the knee. Again, he slaps Carlos twice with blows that sound like gunshots.

He grabs Carlos, sticks a gun in his mouth, and cocks the hammer.

Major Johnson rushes forward.

"Dan, no. That is not the way. Would she want you to do that? Carlos and Antonio will stand trial, and they will pay with their lives."

Suddenly, there is the smell of perfume all around. Carlos screams and covers his eyes, and so does Antonio.

"Get her away from me," he yells and dives for his weapon.

Major Johnson yells to Sergeant Mesa, "Dan, he has a gun."

There is a loud explosion as the guns explode. There is a bright light, and both Antonio and Carlos scream in agony.

Carlos is yelling, "I can't see. My eyes. I can't see."

Antonio is yelling the same thing. It is told later by those present that during the explosion and bright light, there was a face in the light.

As the smoke clears, Major Johnson rushes forward and finds that both Carlos and Antonio are blind. They are handcuffed, and their rights are read to them. Carlos is sobbing and complaining about being blind.

Dan Mesa cocks his pistol, walks over, and once again puts the barrel in Carlos's mouth, saying, "This is for Sonia. I hope you rot in hell for what you did to her."

"Dan, don't do it. He isn't worth the bullet."

"Major, he is responsible for her death. Antonio may have carried it out, but he is responsible."

Carlos is begging and sobbing, and Antonio is shaking like crazy.

"Dan, is that what she'd want you to do? I don't think so. Look at them. They are to be pitied. Please, let them live, and they'll suffer more than she did. They have to live in a blind world."

Mesa releases the trigger and walks away while Antonio mumbles, "It was her face. She did it. She did it."

Sergeant Bonefacio Hernandez asks, "Who are you talking about? What woman?"

"It was that woman I killed, Sonia. She blinded me. She is back, and she is going to kill me."

Everyone stops at the mention of Sonia's name, except Mesa. He limps away and grimaces from the pain in his side. He climbs into his truck and drives away. The prisoners are led away in handcuffs, still mumbling.

At Ranger Headquarters, reporters are asking questions. Colonel Grant has arrived and has been briefed on the situation. Dan Mesa is still absent.

The media has arrived and is demanding to see the prisoners. They are ushered into the briefing room. Jim Landry of the *Phoenix Herald* asks, "It is rumored that the two prisoners are blind. Is there any truth to that rumor?"

Colonel Grant takes over the news briefing.

"Yes, the two suspects are blind," he says, "and you can ask them what happened."

Carlos and Antonio arrive in handcuffs, along with their lawyer.

Laura Denton of *Channel 14 News* leads the discussion: "Carlos, how did you lose your sight?"

With his eyes bandaged, Carlos says, "It was that lady, Sonia. She is back, but she is dead. I saw her face just before that light that blinded me. But she is dead. She burned to death in that house. She has returned to punish me."

Laura turns toward Antonio and asks, "Antonio, what happened to you? How did you lose your sight?"

"It was as Carlos said. She did it. Carlos was reaching for his pistol, when suddenly it exploded in this blinding light. Then my eyesight was gone. Just before I lost my sight, I saw her face, and she was very angry. I confess I did it. I left her in that house, and then I set it on fire. It was me. I did it. Please, now, don't let her get me."

Major Johnson turns to the colonel and asks, "Did he just confess to murdering Sonia on live TV?"

"Yes, Sam. That is exactly what he did."

The door opens, and Mesa walks in. He walks up to Carlos and says, "I know you paid a hit man to kill me. You'd better pray he doesn't miss because if he does, I am coming back to finish the job I started yesterday."

Jim Landry asks, "Sergeant Mesa, are you saying that Carlos hired an assassin to kill you?"

"Yes, a friend in the FBI told me about an hour ago that they found out that Carlos hired a man out of Chicago. His orders are to kill me whether Carlos is alive or dead. He paid two hundred fifty thousand dollars up front and another two hundred fifty thousand is to be paid when the job is complete."

"Ranger, what do you plan to do about it?"

"I plan to live my life but be extremely careful."

Carlos begins to panic and yells, "Ranger, I can stop it. Just get me a phone." He is given a phone. "Please, someone dial seven seven nine five three nine three zero nine nine." The number is dialed, and the line rings. A voice answers, "Leave a message and a number, and you will be called."

"This is Carlos Meana. Cancel the hit. Repeat, cancel the hit. You can keep the payment of two hundred fifty thousand dollars. Call me back as soon as the hit has been cancelled. I will be waiting by the phone at 635-375-8866." He hangs up the phone.

The phone rings, and a voice says, "The hit has been canceled. Thanks for your business." The phone goes dead at the other end and Carlos hands the phone back to the ranger saying, "The hit is canceled. Now please tell her to give me my sight back. Please, you tell her I am sorry."

The cameras have been rolling the whole time, and everything has been broadcast on live television.

Laura Denton finishes her broadcast by saying, "This is Laura Denton, and what you have just seen is real—not a stunt but live from the ranger headquarters here in Nogales. In my ten years as a news reporter, I have never covered anything like what you've seen here this morning. I am Laura Denton of *Channel 14 News*, live from Nogales."

Colonel Grant turns to Laura and asks, "Miss Denton, will you give us a copy of that film? We will probably need it for the trial."

"No problem, colonel. I will personally get it to you. Thanks for the best day of my news career. Where is Ranger Mesa? I wanted to talk to him."

"Miss Denton, if I were you, I'd leave him alone for now. Maybe in a few days you can call for an interview but not now. You'd probably see something that would frighten not only you but the public in general. That lady who was killed was someone special to him, and he is not handling it too well."

The prisoners are escorted to the Tucson Medical Center and imprisoned at the hospital in the criminal ward. The physician assigned, examines both.

"Colonel Grant, these two prisoners are suffering from something we refer to as hysterical blindness. It happens in war a lot but not too often in civilian life. Usually, it happens when someone sees something terrible happen to a close friend or relative. This is the first time I've seen it happen in the manner it happened with these two. If I didn't know better, I'd say they were faking it, but those two are convinced that some lady named Sonia is coming back for them. Their sight may return in a few days or a few weeks or it may never return. It is impossible to say."

"Thanks, Doctor McPherson. You have done your part."

The date is December 22 when Mesa walks into the hospital room where Alana and Matilda are. He kneels and says a short prayer. As he stands, he looks into Matilda's face, and she smiles at him.

"Dan, did you say a prayer for me too?" she asks.

Mesa walks over and gives her a gentle hug.

"I was praying for both of you," he says. "I thought I'd lost you both. Has Alana said anything yet? Look, both of you mean the world to me. I love both of you, and if anything happened to you,

I don't know what I'd do. This is Alana's second injury because of me. I can't allow her to be injured again, and I definitely won't allow anything ever to happen to you again!"

He hears Alana's voice saying, "You don't have to worry, because we are leaving Arizona for a while."

Mesa turns around with a smile, but the smile fades when he sees Alana's face. Her face shows disgust.

"Alana, it is so good to . . . hear your voice. Why are you looking at me with so much hatred?"

"It is because of you that my mother and I were shot. It is because of you that I almost lost my eye! So I want you out of my life for once and for all. Now get out!"

"Alana, what in the world is wrong with you? It isn't his fault. Things just happen sometimes."

"Mother, I am resigning from the rangers, and we are going to Europe for a year or two or maybe to Canada for a while, but we are not staying in Arizona any longer than we have to."

Mesa's face has turned gray, almost totally devoid of color. Slowly, he turns to walk out.

"I . . . I never meant to hurt you or your mom. I am sorry about that, and I wish I could change places with you, but I can't. I will leave now, and I won't be troubling you again. Matilda, if you ever need me you know where to find me."

"Dan, give her time, and I am sure she will change her mind. I don't want us to part like this."

"Neither do I, but I won't be the source of your pain any longer."

Mesa walks away hurriedly. He passes Dr. Burke and doesn't say a word. His face is a mask of pain and anger.

Dr. Burke starts to speak but doesn't. He walks into Matilda and Alana's room to find both women in tears. He looks from one to the other.

"Okay, what is going on here? I just saw Ranger Mesa walking down the hall, and he looked as if he has lost everything he held dear."

"Doctor Burke, my daughter just drove away the one man in this world who could have made her happy. She just gave him the boot. That man you just saw is a damned good person, and he deserves better."

Dr. Burke turns toward and says, "Alana, do you have anything to say?"

Through tears, she says, "I have said all I intend to say."

The holiday spirit has left Daniel Mesa's world as he heads home. As he approaches Amado he stops at the Cow Palace. He walks in and asks for Sylvia Animas.

"I'm the day manager, Jim Fagen. Who shall I say is looking for her?"

"I'm Sergeant Mesa of the Arizona rangers. She knows me."

The manager leaves and returns with Sylvia.

"Hello, Dan," she says. "Is there any news about Sonia's murder?"

"Sylvia, Carlos and Antonio have been captured. They are in jail in Tucson, and they will stand trial for murder. I started to kill them both, I don't think she'd like that, so I will allow them to stand trial. Now, I need to fly to El Paso to visit her parents again. If you need me, you can call any time."

He turns and walks away, never smiling. He climbs back into the truck and leaves. He returns to his place and packs his bags for El Paso. He places a call to Major Johnson.

"Sir, I am flying to El Paso to see Sonia's parents and bring them up-to-date. They deserve to know how things turned out. You can reach me on my cellular phone if you need me."

"Okay, sergeant. Are you okay?"

"Yes, sir, I am fine. I will see you in a few days."

Mesa boards a plane in Tucson and takes an aisle seat. He dozes off, and when he awakens, there is a familiar face smiling at him: Monica Saint Jacque. Mesa starts to speak, but she puts her finger to her mouth and asks him to be quiet.

"It is good to see you again, ranger. I want to thank you for what you did for Sonia. She is so proud of you. Don't look so surprised;

she will be checking on you periodically. See? People do care about you."

She smiles and walks away.

Mesa drops off to sleep again and awakens as the plane prepares to land. He looks for Monica again, but she isn't there. He smiles and disembarks. He rents a car and drives to Sonia's parents' ranch.

Meanwhile Napal and Ophelia are preparing for Mesa's arrival at the ranch. The girls are busy baking a cake and inviting their friends and Sonia's friends to the dinner party.

Mesa arrives driving a new Chrysler Sebring convertible and wearing his traditional western attire. Napal and Ophelia greet him at the door.

"Dan, it is good to see you, but you look tired and your eyes have that faraway look to them."

Mesa smiles his crooked smile and says, "I'm okay. How are you guys doing? Where are the girls?"

"We are great, and the girls are in the house planning a dinner party in your honor. You are something of a hero around here. We saw the capture and confession of Carlos and Antonio on the news. They will have a long time to regret what they did. Sonia would be so proud of you."

"You know, that is the second time I've heard that in less than two hours. I was on the plane and—do you remember I told you about a lady I met on the plane who reminded me of Sonia?—well she was on this plane too. She said, 'Sonia is so proud of you' and then she walked away. Sometimes, I don't know if these things are happening or if I dreamed it all," he says. "Look, I have a few days of vacation coming. I'd like to spend three or four days here if you don't mind. Maybe I could just help you out with the ranch. What I really need is just a few days to calm down before I fall apart."

Ophelia looks into the eyes of this quiet man and says, "Daniel Mesa, you are welcome at this house any day. I think I can speak for Napal and the girls when I say think of this as your second home."

Daniel Mesa just looks at the two of them and smiles and says thanks.

Mardi and Amelia grab Mesa and give him a big hug and a kiss, saying, "That is for Sonia and for us. Thanks for finding the ones responsible for her death. It took a lot out of you, we know, but you kept your promise, and we will never forget it. You have friends in the family for life. Now we have a dinner party planned for you, so don't get all bashful on us. Get rested and get ready for a hot time in the old town tonight."

"I'd like to go riding out there for a while," Dan says. "Will you loan me a horse for a few hours? I will be back."

He saddles a roan and rides out, remembering to take along his pistol.

As he rides, he spies a lone coyote and says, "Old fella, I sometimes wish I was you, and then I would just run free with no worries."

Mesa rides on, enjoying the cool air on his face. Suddenly, the smell of Chanel No. 5 is present. He slows down to a walk and looks around carefully. He rounds a bend, and there sitting on a log is Monica Saint Jacque.

"Lady, you do appear in some of the strangest places. What brings you out here?"

"I came to see you. I knew you'd be riding in this direction. Dan, you kept your promise, and I thank you for that. I will always be there looking out for you. The big guy is worried about you. You need to take it easy for a while." Suddenly, Monica becomes Sonia, and she smile at him. "Yes, it is me, and yes, I know it is confusing, but just accept the fact that some things are not to be understood but just accepted. I love you now as always."

In a flash she is gone. Mesa feels a touch of sadness.

A voice says, "Don't be sad. I need you to smile and remember me as I was."

He rides on until he reaches a creek. He stops and waters the horse. He takes out his pipe and smokes it. Then he rides on at a gallop.

Two hours later, he is back at the ranch. He unsaddles the horse and brushes him down, whispering softly to the horse. He gives him water and some grain and hay.

Mesa goes inside and takes a long hot bath and dresses for dinner in black slacks, a soft beige shirt, black boots, and a white hat. When he walks into the family room, several guests have arrived but no one he knows, so he finds the coffee and pours a cup.

A voice says, "Tis a grand thing they be doing for you. I am happy to be here in honor of you. My boy you don't know it yet, but there are better times in store for you."

Mesa turns to see a very big gentleman wearing a collar.

"I am Father Bishop of Holy Trinity Catholic Church," he introduces himself. "I've known the Perdenales families since the girls were born. Sonia was a special person as are Mardi and Amelia. Sonia had a way of making you smile in spite of yourself. Tis a rare gift she had. There I go, talking incessantly again."

"Hello, Father," Mesa says. "It is my pleasure to meet anyone who was a friend of Sonia's. She did have that rare gift of bringing sunshine wherever she went. For a short time, she brought sunshine into my life."

Amelia sees Father Bishop and goes over to say hello.

"Well, I see the two of you have met," Amelia says. "That is good and as it should be. Father Bishop is somewhat psychic; He has known about you from the very first meeting between you and Sonia, and he approved of you. It seemed as if God had other plans for both of you."

Father Bishop smiles and says, "Young lady, I am not psychic. I am just blessed with a sense of understanding what people need. Yes, I did approve of the two of you," he says to Mesa. "But sometimes the boss has a different plan for us. I do know that she loved you, Dan, and I know how you felt about her. Now, I also know that you have a hair-trigger temper, and you must learn to control it. Stop blaming yourself for what happened. It was not your fault, and there isn't anything you could have done to prevent it. What happened is the fault of Antonio Blackbear, and he will answer to a higher power. Daniel Mesa, you still have a life to live, so get started living it, because that is what she wants you to do. That I have on very good authority."

Father Bishop smiles and walks away to join another group.

Amelia looks at Mesa and sees that lone wolf look in his eyes.

"Dan, what do you plan to do now? You can't just cut yourself off from the world. You are a great guy, and there is still happiness for you if you go and look for it. Sonia was my sister, and I loved her dearly; I know she would want you to be happy. You have to find a way of moving on. We will always be here for you."

Mesa knows Amelia is right but deep down in the recesses of his mind he still thinks of what would have happened if he had done things differently.

He decides to sample the food. Ophelia has baked his favorites: banana nut bread and bread pudding with vanilla sauce. The coffee is excellent and has a strong aroma. He finishes the coffee and walks out to the horse corral and lights his pipe. He stands smoking and watching the horses. He is deep in thought, but he is instantly aware that someone is approaching. He moves to a position so that he may see anyone approaching. Ophelia brings him another cup of coffee laced with brandy.

"I thought you could use this," she says. "Dan, what do you plan to do with your life? I know you won't give up the rangers and I don't want you to. But when I look into your soul, I see much torment, and a man like you needs some peace in his life. You have avenged Sonia's murder. Now what do you do with all that pent-up anger? I am worried about you. I just want you to be happy, and I know she'd want the same thing. You still see and talk with her, don't you?"

Mesa smiles a weak smile and says, "Yes, ma'am, I do. I don't know why, but every time I find myself in danger she is there to warn me. I listen, and I am saved. Suddenly, there is the smell of Chanel No. 5 and she is there, but she isn't always wearing her own face. There is this other person who appears, but somehow I know they are the same. I guess you must think I am crazy. Sometimes I think I have lost my mind, but then she is there and I know better."

"Daniel Mesa, you are not crazy, because we experience the same thing around here. We all know when she is present because we sense the strong smell of Mexican coffee and apple pie. I know my baby is present. It is comforting in a way," she says. "You still did not answer my question and that is what do you plan to do with your life now?"

"I will go on being a ranger and trying to protect the innocent. It is what I do. As for my private life, I just don't know. I have lots of female friends, but it isn't the same. Sonia was special, and I can't think of anyone I'd rather be with. I promise I will try to be as happy as I can. If it is okay with you guys, I'd like to come by from time to time. I like all of you, and this ranch is very peaceful."

"You are always welcome here. What are you doing for Christmas?"

"I am going home to see my mom and visit with my brothers, but come New Year's Eve, I will be back."

Mesa returns home to Nogales to prepare for his trip to see his mother. He has not spent much time in Louisiana these last five years. He arrives in town, visits old friends, and spends days with his mom, brothers, and sisters. To his nieces and nephews, he is something of a hero. To his mom, he is just a little boy, still playing cowboys and Indians. He enjoys the holidays, but he knows he must return and face the future, such as it is.

Meanwhile things are moving fast back in Tucson, and the changes surprise Sergeant Dan Mesa.

When Mesa arrives back in Nogales, he checks in with the major.

"Sir, I decided to check in and see how things are going."

"Sergeant, I am glad to see you, but what I have to tell you isn't easy. Alana and her mother left town. Their lawyer came by and left this package for you. Alana called and said good-bye. She told me to tell you not to try to find them. In time, they will find you. I think you'd better open this package."

Mesa slowly opens the package, which contains several legal papers and documents. One document in particular reads:

> We, Matilda Osborne and Alana Osborne, leave our ranch located in Yuma, Arizona, for Daniel Mesa to oversee in our absence. If anything should happen to us, the ranch is to become the personal property of Daniel Mesa. We, being of sound mind and body, do affix our names to this document in the presence of witnesses. There is one stipulation: Daniel Mesa must agree in the presence of witnesses to never try to find us. If he does, this document becomes null and void.

As Mesa reads the papers, the major notices a change in Mesa's face. That old wolf demeanor returns, and his friend becomes what he feared all along. How can a man with so many people who respect him and like him be so alone?

"Dan, what do you plan to do? Are you going to sign the document and accept the stipulations?"

"Yes, sir. I will sign it. It is what they want, and I won't stand in their way. I wish that I could have been here. There were so many things I wanted to apologize for."

Mesa signs the document, and Major Johnson witnesses it along with Sergeant Bonefacio Hernandez who has been standing by observing. Mesa walks away into the night.

In an apartment in Tucson, the girls are gathered around Marilyn's bed, and all eyes are filled with tears.

Marilyn speaks in a weak voice, "It has been grand knowing you guys. Please don't cry for me. I've had a good life, and this is just the beginning. Now promise me you will not fall apart. Also, no more banks. I want your promise."

"We promise to go straight, and we also promise to visit you often."

Dr. Burke walks into the room and ushers the girls out.

"Marilyn how are you feeling at this moment?" he asks.

"Doctor, I don't hurt anymore. I am at peace. Thanks for everything you did for me. I guess sometimes it just has to be this way. Tell the girls good-bye for me. I love them all."

Suddenly, she is gone. Dr. Burke becomes very sad, and he knows why. He has seen too much death and hurt in his life. He walks out of the room with gloom.

Susan, Jane, and Sophia are crying softly as they look into Dr. Burke's face.

"She is gone," he says. "She said to tell you that she loved you all dearly and good-bye."

The girls are sad and they lean on each other for support as they leave the hospital. They must contact Marilyn's parents. When they arrive at Jane's place, Susan places a call to Marilyn's parents.

Funeral arrangements are made for Marilyn for after New Year's.

In Yuma at the Osborne's' ranch, Daniel Mesa is watching the sun set over the desert. He remembers the faces of Matilda and Alana. He especially remembers how much hatred Alana had for him the last time he saw her. A tear rolls down his cheek though he is unaware of it.

EPILOGUE

Mesa awakens to what he thinks is December in the present day and walks outside, but it is a strange day. It is not the present. It is the year 1904, and it is approaching Christmas. He rushes back inside and looks into the mirror. He discovers he is still Daniel Mesa, but he looks different. He is wearing brown jeans and a faded green shirt with a star pinned to his chest. He is carrying an old .44 single-action revolver.

Another ranger walks in and says, "Dan, the captain wants to see you right away, something about a bank in Tucson that was robbed and the teller killed."

Mesa walks into the room and sees a familiar face. It is Colonel Grant, but he is not Colonel Grant. He is Captain Josiah Grant.

"Sergeant Mesa, I want you to go to Tucson to investigate that bank robbery. The robbers were the Russell brothers. There are five of them, and they have hit banks as far east as San Antonio. I want them stopped."

Mesa saddles up his horse and heads out to Tucson. The terrain is totally different. He is trying to get used to his new surroundings when suddenly there is a fragrance that is familiar to him.

A familiar voice calls out, "Hey, ranger, wait a minute."

He turns, and there is Sonia.

"Yes, ma'am, what can I do for you?"

"I am Monica Saint Jacque, and I am the editor of the *Nogales Sentinel.* I would like to accompany you to Tucson to cover that bank robbery. I spoke with Captain Grant, and he said it was up to you whether I go or not. So, what is your opinion?"

Mesa is aware that all this must be a dream, but he plays his hunch.

"Ma'am, I don't mind you going along, but are you aware that it is a sixty-mile trip, which is rough enough for a man on horseback but even more so for a lady?"

"Yes, I am aware of the distance, but I have a spring wagon, and that will make it a bit easier, but I am willing to take the chance. I am a crack shot with rifle or pistol."

She smiles at Mesa, and his face lightens up a bit.

Mesa looks at the lady for a moment and smiles, saying, "Okay, you can come along. Do you need help with your wagon and supplies?"

"No, it is packed and ready to go. I packed with the hope that you'd say yes. I didn't want to hold you up."

"Lady, I like the way you think about things. If you will get your wagon, I will wait here for you. It is cold, so I hope you have dressed for the trip. I have coffee and some beans and bacon. I'm not much of a cook, but I get by."

"I'm a great cook, and I've brought along enough food to last for the trip. I even brought along some doughnuts. The captain said you have a taste for them. He thinks very highly of you."

"Ma'am, your face is very familiar. It is like a blast from the past or a blast from the future."

THE AUTHOR

I thank you for buying this novel and reading it. Someone once said "you should write about things and situations you are familiar with." I write about things and people I am familiar with. I hope you will continue to read about the characters in this novel. There are other books on the horizon about Dan Mesa. It is a joy to develop the character of each person in the novels. As a retire Air Force Officer and now a retired teacher, I find I have a lot to write about. Best wishes.

Dan Sears